Shot Through
the Heart

Shot Through the Heart

Ms. Bam

www.urbanbooks.net

Urban Books, LLC
300 Farmingdale Road, NY-Route 109
Farmingdale, NY 11735

Shot Through the Heart

ISBN 13: 978-1-60162-108-5
ISBN 10: 1-60162-108-6

First Mass Market Printing February 2019
First Trade Paperback Printing July 2018
Printed in the United States of America

10 9 8 7 6 5 4 3 2 1

Distributed by Kensington Publishing Corp.
Submit Orders to:
Customer Service
400 Hahn Road
Westminster, MD 21157-4627
Phone: 1-800-733-3000
Fax: 1-800-659-2436

Shot Through the Heart

Ms. Bam

Preface

Dear Readers, thank you so much for taking a chance and purchasing your paperback copy of *Shot Through the Heart*. I've been told by many of my supporters that what they like about my writing is the realness. They know I may throw an unexpected curveball into the story. Yet, they're willing to take the journey with me anyway, knowing that when they reach the end of the journey, they may not exactly like the way things went down, but they understand why I did it. No one knows this more than the characters in my head! Trust me when I say, sometimes I'm sitting there thinking certain characters are cruising their way along slow and steady to their happily ever after—then *Bam!* I throw them the same twists and turns we all experience in life. In two of my previous book series, you met two individuals, Nicole Evans, *Hoes Be Winning*, and Jeremiah Wilson, *Ballad Of A Bad Bitch*. Readers were upset with me about the way things ended for these two characters. When I was writing, I knew readers would be upset, but as a writer, I have to admit it made me smile because that, in turn, meant I'd created characters readers cared about. They got to the end of the story and felt these two people deserved something good for being good people. For being loving, faithful, dedicated partners in their relationships, shouldn't they have their happy ending? Of course. Though in real life, we all know that you can give your all to a person, be everything they need, when they need it, and still, in the end, get screwed over. Even when you've done everything right. You can be left an emotional wreck because you followed all the "rules"—and still be left with nothing.

In those moments, it's hard to look ahead and know that God just may have something better planned for you than you planned for yourself. Or, in this case, the author had bigger plans for you. I hope you enjoy the story, and as always, thank you for your support.

~ Candace, aka Ms. Bam

(Let's get started!)

"*Sometimes you meet someone and it's so clear that the two of you, on some level, belong together—as lovers or as friends, as family or as something entirely different. You just work. Whether you understand each other or you're in love, you're partners in crime. You meet these people throughout your life, out of nowhere, under the strangest circumstances, and they help you feel alive. I don't know if that makes me believe in coincidence, fate, or sheer blind luck, but it definitely makes me believe in something.*"

~ *Unknown*

Jeremiah

Damn! How the hell did this happen? Here I was being held hostage in my own bedroom. I lowered my eyes, glancing downward.

Paige, a casual friend of mine with benefits, had her arm thrown possessively over my chest as if she was scared I was going to try to escape while she was asleep. Anyone else may have thought it was by accident. After all, she *was* sleeping. But I knew better. So did Paige. I'd pulled disappearing acts on her more than a handful of times over at her place during the course of this "friendship."

Here we go with this shit again, I thought to myself, moving about my bedroom, intentionally making as much noise as possible. If Paige slept any longer, she was going to think she was in the midst of the Mardi Gras parade by the time I got done banging around this room. I was annoyed as hell, but I couldn't stop the grin from playing at the corners of my mouth as I looked around my spacious bedroom. Despite the last year and a half of my life, sometimes I still couldn't believe my luck. I'd been struggling all my life, and now, here I was, laid up in a 3,000-square foot warehouse apartment in New York City. My eyes traveled over to the expansive California King platform bed. My on-again, off-again "friend" of the moment, Paige Durant, was sprawled a little too comfortably across my damn bed.

Paige had shown up late last night unannounced, and against my better judgment, I'd let her behind in. I knew when she sashayed that round ass through the door I was making a mistake, but what the hell? It had been about a week since I'd seen her, despite the obvious attempts and daily phone calls to snag my attention. Paige had, in fact, damn near bullied her way into staying the night. I usually didn't allow anyone over here, but after two rounds of tears, and some bomb-ass head, I figured I'd go ahead and let her stay.

I knew damn well Paige was laid out in my bed trying to pretend she didn't hear all the noise I was making. I was intentionally being so loud how could she not? Playing possum. I'd just stepped out of the shower. I finished drying off and threw on some sweats. I was getting on a plane headed to Virginia later this afternoon and had some business to handle around the house and at my club before I left. I planned to be gone about a month. Things were going so well with the Club Dip, and I opened in New York, Club Azure. The venture had been so profitable we were now opening up another location in Virginia. The club, Table 51, was already open, but the owners didn't have the funding to keep it afloat from what we'd been told, so they wanted to sell, and we were interested in taking it over. Table 51 was already making a buzz all over social media. So we figured instead of expanding with a club from the ground up, why not just jump in on this deal. We'd keep what we liked and make any changes we felt necessary.

"Paige . . ." I called out as I walked over to the window, grabbed the remote, and pushed as I watched the navy blue and gold curtains retract, flooding my bedroom with natural light from the only windows in the entire place. Shit, let this sunlight hit her and she'll wake her behind up. Enough was enough. It was time for her to exit stage left. I turned around, and now all her naked ass was out for me to see. Five minutes ago, she was covered like a mummy wrapped up in my thick gold satin comforter as if she'd paid for it.

"Jeremiah! The light! I'm sleeping, bae," Paige whined, tooting her ass out even more. I didn't give a damn about her being sleepy. Paige could get all the rest she wanted . . . at her own damn house.

"Well, you need to get up and make your way home, then. You can sleep as much as you need to at your place. I got shit to do."

Paige sat up straight in the bed, suddenly wide awake. Not a trace of sleep in her voice. I knew her behind was awake the whole time.

"Why do I always have to go to my place to sleep, Jeremiah? I mean, damn, what's the problem with me staying here? I mean, we've been together four months now. Besides, I thought I'd make you breakfast before I went home. At least let me do that," she complained, arms in the air stretching as she showed off her bare breasts. Paige didn't have much to show, but her big ass made up for it.

"You have to sleep at your place because that's *your* home. Don't you pay rent for the privilege of sleeping in that muthafucka? Look, I'm on a plane out of here this afternoon. I have a lot I need to take care of today before I leave. And another thing, Paige, please stop saying we're together. We've gotten together every once in a while over the course of four months. We ain't been together. Stop twisting the facts, ma; you gon' end up hurting your own feelings."

"Well, when were you going to tell me you were leaving town? Are you taking me with you?"

I took a deep sigh trying to compose myself before I really hurt this girl's feelings. I took notice of the fact Paige conveniently left out the most important thing I'd said. The last thing I wanted was hurt feelings and an argument before I headed out of town, but Paige and I had been bumping heads about this issue heavily for the last two months. I wasn't interested in a relationship with her—or anyone else—at the moment. I'd tried the whole relationship thing once after Mia and I broke up, but I realized my head and my heart weren't ready for that. At this point, I was all about business. I wanted to build an empire for myself, and as far as women went, it was all about getting my needs met. Paige was a prime example to me that the whole casual dating thing didn't work. Yeah, I'd taken her out on some dates, chilled with her a little, but she took that to mean we were in a relationship of some sort.

I wasn't out here leading women on or no shit like that, but I felt like I was very clear about my intentions. Paige played the role like she understood, but she still over here acting like a bandit trying to creep into my heart. Twice, I'd cut her ass off completely. We went a week or two without talking but always found ourselves back in bed together.

"Shit, your ass is lucky I'm telling you right now. And even that's only because you just happened to be here. Go 'head and get up and outta here, ma. Like I said, I have some things to wind up today before I head out."

"Well, at least tell me how long you'll be gone. Why do you treat me like this, Jeremiah? You act like I'm the enemy or something. I'm so good to you, and you act like it means nothing. Am I *nothing* to you?" Paige asked. When I looked at her, she had the nerve to have a tear falling down her cheek, but I was not falling for that shit.

"See, this is the reason I keep saying we don't need to sleep with each other . . ."

"Well, why do you keep doing it? Why play with me when you know how I feel about you?"

"Why do you keep calling me when you know I don't care about you is the bigger question? I keep doing it because the pussy is good, and you keep throwing it at me, even when I tell you straight up I'm not going to be your man. Paige, look, I'm not trying to be cruel. I'm straight up about what this is and isn't but take responsibility for your own emotions. I ain't the keeper of your heart. I don't want the job, and I keep telling yo' ass that shit."

Paige pulled her knees to her chest gazing at me forlornly.

"Well, can I ask how long you'll be gone? At least let me know that."

"I'll be gone a minute, Paige, about a month. Let's not get into this, okay? I'm kinda tired of going over the same old thing with you. You're a good girl. Find someone that wants the same things you do. I'm not there yet. I know you've been waiting on me, but it's just not happening for me right now."

"What? A month! What am I doing wrong, though? I fuck you good, I cook for you . . . at least I do when you let me in long enough to do it—"

"I don't care what you cook! You ain't the first female to fuck me good and make me a nice hot meal," I yelled, interrupting her. A nigga was trying to keep his composure but, damn! When the writing is on the wall, read that shit!

"Jeremiah, at the very least, we're friends. Look, I need some help right now . . ."

I stopped dead in my tracks, lips turned down into a frown. My eyes rolled to the back of my head before I slammed my dresser drawer shut and turned around to face her, my arms folded across my chest. Damn! All I wanted to do is grab some socks—not all this extra conversation.

"What do you need from me?" I asked cautiously.

"Well, you know, I've been telling you I'm having problems with my roommates. Do you think I could stay with you for a while? Just on a temporary basis while I find my own place? I respect what you're saying, I know we're not together. I just need to regroup and get myself together. Besides, you just said you'll be gone a month. I could watch the place for you," Paige stated, trying to look at me like she had all the sense in the world.

Hell to the muthafuckin' no! is what my head was screaming. People were too fucking shady, and I knew all she wanted was a way in. I was not about to have a squatter on my hands that I couldn't get rid of.

"You know what, ma, I'm sorry you're going through it, but I'ma have to say no to that. I just ain't feeling it. Also, I'm leaving here today. Even if I was to consider it, you haven't even given me any time to think about it. So it's gonna have to be a firm no for me. Your entire family is in the Bronx. So why can't you go home? Or stay with one of your three sisters? Nah, baby girl, it's a no for me." I waved my arm around the room real fast.

"Go 'head and get all your things together. I'm calling you an Uber."

Paige

I stood in Jeremiah's bathroom seething! What the hell was I supposed to do now? Then I sat down on the toilet, frustrated as hell. Something has got to give. I've been chasing this man for four goddamn months, and he was sticking to his little proclamation of not wanting to be in a relationship. Yes, he'd cut me off a few times, but I always managed to get back in his good graces. Or more to the point, his bed.

I stood up and looked at myself in the mirror. I was a baddie by any man's standards. My auburn hair hung to the middle of my back, granted that was with the help of a weave, but I made sure my stylist had my hair laid and slayed every two weeks. It perfectly complemented my light brown complexion. I'd starve before I missed an appointment. If my light bill was late, so be it. Which was part of the reason my roommate wanted me out. I had a great sense of style and made sure I always looked good. I

never brought it up because I didn't want to
sound like a groupie, but I knew who Jeremiah's
ex-girlfriend was. How could I not? When all
that shit went down with the R&B singer Mia,
her mama, and that fine-ass nigga she ended up
marrying, Quinton, it was the talk of the blogo-
sphere. I felt like I looked just as good as—if not
better than—Mia. I mean, I didn't really have
any talent. But neither did any of these hoes on
damn near every reality TV show on right now.

I met Jeremiah one night at his club, and
when I found out he was one of the owners?
Baby, I knew I had to have him. His club was
always packed with celebrities in the VIP section,
and I knew the circles he ran in. I wanted to be
a part of that. Don't get me wrong, I want this
nigga bad as hell! Jeremiah is cool as a fan, he
can hold a conversation about anything, make
me laugh, and the dick is the truth. I feel like
physically I have him where I want him. I don't
think he's sleeping with anyone but me. But
mentally? I can't get in his head or heart for
shit. Hell, Jeremiah's bathroom alone was larger
than my apartment. And I was sharing that with
a bitch I could barely stand. I did lie, though. I
wasn't being put out . . . yet. But, damn, I felt like
I had to start pulling out all the stops and taking

drastic measures just to get on another level with this nigga.

What was I missing? Ugh!

There was a loud banging on the door.

"Let's goooo! Ya Uber is outside," Jeremiah yelled on the other side of the door.

Let me just go without a fuss. When he gets back in town, I'm locking this nigga down! I've spent four months chasing him, and I will *not* have all this time and pussy go to waste. Besides, I've already told my girls Desiree and Chantal we're damn near engaged. I'll look like such an idiot if this doesn't work out. Maybe I shouldn't have embellished the situation with Jeremiah the way I had, but it was too late to take it all back now! I just have to go for what I know at this point.

I quickly brushed my teeth and ran my fingers through my hair. When I opened the door, Jeremiah was standing there holding my bag for me, packed to the brim, and my coat was dangling from his other arm.

"Dang! Are you that anxious to get rid of me? What's all that in my bag?" Shit, I had to ask. It was stuffed! I knew damn well when I came over last night I barely had anything in there.

"Ask me no questions, I'll tell you no lies. This is all of your stuff you left behind each time you've stayed the night. I took the liberty of gathering it all up for you."

The look he gave me made me wish I hadn't asked. I shrugged my shoulders into my jacket and stood on my toes to give him a quick peck on the lips.

"We'll get together when you get back. When is that exactly?" I asked, hoping he'd soften a bit and tell me. I'd asked his ass what seemed like ten times when he'd be back, and Jeremiah had yet to answer.

"I'll be back in a month."

My heart felt like it dropped to the pit of my stomach. A month? Was he fucking *serious?* What the hell did he have to do that would take so long? Not seeing him for thirty days would feel like I was starting from scratch with him when he got back. Then again, maybe we needed this bit of space. Lord knows I didn't want it, but there was nothing I could do about it.

"Wow. That's a long time but good luck on your business deal. Be safe," I said, trying to check the tears threatening to spill down my cheeks.

"You too. I'll holla."

I just walked out the door. Would he, though? Holla, that is. Jeremiah rarely, if ever, reached out to me. I was always the one initiating contact with him, and wasn't shit about that going to change. If he didn't call me, I would *definitely* be calling him. If I was anything, it was persistent.

Jeremiah—Virginia, Thursday Night

By the time I got Paige out of my place, did a bit of cleaning, made sure my security cameras were on, and locked up, I was exhausted. I napped on the plane, and when I arrived in Richmond, Virginia, and rented a little Cadillac Escalade to get around in and checked into an extended stay suite, I was beat. It was Thursday night, and after I took a quick nap, I planned on heading straight to Table 51 to start getting a vibe on the entire establishment. Tonight was Ladies' Night. I wanted to see exactly how many women they actually pulled into the club. I also wanted to see how many men followed the ladies there. I was leaving no stone unturned in my assessment of Table 51. After all, Dip and I were dropping a ton of money into this club. If it wasn't beneficial, we were pulling out. Monday was the final meeting to sign papers, but it was already known that nothing was set in stone until we signed on the dotted line.

No one even knew I was flying in. I was walking into the club tonight strictly undercover. By the time I walked into Table 51, I was surprised to see the parking lot was packed. I spotted a small corner table in the back where I decided to park myself the entire night. I took in the entire vibe of the club and had to admit, I was impressed. The whole place was decorated in black, red, and white. Classic lines and the furniture was edgy futuristic-type shit. I knew it had to be expensive. Damn club going under because the owners wanted to spend too much on their decorating budget, I thought to myself. Every waitress my eyes landed on was an attractive woman. The bar was packed, though I didn't like the fact I only saw one bartender. Shit, based on the size of the place, I didn't like the fact there was only one bar. That would have to change. I was even more pissed when thirty minutes passed before a waitress came to take my order. Shit, at that point, I wasn't just checking the place out, a nigga was actually thirsty!

"Hey, love! I'm sorry it took me so long to make my way over here. What can I get you to drink?" the waitress asked. The uniforms consisted of a crisp white button-down shirt and short black skirts. This lady knew damn well she had way too much ass for this short skirt.

"What's your name, ma?" I asked since there wasn't a name tag in sight.

"Ooohhh, I detect an accent! You sound like you're from the South, but I detect a little New York swag too. I'm Tiny," she said, grinning from ear to ear. Her smile would have been cute if it wasn't for the chipped tooth in the front. It was an immediate no for me since I was a smile guy. Pretty teeth and a sexy smile would win me over every time.

"Yeah, I'm from Texas, but I've been living in New York for a few years now. It's kinda growing on me. Say, let me get two shots of Hennessey and a Heineken."

"I got you, boo! Now, do you want a basket of wings to go along with that? We also serve food until eleven if you get hungry," Tiny explained, handing over a menu I quickly glanced over. It was cool, simple finger foods that wouldn't take much time. We didn't serve food at our spot in New York, but this might be something we needed to add on to our establishment. I'd talk to Dip about it once we went over the numbers to see if it would be a profitable move to make.

"You know what, Tiny, I think I will take a ten-piece lemon-pepper wings and some fries.

Heavy on the lemon pepper. Thanks for the suggestion," I said, giving her a quick smile. Tiny was a smooth chocolate sister, and I could see a blush coming through her richly hued skin tone up to her cheeks.

"I'll be right back with your drinks. What's your name, by the way? I've never seen you in here before. I'm sure glad you found us, though," she said flirtatiously.

"You can call me Jay. Tiny, do me one more favor. I see y'all packed up in here tonight. Can you get me a reserved sign for the table? If I get up and move around, I'm not trying to lose my spot."

Tiny looked around nervously. "I'll see what I can do, Jay, but my manager really doesn't like us reserving seats for people. He said if you want to make sure you keep your seat, you need to pay to be in the VIP," she revealed shyly. I could tell by the way her whole demeanor changed she didn't too much care for the manager.

"Okay, then, escort me to the VIP section. I'm paying to sit in there solo. Make sure you're still my waitress, even though I won't be in your section anymore."

Tiny's smile lit up. "Okay, let me take you over there and get your order in."

Five minutes later, I was sitting in the VIP section, and all eyes were on me. It wasn't exactly the way I'd planned to check the place out. I knew people were wondering who the hell I was, and why I was in there alone, but fuck it. I spent the rest of the night chilling in the VIP. I even invited a few ladies over and bought them a few rounds of drinks. All in all, Table 51 proved to be a good night. I also snagged a few numbers. I figured, why not? I was going to be here a month, so I might as well meet a few people. I actually had a good time mingling, aside from the fact Paige was blowing my phone up with texts stating how much she missed me. Eventually I stopped looking at my damn phone since I knew it wasn't no one but her.

Ladies' Night at Table 51 was poppin'. I couldn't wait to see what Friday night would bring.

*****Remember that time you confused a
life lesson for a soul mate?*****

Nicole—Friday Morning

It was 7:15 a.m., and as sure as the sky is blue, like clockwork, my alarm sounded off, buzzing loudly in my ear. Unlike the other four days of my workweek, my hand didn't quickly shoot out from underneath the covers to quiet the intrusive noise steadily invading my brain with the loud, staccato buzzing of the alarm. This morning, I just let the damn thing buzz. Any distraction right now was a welcome one. Even the most annoying invasion of my peace was better than the slow, dull, aching pain my heart carried around every waking minute of the day. Today was an anniversary of sorts for me. A sick, tormenting counting of the days I happened to perform unconsciously . . . or consciously every single month. The twenty-third day of the month.

After two minutes of the constant, nondescript, blaring buzz, I finally reached over and turned it off. I threw my forearm over my eyes, still refusing to open them at all. When my arm was soaking wet, I used the back of my hands to wipe away the tears that, no matter how much I tried to keep at bay, always seemed to find their way each morning to slow dance a permanent path down my cheeks the minute my eyes opened every day.

Well, I thought, *at least it's Friday. I can stay in bed all weekend, turn my phone off, and not talk or look at anyone. Just the way I like it,* I thought.

I sat at the edge of my bed gathering my thoughts quickly in order to go about the day. Toilet, shower, teeth, then dress. You can do this, Nicole, I told myself for motivation. I repeated it several times. What kind of shit is this? I'm twenty-four-years-old having to give myself a pep talk to go to the bathroom. "Get up! No wonder Kendrick didn't want you. You're a weak bitch. I'll bet Tierrany never had to say this shit to herself, even with all she's been through. She's strong. That's why Kendrick chose her over me. Hell, it's why Don Travious walked all over me too and cheated all the goddamn time," I bitterly said to myself as I willed my body into a standing position. *Stand your fuckin' ass up!* my brain silently screamed. My body always did everything I asked of it. I just wished my heart listened more. If it had, I wouldn't feel this way.

I walked into my bathroom and started my day. After letting the soothing, warm water run over my body for twenty minutes, I stepped out of the shower wrapping the towel tightly around my body and looked at myself in the foggy mirror. How could I have ended up like this? Pathetic.

The person I saw looking back at me, the loneliness I felt every single day, wasn't supposed to be my life. I used to be happy. Optimistic and motivated. I should be smiling, married to Kendrick and the mother of his sweet baby girl . . . a bouncing baby boy . . . Hell, it didn't matter as long as it was Kendrick's. Yet, here I was. Alone. Kendrick had all of those things. Just with someone else. That graveyard bitch Tierrany. I didn't give a shit that only moments ago I'd been praising her supposed strength. I hated Tierrany. That bitch had stolen my life. Fuck.

I opened the medicine cabinet and pulled out my bottle of Xanax. I could see it was going to be one of those days. My normal dosage was one pill, but I took two. Over the course of the last year, my tolerance with these pills had dulled. One barely took the edge off my anxiety. So on days like this— and there were many—I needed two damn pills just to get my mind right. I swallowed my "medication," finished dressing, and walked out the door to my job as one of the best trainers Health Call Solutions had ever seen. I made it a point to excel at my job because the reality was that it was all I had. Six months ago, I'd left my job with the state. I'd barely graduated with my master's after my breakup with Kendrick, but I managed to get the bare minimum done to still attain my degree. I thought a job change and higher pay would be just what I needed to get me out of the funk I'd gotten myself into. It didn't. So, for exactly eight hours . . . and eight hours only . . . the world would get to see Nicole Evans. The calm, cool, and collected woman at work. Tastefully dressed and beautiful . . . always on her game. If only they knew what a carefully crafted facade—no, let's not pretty it up—*lie* . . . my life really was.

This morning, my mind was still sharp and didn't miss the exchange between the two male trainees. I'm glad I felt a little mellower because these two brothers were working my nerves to the ninth degree. I was on the verge of putting both of their asses out of the training class.

The guy Jordan looked like a deer caught in headlights and shrugged his shoulders quickly at Khalid with a look that screamed, "Don't get me in trouble too! You're on your own!"

"Okay, class . . . *Most* of you have been doing great!" I said, eying Khalid. "Why don't we take a quick fifteen-minute break, refill your coffee cups if you need to, and let's get back at it. We have a busy day, and there are a few more key points to go over this afternoon because, tomorrow, ladies and gentlemen, you will begin taking live calls! See you back here in fifteen minutes. *Not* sixteen minutes," I said, smiling. I was serious as hell, though. Anyone walking back from break even one minute late would find the class door locked. Several of them found out the first day of training when they were standing outside the class looking crazy. I'd told them to set their watches and phones to the class clock. I was not fucking around with these people.

Everyone scrambled from their seat, happy to have an extra break.

"Mr. Carson, I need to have a word with you for a moment."

Khalid Carson threw his head back as if he was pissed I'd called his name and was cutting into the break time I'd so graciously given him. His ass better be lucky I was taking the time out of *my* day to say anything to his ass. The scuff marks on his shoes told me he really needed this damn job. As a trainer, I'd invested too much time and company money into trying to prepare

him to go on the floor, but it was at my discretion
if he made it through. The way my fucked-up
attitude was these days toward black men after
the foul way *I'd* been treated, I didn't give a fuck.
Then again, my short stint into white men didn't
have me feeling any better toward them either.
Matter of fact, I was at a fuck men stage. Period.
Every race. The only exceptions was my daddy.
Shoot, I knew my brothers had some doggish
ways too, so even they didn't make the cut.

"Mr. Carson, do you plan on making it through
this training? The company puts a lot of time,
money, and effort into training our employees,
and if you can't give me the common courtesy to
pay attention when I'm trying to equip you with
the skills you need to successfully perform your
job duties, why waste your time, the company's,
or mine?"

"I apologize for the one time all week I got
distracted, Ms. Evans. It won't happen again."

"Well, I certainly hope not . . ." I replied, just
getting wound up. There was something about
him I just didn't like. I knew his type: good-looking and arrogant. I bet he's looking me in my
face thinking just because he's standing in front
of me fine as hell I think he's cute, I thought,
folding my arms across my chest and looking up
at him. I took a step back to avoid the piercing

stare Khalid Carson was giving me. I couldn't quite pinpoint the look he was giving me, but I'm sure he was pissed. Black men always thought a sista couldn't say shit to them. Well, news flash, Negro. I was running shit over here!

Khalid

If this bitch don't get off my goddamn back!
I thought, swallowing slowly, my temples were
now throbbing. I couldn't afford to cuss her ass
out and walk off this job like I'd done the one
before this. Since being laid off from the plant,
I'd had several menial jobs that hadn't worked
out for one reason or another. This was the best
opportunity to come along in months. I couldn't
afford to lose this job.

"Will there be anything else, Ms. Evans?" I
asked. I felt like any minute I could snap, and
at this very moment, what I really needed was
a real cigarette. Not the fake shit I had in my
pocket, either. Damn, do I need to bring a flask
up in this muthafucka just to make it through
the day? I guess it's true what they say about
black women in power positions in the workplace. She's riding my ass hard. I don't know
why, though. I've followed everything perfectly
all week.

"That's it, Mr. Carson."

I walked out to the break room with a frown etched across my face. Ain't this some shit? This lady took up five minutes of my fifteen-minute break behind some bullshit. My nerves were so wrecked at this point I was for damn sure feenin' for a real cigarette. I walked outside to the smoke area to see if someone would show me a little mercy and let me bum one, though I knew I'd have to really beg to get it. As high as cigarettes were these days, people would turn their nose up at you quick at the mention of "can I borrow." Oh, well, fuck it. I'ma beg, borrow, and plead for one. I need it.

Goddamn! I wanted to turn my ass right back around when I saw my coworker Renee Smith was the only one standing in the smoke shack.

"Hey, Khalid. How are you this morning?" Renee asked. Every morning since the first day of orientation, this woman has been skinning and grinning up in my damn face. I loved pussy just as much, if not more than, the average brother, but at this stage of the game, I needed this job more. This woman was going to have to bring more to the table than all her titties hanging out to turn my head, I thought, giving her a slow, easy smile.

"I'm good, Renee, how are you this morning?" I asked in an attempt to be polite. Training lasted another two weeks. I didn't know if I could stay polite much longer the way this woman kept coming on to me. Ain't nothing worse than a female who can't understand when a man isn't interested. Renee bought me drinks during our breaks, daily invites to lunch. Damn! Why did women make it so easy for men? Then the minute shit wasn't going their way, they wondered why a nigga was dippin' on they ass. Every man liked to be approached every now and then, but at the end of the day, a man wants to feel like a man. We want to take the lead.

"I'm doing good, Khalid! Blessed and highly favored as usual," Renee said, smiling at me as she placed her manicured hands at the nip of her waist, accentuating her ample hips. No doubt Renee was fine, but this sista wasn't on my radar at all. I like my women classy, reserved . . . Nah, let me keep it real. After spending the last four years with my half-dead-ass baby mama, my next woman is going to be classy, sophisticated, and demure. I'm not falling for anything less than that this go-round, I thought smiling down at her. Shit, I may not be exactly where I want to be with my career, but I know damn well I'm a good man. Hell, I can be even better with a good woman by my side.

"Well, Khalid, I wanted to know if I could finally take you to lunch today. You know, to celebrate our first week of training. I mean, we have two more weeks of training left, and then we'll be on the floor together. So I thought, why not try to get to know my new coworkers better?" Renee asked coyly, looking me dead in my eyes. I almost laughed in her face. *This woman ain't got no shame! None at all. Females got the game all fucked up, I see. I got something for her ass, though,* I thought, my head turning toward the smoke shack door. I saw a dude named Jordan Davis walk through the door. Jordan was cool. We'd been kicking it in class the last week. "Hey, Jordan! Come have lunch today with Renee and me . . . her treat! Renee said she wants to get to know her new coworkers," I said, giving him the unmistakable man code look that said, "My nigga, don't leave me alone with this bitch!"

Jordan quickly picked up on it. "I'm in. As soon as you said free lunch, I was in!"

Renee tried to quickly object. "Oh no, wait . . ."

"That was a good idea, Renee. I'm glad you suggested it," I said, giving her my sexiest smile. I even followed it up with a wink.

"We'll decide who drives, Jordan or I, a little later since you're treating. The least we can do is drive. I'm going to the bathroom real quick. I don't want to be late back to class."

"Okay," Renee replied dejectedly.

I walked toward the building, laughing inside. Bet your ass you won't force yourself into a lunch date with me anytime again. I can already tell I'm good and hungry too!

Nicole

I had almost made it to my office when I heard Cherell's voice calling my name.

"Uh-uh! I know your behind ain't trying to avoid me! Please tell me that ain't what your ass is up to, Nicole Evans!" Cherell practically hissed.

"Hush, girl, I'm not trying to avoid you! And stop calling my name like you're my damn mama," I said, trying to quickly cover up the fact I was lying my ass off. Cherell was one of the few coworkers I actually called a friend. Hell, at this point, she was more of a best friend to me than my childhood friend, Meka. Not that Meka was a bad friend . . . I guess. But since Meka had her baby, and I'd changed jobs, our lives were just going in two different directions. Meka was too busy running down her baby daddy, who was ducking and dodging his child support. I had my own issues. We did play catch-up on our weekly phone calls to each another, though. Cherell, on the other hand, had caught the tail end of the demise of my relationship with Kendrick. I'd called myself trying to go antiblack man right after, but that damn Scott wasn't any better than Don Travious or Kendrick.

It took me a long time to function after Kendrick, and I'll be the first to say, I'm still not over him. I'm still mourning the death of that relationship. Now, Cherell had made it her personal mission to find me a new man. She held fast to the age-old adage that the best way to get over an old man was with a new man. I just didn't think anyone compared to Kendrick Taylor. My heart and mind wouldn't allow me to think there was another man created that was better than him—which I knew was pathetic given the fact I was now literally obsessing over another woman's husband.

"Look, don't play with me, Nicole. I know your ass is ducking and dodging me because you already know we've had plans for the last two weeks to go to Table 51 after work today. Don't think I ain't picked up on the way your moods get on the twenty-third of the month, either. Breakup day. Hell, you get to acting so damn funny every month, I halfway feel like the nigga broke up with me too! I'm making it my mission to get you over this old bullshit. Fuck Kendrick

Taylor. That nigga ain't all that. So your ass better be ready to go tonight. I'll be by your place to pick you up at seven on the dot!" Cherell said, rolling her eyes at me.

"Cherell, my head is kinda hurting. I think I may have to pass—" I began.

"Well, lucky for your black ass it's only 11:00 a.m.! Take something for that shit and have your ass ready on time. You about that bullshit, Nicole! I'ma wait and cuss you out and tell you about your damn self when we off the damn clock. Oh! Before I go, girl, what's up with that fine-ass brother in the training class? I believe his name is Khalid. I heard one of the trainees in the bathroom talking about him," Cherell whispered, leaning in conspiratorially.

I leaned back and looked at my friend. I couldn't help but laugh because Cherell didn't give a damn about going after who she wanted. Workplace or not.

"Now, see, bitch, you outta order! That man is a trainee. I'm his supervisor. I'm not looking at him like that," I said, lying, knowing damn well I'd taken notice of how attractive Khalid was.

Cherell cut her eyes at me.

"I don't give a damn what he is. If the nigga is a trainee, retiree, parolee, that brotha is fine. See, *that's* your problem. You worry too much about a nigga's title, or what's on the outside than what kinda man he is underneath all that. Where did that get you last time?"

My eyes smarted with tears at the low blow my friend had just issued.

"Now I know I didn't have to go there with you just now, Nicole, but I only did it because I'm your friend. You need to stop judging people so harshly. You could be passing over your soul mate just because he doesn't live up to your preconceived standards, and that's not right. Anyway, let me go. I have to run a team meeting. Be ready at seven!"

I slowly exhaled. I may as well go out tonight and get this out of the way so I can dodge her ass for the next two months.

"I'll be ready," I said, my voice tight. Cherell made me sick sometimes.

I quickly looked down at my watch and made a U-turn back down the hall toward the training room. Lord, help me. I knew when I got out of my damn bed it was going to be a hell of a day, I thought, frowning.

***I have loved to the point of madness. That which is called madness.

That which, to me, is the only sensible way to love.***

Later That Night . . .

I rushed around my bedroom putting the finishing touches on my hair and makeup. I definitely wasn't looking forward to the evening out. Another dose of Xanax—one this time since I did intend on having a drink, and my pillows were calling my name, but Cherell was relentless. I knew there was no way I was getting out of going to Table 51 with her tonight. So I'd made up my mind to make the most of it. Hell, it had been ages since I'd gone out anyway. I could get Cherell and my mama off my back in one fell swoop. My mom felt like I was turning into a recluse, and I couldn't honestly say it wasn't far from the truth.

I smoothed down the short red peplum dress. It stopped midway, showcasing my thick thighs and cupping my voluptuous backside. My C-cup breasts were prominently displayed with a scooped neckline. I had dusted my collarbone with a little gold shimmer powder. Red lipstick adorned my full lips along with smoky eyes. By all outward appearances, I looked fabulous, but inside, I felt ugly. People tell me all the time how beautiful I am, and my personality used to reflect that. I didn't care about any of that, though, because none of those positive attributes made Kendrick love me enough to choose me over Tierrany, I thought, turning away from the mirror and grabbing my gold-sequined clutch. My cell phone was ringing, and I knew it wasn't anyone but Cherell calling for me to come out.

Well, let's get this night over with, I thought, locking my door. I tried to shake the thoughts of Kendrick out of my mind. At least for one night. Please, God, just for one night, let my mind be clear. Remove all thoughts of Kendrick Taylor and the way he made me feel for just one night so I don't feel like such a loser. So alone and unwanted. Please, just one night.

"Girl, it is packed in here tonight! Now, aren't you glad you came instead of sitting in that little hovel of yours?" Cherell smirked.

"Umm, *excuse* me, bitch? My condo is 1,500-square feet of pure luxury. Now *your* place . . . *that's* a hovel. Your whole place fits inside my closet, okay, boo-boo?" I said, laughing genuinely for the first time all evening. This bitch really tried it!

Cherell burst out laughing. "There she is. The bitch is back! That's my friend right there. Come on back to the light, ho!" Cherell said, laughing as she walked over to an empty table she'd spotted on the other side of the room. I followed behind her taking in the crowd. Damn! They *are* crowded tonight. Maybe this *is* what I need. To get out and be social instead of crying over a man who obviously didn't want me and popping pills every night. A waitress came by and took our order. I decided to go light and order a white wine spritzer given the fact I had another Xanax when I'd gotten home from work just to make coming out tonight tolerable.

"Uh-uh, baby . . ." Cherell leaned in whispering, ". . . I don't give a damn. I'm taking one of these honeys home with me tonight, so be prepared to get dropped off as soon as I lay eyes on the lucky Negro I'ma let taste some of this sweet pussy tonight," she said, smacking her lips.

"Cherell! Oh my God! Why are you so nasty? This is 2016. You can't just bring people home like that."

"Shit, I don't know what you're talkin' 'bout! As long as I can put a condom on his dick, I can ride that shit," Cherell said, rolling her neck at me like I was the one talking crazy.

"What about Travis? I thought you guys were getting along so good. You said y'all were discussing marriage. He's really nice too. Don't do that man like that."

"Look, I'm trying to have a good time tonight; don't even speak that nigga's name."

I gasped. "Girl, is he cheating?"

"Cheating? On me? Chile, please . . . I wish he would!"

I burst out laughing, and her hand flew to her mouth to stifle the laugh.

"No, seriously, bitch. I *wish* the nigga would cheat on me and fall head over heels in love with another woman. I get on my knees every damn night and pray for another bitch to take this weak-ass nigga off my hands. Girl, you don't even know. God ain't listening, though . . . He ain't hearing my cries."

"What is he doing? I know the Negro ain't putting his hands on you!"

"Travis can't fuck worth a damn. I cheat on him every chance I get. Don't look at me crazy either. Shit, you don't know my pain."

"What? Not at all?"

"Not at all. I feel bamboozled. The one time I waited to be in love with a man, held out for sex until we were in a fully committed relationship—and a limp dick. Vienna sausage-ass nigga is what I get stuck with. Don't get me wrong, I feel so torn over the whole situation. I know I'm dead-ass wrong for the times I've cheated on Travis, but I feel so cheated," Cherell said, sighing as she downed her drink and motioned for the waitress to come back over so she could order another.

"I mean, Nicole, trust me when I say before I got with Travis I got good dick! Please believe me when I say . . . I've had good, long, strong-ass dick in my life. So it's hard to know what I should be getting sexually and to know I'm *not* getting it. Girl, I literally go to sleep at night with my pussy aching, and here this nigga is snoring like a damn bear after he gave me three pumps and done nutted. All I'm getting up with is a damn wet ass. So I just made the decision to get my dick elsewhere. I've tried talking to him about it, but he isn't willing to do anything to make the situation better for me."

Damn! I didn't know what to say. My relationship with Kendrick had ended badly, but the one problem we never had was sex. Hell, half of my issues now was the fact I didn't think I'd ever meet another man who would satisfy me sexually the way Kendrick did. I was scared to try a new dick. Yet another reason why things didn't work out with Scott. I heard white guys were supposed to be all romantic and shit. Scott's ass wasn't nothing but a pussy hound. When I wouldn't sleep with him right away, he hurried up and broke things off.

"Well, girl, that's a sad position to be in, but I will say this as your friend. You're playing a dangerous game right now. I mean, you never know what could happen with these men you're out here hooking up with—"

"*One* man, Nicole! I only cheated with one man. Now, granted, I fucked that one man several times before he caught feelings and I had to cut ties with his ass, but it was *one* man!"

I rolled my eyes. "Whatever, bitch. The other thing is this: if Travis finds out? Girl, you're gonna be in a world of trouble!"

"Don't I know it. That man is jealous as I don't know what. But until I decide on if I'm going to live my life fuckin' a dildo or to leave his ass permanently, this girl's gotta do what a girl's gotta do! Now, in the words of Kendrick Lamar . . . Bitch, don't kill my vibe because I have a feeling there's plenty of good hard dick in this room," Cherell said, smiling.

"You are just terrible, Cherell," I said, laughing as I raised my wineglass to my lips. Just as I was swallowing, I felt my stomach clench and my hands began to shake. Kendrick Taylor. The only man I'd ever felt truly loved me had just walked through the door of Table 51.

With his wife.

"What's wrong with you, girl? You're shaking like a leaf." Cherell turned her head in the direction of my gaze.

"Aww, hell. Don't start no shit with that man tonight, Nicole. Just leave his ass alone. That nigga was never any good for you. Be glad things played out the way they did, when they did. Hell, like my mama says, 'It's better for you to cry now, than cry later,' so just keep it moving."

I couldn't tear my eyes away from him.

Kendrick was the epitome of male beauty in my eyes. I loved everything about this man. Even the things about him I hated, I'd grown to love because they were a part of him. Even when he was destroying me, obliterating my heart with his careless actions, I loved him. I could feel my forehead becoming moist with nervousness and my breathing coming shallow.

"Umm, maybe you need to go to the bathroom real fast and get yourself together," Cherell said, looking at me with concern. The last time we'd run into Kendrick in public hadn't gone too well for me. I mean, unless public humiliation was your thing. I had shown my ass demanding to know why he'd broken up with me, what he saw in the woman he'd left me for, and a million other questions. All the while, Tierrany, Kendrick's new woman, now his wife, had been there contributing to the conversation. She'd gone in no-holds-barred on me. Basically handed my ass back to me for questioning her husband. The whole scene got really ugly and only left me looking foolish.

It was such a fiasco I knew Cherell had no intention on repeating it tonight. If I chose to take the same route with Kendrick tonight, I would be on my own. Hell, the way Cherell was talking, she had bigger things on her agenda tonight than arguing over some dick that wasn't hers . . . or mine . . . anymore, for that matter.

"You're right. Let me just get myself together real fast. I promise you there won't be a repeat of the last time. I'm not saying shit to his ass." I grabbed my clutch and on trembling legs made my way to the bathroom.

I was glad there wasn't anyone in the ladies' room when I walked in. The last thing I needed were witnesses to my mini meltdown. I splashed water over my face and patted down with a few paper towels. *You've got this, Nicole, it's been over a year. Get over it, Kendrick never deserved you,* I sternly told myself in the mirror. I didn't know why it was taking me so long to get over him. Kendrick had humiliated me. I should have hated him with ease, but my heart somehow kept making me feel he was the one who'd gotten away.

I couldn't bring myself to even leave the bathroom just yet thinking about what a fool I'd been concerning Kendrick Taylor. Granted, I'd literally met him the day I'd ended another bad relationship with my long-term boyfriend Don Travious, but Kendrick was something different. He'd made me feel things on a whole other level. From day one, Kendrick made me believe I could trust him; he'd shown it as well. He'd made me promises that I'd readily believed. Then almost five months later, it all came crashing down around me when his childhood sweetheart Tierrany stepped back on the scene. Without a day's hesitation, Kendrick had swiftly ended things with me. He didn't give what he'd built with me over the course of five months a second thought when it came to making a choice between her or me. It was a blow to my heart and self-esteem. So much so, that over a year later, I still hadn't recovered from it. Even now, if my mind strayed to thoughts of him, it was physically debilitating to me. I literally used sick and vacation days up in bed, mourning the loss of this man, and it's not like he was dead. He just didn't love me.

I had just lost my case against my ex who attacked me and attempted to rape me in my home. The very same day, I'd introduced Kendrick to my family, thinking we were going to really build a life together. For months, I asked myself, had I made our entire relationship up in my head? Was I the one making more of the months we spent together? I know it wasn't just me. Kendrick had built me up just to tear me down, leaving me in a worse state than I was in when we'd met. At least when things ended with Don Travious, I knew it was coming. I knew he was a liar and a cheater. My heart was ready for a betrayal coming from him. With Kendrick, I was wide open. A moving target, and it shot me right through the heart. *Shit, I should have taken that damn out-of-state job,* I thought, looking at myself in the mirror.

I smoothed my dress down before leaving the bathroom; then I headed straight for the bar. Fuck a white wine spritzer. I need something stronger to get me through the night. I stood at the crowded bar waiting to get the bartender's attention. The bar was crowded as fuck, but I didn't give a damn who was standing in front of me at this point. On all I love, I felt like I was on the verge of a nervous breakdown.

"Excuse me . . ." I called out, shoving myself in between two men seated at the bar. ". . . bartender? Yes, you. I need two Hennesseys on the rocks, double shots, please. ASAP." My hand was already in my purse ready to wave a nice tip in his face to expedite the service.

"Damn. Two doubles on the rocks? I hope you're ordering for a friend too!"

I heard these words from the man whose space I'd encroached on. I barely digested his words before I was ready to go off.

"Not that it's any of your business, but they're both for me, and unless you're paying for them, I suggest you shut your mouth," I damn near growled. My face was frowned up something terrible. I couldn't fight with the one man I really wanted to go off on, so whoever this Negro was all up in my business would be a welcome substitute, if need be.

The man speaking just so happened to be sexy as hell, and the smell of his cologne wafting up to my nostrils was throwing me off a bit. The tip of his tongue flicked across his bottom lip, rendering me momentarily speechless. The waves adorning his closely cropped head had me spinning, and I was sober . . . well, aside from the Xanax earlier. I was going to be seasick if I stayed here looking at him after I tossed these two drinks down my throat.

"That's not a good look, ma. An alcoholic and an attitude. You can't have both. You gon' need to choose," the man said, laughing at me openly. I couldn't detect the accent in his voice. It was weird, a mix of North and South. He sounded good, though.

"It's a good thing you're cute. I mean, if a nigga can look past your nasty disposition," he said, picking up his beer bottle and taking a long sip.

"Umm, *excuse* me? Who the fuck are you?"

"Ugh. Nasty mouth too. I'm Jay. Who the fuck is your rude ass? Busting all over here, damn near knocking me off the damn stool. Barging your way in, throwing out drink orders. It ain't even your damn turn."

I was ready to tear this fool a new asshole. He'd struck a nerve with me. I *was* rude as hell. I didn't used to be this way prior to my breakup with Kendrick. But since then, I was damn near confrontational at times. With everyone.

The man sitting on one side of this Jay asshole got up, and I quickly sat down on the stool next to him. I hated to get really obnoxious with the bartender since it *was* crowded and he seemed to be the only one working, but I needed my drinks fast so I could get away from this Jay person. Maybe if I sat down and displayed a tiny bit of patience, he'd get to me sooner rather than later.

"Hello, Nicole," I heard the familiar voice behind me speak. The voice that still, over a year later, haunted me.

I felt like dropping through the floor. Shame and embarrassment suddenly enveloped me, and I couldn't speak. My back stiffened, and I just sat there for a moment with my eyes pinned on this Jay guy blinking uncontrollably, too afraid to turn around and look into the eyes of the man I loved more than anything in this world. The man who had betrayed me. Lied, and who had completely shattered my heart. Don Travious fucked around on me, yes, but all the credit for the pain I've walked around with for the last year went exclusively to Kendrick. Lord have mercy. I can't just sit here looking like an idiot. *Why did he have to even speak to me at all?* I thought to myself, knowing damn well I would have been crushed if he'd acted like I didn't even exist and ignored me. Lord knows right after we broke up I acted up enough for him to *want* to ignore me completely.

I took a deep breath and turned around to face Kendrick. He was as handsome as he'd always been, and the dull ache in my heart for over a year now seemed to bloom as fresh as if he'd dumped me this very morning.

Jeremiah

***If you're a gem, you have to understand
you were made for a king. Give a diamond
to a bum and watch him pawn it for a crack
rock.***

Now, this is interesting, I thought, looking at
the exchange taking place right in front of me.
Ms. Rude Ass was reduced to damn near silence
in front of whoever this nigga was. Ol' girl was
saying hello, and this guy was asking how she
was doing. Voice all sweet and shit when just
seconds before she looked ready to cuss me
out! I mean, the nigga sounded nice enough,
but I could tell just by the way she was shifting
nervously around in her seat, the shaking of her
hands, something was wrong. Her ass was ready
to loud talk me for no reason at all; now with
this nigga right here, she was talking all soft.
Meek as hell. Damn right I was being nosy. Why

not? I may as well enjoy the show. Shit, I didn't have anything else to do. Besides, I couldn't stand a loud, boisterous-ass woman. I was here incognito again tonight checking out the vibe of what would be my latest club acquisition in Virginia. I thought maybe Tiny would be working again tonight, but I guess she was off.

I turned back in my stool and grabbed my beer. Shit, let me sip and listen.

Ol' boy was still waiting for the bartender to take his order. Just as I turned around to look at her, I caught something that stopped me dead in my tracks. My beer bottle was stuck midair. I saw ol' girl turn her head from him slightly and raise her hand quickly to her face. Damn, is that a tear sliding down her face? I could see she was really shaken up. I didn't know what this guy meant to her or had done, but whatever it was had reduced loud-mouthed bae to tears. I suddenly felt bad for her. I don't know why. It's not like she'd been particularly nice to me, but I did hate to see a woman cry. I didn't even view women the same as I did prior to my breakup with Mia, but I was a gentleman at heart.

"Baby, when your drinks come, do you want to join your friend back at the table or stay here?" I asked her pointedly. Hopefully, her dumb ass knew how to play along. She looked at me wide-eyed before nodding her head slowly.

"Yes, that would be nice. We already found a table," she finally said, her voice slightly fumbling over the words.

"Oh, are you two together? My bad, man. I didn't mean to intrude," this Kendrick nigga said. I could tell the nigga was immediately sizing me up. What for I have no idea since I spotted the nigga when he walked in Table 51 with a bad sista on his arm. This nigga looked like he was suddenly trying to flex in front of me, so I stood up at the bar to my full height and looked down at his ass.

"No intrusion at all," I said, never taking my eyes off him.

Nicole cleared her throat lightly, and I cut my eyes at her real quick. Don't be trying to cut in when two men are sizing each other up! Two seconds ago you didn't have a word to say. So stay your ass quiet now and let me handle this.

"Kendrick, this is Jay; Jay, Kendrick," Nicole said, introducing us nervously.

"Oh . . . This is the Kendrick you told me about?" I asked, immediately deciding to be messy. My inner "mitch" was on alert. Something in me was telling me the nigga fucked her over bad. She looked ready to cry right now, matter of fact.

This nigga Kendrick took a step back and cut his eyes between the two of us. "You know what, Nicole? It was nice running into you today. Enjoy your night," he said before leaving the bar without placing his drink order.

I leaned against the edge of the bar gazing down at her. I couldn't tell if she was glad he was gone or sad. She was rubbing her damn neck and looked like she'd broken out into a sweat. *Maybe I should throw my last sip of beer in her face, teach her how to be nice to a stranger who just helped her crazy ass out in a tight spot!* I thought quickly but changed my mind and went a different route.

"Just breathe, deep breaths, that's it . . ." I whispered softly in her ear.

"Thank you. Thank you so much, Jay," Nicole stammered, taking deep breaths as I'd instructed.

"No problem. Just play along . . ." I whispered ". . . They're sitting at the other end of the bar still checking you out, you know. Put a smile on your face and fake it until you make it, baby girl. Never let 'em see you sweat," I said.

Shit, I knew about that all too well dealing with Mia's trifling ass this past year. I was trying to put all that behind me as well, but sometimes that whole situation still ran me hot how she fucked me over. It didn't help Mia had really blown the fuck up. I couldn't escape her on the TV talk shows, radio—hell, the Internet. If it wasn't for the fact I worked with the public, I would have damn near turned into a recluse just so I wouldn't have to hear about her ass. Period.

Nicole cut her eyes to the left, and sure enough, Kendrick's wife, I assumed it was his wife, at least, was looking dead in her mouth.

"What the fuck is that bitch's problem? You would think *I* was the one who walked in and destroyed her life. That bitch fucked my world up, not the other way around," Nicole hissed under her breath. I cut my eyes quickly to the end of the bar. The woman was fine, I couldn't lie, but I could tell Nicole wasn't trying to hear that at all right now. There was definitely bad blood between the two of them.

"How about we just get our drinks? I think I pretty much owe you drinks for the rest of the night. My girlfriend and I have a table. Why don't you and your friend join us?" Nicole asked.

"What friend?" I asked, confused.

Nicole pointed to the guy who had been sitting on the other side of me. I didn't know his ass from Adam. But what the hell? The nigga seemed to be there alone and was all in our conversation.

"Hey, my man, you wanna sit at the table with us? She has a friend with her," I asked, pointing to Nicole. Despite her nasty attitude, Nicole was pretty. Hopefully, her friend wasn't at the table looking like a bugga wolf!

"Who me?" the guy asked, pointing to his chest.

"Yeah, man, come on."

"I'm down. I'm Carlos, by the way," the man said, grabbing his drink and standing up.

"You mean you don't know him?" Nicole asked, her lips turned down. Just that quick, her nasty attitude was back.

"No. But I don't know you either, so what's the difference? Where's the table? Stop acting stupid. Ol' boy and his girl still looking this way," I goaded her along. Nicole looked mad as hell, but I gave zero fucks. Her arms were folded across her chest, eyes narrowed, ready to challenge me. I could see it in her whole demeanor—after I'd just come to her rescue. *This* is the thanks I get?

"If you don't want us to go sit with you and your friend, it's cool. But like I said, his girl is checking you out on the low. It ain't shit to me. *You're* the one in here looking lonely on a 'girls' night' while he's over there happy with the woman who snatched him from you," I said smartly. Granted, I'd stepped in to help on my own, but if she was going to start tripping, I could sit my black ass down and mind my own business. My mind hadn't changed about her at all. This Nicole was a class-A bitch if my first impression of her was any indication.

At the same time, she didn't owe me anything. I could have let her stand there and get clowned, but it just wasn't in me to leave a sista hanging in the wind like that—even though I wanted to after all the shit she's talking only seconds before. And with all the women coming in and out of Table 51, it should have been easy for this nigga Carlos to find a female to chat up. Evidently, he'd come along and needed a wingman and had found one in me. I didn't have to ask that nigga twice. He was at the table ready to sit down before Nicole and I made it there.

We arrived at the table, and her friend glanced up at us and smiled. "Well, hello, there. Who do we have here?" Nicole's friend asked.

Nicole quickly . . . and awkwardly . . . made introductions all around. I signaled a waitress over to refresh our drinks. Not for a second did I forget I was actually working. I was seeing what staff we needed to get rid of and who could stay. The bartender Javier was definitely in need of a raise. He was holding the bar down like a champ all on his own, and this place was way too busy for him to be working alone for the second night in a row.

"Well, the more the merrier! Have a seat, everyone," Cherell said, smiling, patting the chair next to her as a not-so-subtle invite to

Carlos. He was as good-looking as the rest of the brothas she'd seen in there tonight. Cherell wondered what he was working with.

They all sat down, and it wasn't long before Cherell had used her feminine wiles to lure Carlos under her spell. Their lips were so close while talking they might as well have been kissing. It happened so fast I wasn't sure who was seducing whom!

"Thank you for that back there, Jay. It's kind of a sticky situation with my ex and me," Nicole said, nervously smoothing down her skirt.

"Oh yeah? Is ol' girl his wife?" I asked. I wanted to know just how "sticky" shit was. Since the whole thing with Mia and her fuck-boy of a husband Quinton, I didn't have no time for games. Granted, I wasn't interested in this woman at all. I just had a low tolerance for bullshit. Period. I wasn't the laid-back type of guy I used to be. Whatever question popped into my head, I asked. Rude or not, I didn't give a fuck.

"It's his wife," Nicole answered, her voice so low I almost had to lean in to catch it.

"Well, what's 'sticky' about that? I see you cuttin' your eyes over there looking at the nigga like he can still get it. No wonder his wife is looking at you like she ready to lay hands on your ass. Respect that man's marriage," I said, taking a swig of my beer.

That's what was wrong with society today. No one had any respect for one another. No decency or boundaries.

"Hold up. You do *not* know the situation and what went down between us, okay? That bitch Tierrany didn't respect *my* relationship! She stepped on *my* toes. *Not* the other way around," Nicole seethed.

"So explain it to me, then. Seems to me the man made his choice. You didn't make the cut. The better woman for him won his heart."

I couldn't quite keep the edge off of my voice. Especially since I knew all too well exactly how that felt, but I'd faced it. Typical-ass female. I should have just let her ass twist in the wind so she could look even more pathetic than she already did when she was talking to ol' boy. If I had given it five more minutes, she could have been in complete tears. *That's what I get for trying to help a bougie bitch out*, I thought angrily. As much as I loved women, I swear to God sometimes I couldn't stand them. Well, like they say, can't live with them, can't live without them.

Which is exactly why I kept Paige where she was in my life. It wasn't even hard to do with Paige because it wasn't like she was a good girl anyway. I peeped game the second I met her ass.

I mean, I could understand being in love with someone and caught up in your feelings because the shit didn't work out. Hell, I was at that point my damn self. But ain't no way in hot hell I would let the next man see me sweat! I'd walk barefoot through fire before I let Mia's husband see me sweatin' Mia in public. Shit, or anywhere else, for that matter. It's the main reason I'd basically cut her off clean. I can't say it actually helped the situation, but at least I wasn't out here looking bad.

Nicole sat stonily looking at me, her lips opening and shutting several times, as if she was deciding on exactly how to answer my question, or if she *should* answer me at all. Seconds later, she flooded my ears with the story of her and Kendrick, her low-down ex-boyfriend Don Travious, and Tierrany rising from the dead and coming to claim her man.

Honestly, listening to it all, I didn't think Tierrany had done anything to her. It was just as I'd stated. Kendrick made his choice, and it didn't end up being her. I will admit, it was a fucked-up situation, and she'd gotten the short end of the stick. I knew about that shit all too well, but I wasn't about to spill my guts to a stranger. Evidently she needed to. I didn't have anything better to do, so I listened.

"Why did you help me? I haven't been exactly nice to you, Jay. Why would you go out of your way to help me?" Nicole asked earnestly.

"Well, at the time, I didn't know exactly what it was I was helping you with. But I can say I've been there before, cheated on and humiliated. Feeling like a fool. You actually looked like you were about to lose your shit right then and there and start crying. I saw ol' boy when he walked through the door with his wife, so it wasn't too hard to piece it together. Now that I know all the details, I'm glad I could help a sista out in a tight spot," I answered with a smile. I meant it too. I mean, I was kinda fucked up toward women after the whole Mia situation, but deep down, I was a good dude.

"So I guess when I saw it happening to you, my own situation was fresh on my mind. It's his loss, by the way."

"Excuse me?"

"That guy Kendrick. If it makes you feel any better, I think he downgraded. You're better off without him," I said seriously. Kinda. I know damn well I was lying because the sista at the end of the bar with this Kendrick nigga was fine as frog's hair. But it just seemed like Nicole could use a little ego boost, so why not? I mean, it ain't like Nicole wasn't fine in her own right but didn't no woman want to hear that shit when her heart was hurting.

A wide, genuine smile spread across her face. Probably the first one all night.

I guess since I'd given her the green light, and more than likely due to the fact she didn't know me and we were at a bar drinking, Nicole proceeded to tell me the entire story in more detail, all of a sudden spilling the beans on her personal situation. Ms. Nicole gave me quite the earful. Despite all she knew she had going for her, the whole incident with Kendrick cheating (Nicole's words, not mine; it sounded to me like ol' boy cut her ass right off!) made her question her entire being. Nicole berated herself endlessly about what she should have done differently . . . She shouldn't have let her friend Meka talk her into pulling some pregnancy stunt or run into his house causing a scene. Maybe she should have given Kendrick time to really feel like he'd made a mistake leaving her. Instead, she acted a fool and made him glad he did leave. The list she'd drawn up in regards to what she could have/would have/and should have done was endless.

The entire time telling me this she was throwing back the drinks. Just tossing them back.

"Okay, Jay, so spill it! Tell me what happened to you. You just rescued me from complete humiliation. Now tell me something. Don't think I didn't hear you say you went through a recent breakup as well," Nicole said, smiling.

I couldn't believe this shit. I guess Nicole felt like she wanted to keep us on the same playing field. Sometimes I felt like a sucker for all the shit I'd put up with from Mia, but I was stuck between a rock and a hard place.

"So, um, Jay, I'm sure I can depend on you to give my girl Nicole a ride home, right? Thank you!" Cherell practically sang. Thank God, I thought rolling my eyes to the heavens. Cherell stood up quickly with Carlos right on her heels.

"Where are you going, Cherell?" Nicole asked, shocked. Even though Cherell had confessed to her bedroom issues with her man, Nicole couldn't believe she was going to actually take off with Carlos. She'd just met this man tonight!

"We're going somewhere where we can get to know each other a bit better. All this loud music is interfering with us getting to know each other," Carlos piped up and said, never once taking his eyes away from Cherell's DD-cup breasts.

Nicole and I looked at each other, both holding in our laughter.

"No problem. I'll see Nicole home. It was nice meeting you, my man," I said, slapping hands with Carlos.

"Are you sure, Jay? I don't want to impose. I could catch a cab," Nicole said, her eyes darting toward Cherell who was so caught up in Carlos she didn't notice her at all.

"Nonsense. I got you. Besides, I couldn't let my woman leave in a cab. What would the haters think?" I asked, slightly nodding my head toward the dance floor where Kendrick's wife was glaring at Nicole.

"What the hell is her problem? She's all up in your mix. You know what that is, right?" I said, laughing.

"No, what?"

"Well, you never know. Maybe they aren't living so happily ever after as you thought. You never know what goes on with people behind closed doors. For all you know, maybe that man is regretting not giving you a chance," I said.

Nicole scoffed. "I doubt it. I know it may have seemed like I was really running my mouth, but I left out a lot to the story. Those two are soul mates," Nicole said, standing and extending her hand to me.

Jeremiah

Nicole and I spent the next two hours dancing, laughing . . . and drinking. She said she hadn't had this much fun in so long, she wasn't ready for it to end. There was an awkward moment for me during the ride to her house when Mia's song "Slow Ride" came on. Nicole whooped loudly shouting "That's my sooong" and began gyrating in her seat, snapping her fingers. I turned that shit off so quick it wasn't even funny. Nicole just pouted and started talking about something else, thank God. I think she was too drunk to even notice. I mean, she wasn't sloppy drunk, but she'd had enough that she was feeling good.

"Jay, I want you to come in. I can, you know, make you some coffee for your ride home, and we can still talk," Nicole offered, turning to look at me. My mind was a bit skeptical on if I should take her up on the offer. For one thing, the flirting between us had begun about two hours ago.

I knew if I stepped inside this woman's home, there would be not a drop of coffee touching either one of our lips tonight. I, for one, don't even like that shit. By the time we arrived at her spot, she'd convinced me to come in.

Nicole inserted her key into the lock, and we both stepped inside her dark condo. We barely made it inside the front door and turned the lock before we were on each other. All that coffee and talking shit was out the window. Lips upon lips, tongues deliciously tangled and tasting each other.

"Jay, I'm so turned on right now I could lick you . . . everywhere, and I just might. Confession time. I've been thinking about what it would be like to fuck you for the last three hours. I mean, I know I don't owe you anything, but the way you just stepped in and helped me out of nowhere just turns me on. It makes me wonder even more what kind of man you are," Nicole said between kisses, her hands caressing the span of my muscular chest and dipping lower until they were at the top of my unmistakable bulge. "I want to find out all about you tonight, Jay," Nicole whispered huskily, running her hands over my thick hardness.

"Okay, we're both rational adults, so we need to be clearheaded for a minute. I'm a single guy.

When we get out of your bed and it's all said and done, this is all it is. I'ma still be single. Don't place no expectations on whatever goes down between us. If you want me tonight, and I damn sure want you, we're two adults that have needs we both want met, right?" I said. "So there's no judgment involved here at all, Nicole. I just want you to know that."

"I totally agree. I haven't asked you for anything. That was all nicely laid out, but I wasn't putting up any arguments about us being together, you know. I *want* this," Nicole said, leaning in for more of my sweet kisses.

My lips met hers, and I melted. Her kisses were perfect. We kissed for what seemed like an eternity. Our tongues intermingled and danced in intimate circles . . . sucking, licking, and biting until my lips were sore. My hands gently filtered down Nicole's chest. Her already-raised nipples were poking out through the fabric of her dress.

Things between us heated up quickly but a moment of doubt did cross my mind. Fuck it. There was no going back now. I quickly raised her dress above her hips and over her head, tossing it to the floor. I ain't gon' lie Nicole's body alone took my mind off any troubles I thought I had. Mia had more titties, but that

wasn't shit. Nicole's were just big enough to fill
the palms of my hands, and she had the prettiest
nipples. Why the fuck am I comparing her to
Mia any-damn-way?

*Decide now, nigga! This girl might be crazy.
You can already see she's still hung up on that
married man!* I thought again. I was getting
mad at my own damn self for not just going for
what I wanted and being done with the shit. It
wasn't like she was protesting, but here *I* was all
in my head.

*You're not a child. Do you want this or not?
I do. No doubt about it. I do!* Nicole's lips, the
very lips I'd watched her lick over the rim of
her glass at the club, took one of my nipples
into her mouth through my damn shirt! Nimbly
licking and tugging it until I felt like I was on
the verge an orgasm right on the spot. No pussy
needed. *Fuck it. I'm doing this.*

I wanted us to be skin to skin, so I started
unbuttoning my shirt and stepped out of my
jeans. Nicole stood there looking me over, then
proceeded to step out of her last remaining
piece of clothing, her panties. I climbed onto
her until I was straddling her. Easing my weight
on top of her, I ground myself into her pussy,
trailing kisses down her neck until I was tortur-

ing her nipples in the same manner she'd done mine. Nicole's nipples appeared to be a weak spot for her. I could see her visibly shaking with want as my hot tongue circled her nipples. I could feel the length of my erect dick rubbing against her pussy.

Nicole

"Do you have a condom with you, Jay? I don't have anything on me," I whispered huskily. Dammit, sex had been the last thing on my mind for so long I didn't have anything here in the house with me. I was losing the little bit of sense I still managed to hold on to. The last thing I wanted was a baby—or worse—from a man I didn't even know.

"It's not a problem; I have some," Jay said, reaching down to grab his jeans and pulling a condom out of his wallet.

"Goddamn, you're beautiful," Jay said. I got wetter just hearing him say that.

"I'm glad you like it," I said, smiling as I walked over to him. I took the condom from his hand and set it on my nightstand.

"I more than like what I see, Nicole."

"Sit down, Jay," I instructed, and he willingly complied.

I kneeled before him and took his thick dick in my hands, giving it a slow lick from the base to the wide, mushroom-tipped head of his dick. Besides his dick being hard as granite, the head of his dick was slick with the evidence of his excitement. I cleaned him up . . . with my hot, wet tongue, the salty taste of his essence turning me on even more.

"Shit, that feels good," Jay murmured, rubbing his hands through my hair until he had a gentle yet firm grasp of my hair and slowly gyrated his hips in time with my mouth. With the right dick . . . I love face fucking. Scratch that, I'd loved it with Kendrick, but he was the last person I should be thinking about. Especially right now.

"Lie on the bed," Jay said. "I just want to look at you for a minute."

"Sure," I said, easing myself onto my fluffy pillows at the head of my bed. "What can I do for you, Jay? Do you see anything you want?"

"Everything I'm looking at I want, Nicole. Spread your legs and touch yourself."

"I can do that as long as you know I like to watch too," I said with a sly smile.

Jay's eyes seemed to flash with desire. "Whatever makes you feel good tonight, Nicole. I'm willing to do it all."

Jay seemed to have said the magic words because before I knew it, my legs were parted like the Red Sea, and it was showtime! I spread my legs, bending my knees up to a comfortable open stance.

"Goddamn," I heard Jay rasp. Teasingly, I ran my fingertips over myself, then sank two fingers deep inside. I moaned at the sensation and slid down a little in the pillows, my hips thrusting forward as I slowly drew my fingers in and out before I placed them in my mouth and tasted myself.

"Would you like to taste it, Jay?" The words were barely out of my mouth before Jeremiah's face was planted between my thighs.

Jeremiah

Within minutes, Nicole had come in my mouth, and I positioned the large, mushroomed-tipped crown of my dick to her entrance and slowly eased inside Nicole's tight wetness. She moaned loudly as I slowly and gently penetrated her pussy. Damn, she was tight! I damn near screamed out loud myself, she felt so good. Inch by slow, delicious inch, I pushed inside her, slowly stretching her walls until I was balls deep, and she was panting, it felt so good.

"Oh shit, Jay! You feel wonderful!" Nicole cried out. Grasping her hips, I pulled out of her and pushed back in, shafting her slow and deep.

"I'ma make this pussy feel so good to you. You gon' ask me to keep coming back," I said confidently, knowing I was driving her crazy.

"Faster, Jay, please! You feel so good I can barely stand it," Nicole rasped. "Harder. Please. Now!"

I increased my pace, giving her exactly what she wanted. My dick slid easily in and out of her despite my size because she was so nice and slick.

Nicole moaned loudly, and I caught it in my mouth as my lips covered hers. Her hands grabbed my back tightly and ran down to my ass, gripping me tightly and pulling me into her. Our bodies were one. Pleasure coursed through every part of my being. Being inside of her was pure divine bliss. I'd fucked plenty in the last year, but this felt different to me, and I couldn't figure out why in the moment. I bent my head and took one of Nicole's breasts in my mouth, then reached up and played with her other breast, rolling her nipple between my thumb and index finger as my dick rhythmically eased in and out of her.

"God, Nicole . . . Your pussy feels so good. You gon' keep giving me this pussy? Don't let nobody else in this pussy but me," I demanded. Fuck it, as long as I was in town, this was gonna be mine. I placed my hand between her thighs from the front, found her clit, and stroked it while I pounded her pussy. "Answer me, Nicole!" I said, pumping into her, stroke for stroke, while Nicole bucked her hips into me meeting my dick stroke for stroke. "I want this pussy to be mine. Tell me it's mine, Nicole," I growled. Every single thrust of my dick rocked her swollen bud, bringing her orgasm closer and closer until it flooded over her.

Nicole's head flung back as it overtook her body, making her scream out, "Yes! Yes, this pussy is yours!" The muscles of her pussy pulsed and contracted around my thrusting dick. I continued stroking her clit, drawing a longer, more intense climax from her. Suddenly, I groaned low, and my dick jumped deep inside her, spilling my seed into the condom.

I collapsed on her, both of us breathing heavily. There were several moments of silence before I could think, let alone speak.

"I think Virginia might be okay," I gasped rolling over on my back and pulling Nicole with me. Her body was limp, and all I heard was the sound of her breathing deeply as she snuggled onto my chest.

"You good?"

"Uh-huh, I'm great," she moaned.

Jeremiah—Monday Morning

At 9:45 a.m. sharp, I strolled into the building.
My meeting with the current owners of Table 51
was at 10:00 a.m. sharp, but I was never "just on
time." In my book, if you were simply "on time,"
you were late. I checked in with the secretary
and was escorted into a large conference room.
Damn, these niggas just as diligent as me, I see.
Noticing the conference room was already filled.
I was a little taken aback to see ol' boy from last
night. The Kendrick dude that had that basket
case Nicole all in her damn feelings. I was still
pissed about the way she'd put me out of her
house only hours before.

When his eyes landed on me, I could see the
immediate recognition registered there as well.
He simply gave me a slight head nod, and I sat
down as we began to hash out the details of me
taking over the club.

I quickly found out that I'd been misinformed
about a few details, but they were of little con-

sequence. Kendrick and his partner Antonio, who was also in attendance, weren't in financial difficulty at all in regards to the club. They were simply more interested in real estate. To be exact, they were building subdivisions all over Virginia. Their accountant was there to answer any questions I had, and after going over all the paperwork with my lawyer and accountant via conference call, that included Dip, a deal that was satisfactory to all parties involved was made, and Table 51 officially belonged to Dip and me. Just as with Club Azure, Dip and I both had an equal stake in the club.

People started slowly dwindling out of the meeting since it was a done deal. I could hear Antonio saying he needed to leave to get back home to his wife who had apparently just had a baby from what I could gather. It left just Kendrick and me in the room. I always came early, but if I could help it, I was the last to leave. You never knew what shit was said during business when you decided to leave early, as if you had something more important to attend to than the business at hand.

"Say, man, why don't I take you out for an early lunch and a drink? We both got what we wanted out of the deal, and I couldn't be more pleased," Kendrick said.

"Sounds good to me. I'll follow you," I said, placing all the documents and contracts into my attaché case. Thirty minutes later, we were seated at a classy little spot on the beach. I'd barely taken a sip of my drink when Kendrick cut straight to the chase.

"So, you're dating Nicole, huh?"

I ain't gon' even lie. I was caught a little off guard. Not that it was any of his business what I was doing with her, but I didn't see the sense in lying to him, especially since the nigga knew I didn't even live here. He knew I was just in town to land this deal.

I lowered my head and laughed.

"Uh-huh, nigga, when I seen your ass walk through the door this morning, I knew y'all was on some bullshit last night," Kendrick said, joining me in laughter.

"Now, man, on some real shit, I just stepped in and helped her out because I could see her sweating bullets when you came and spoke to her. She looked like she was about to pass out," I said.

Kendrick shook his head silently before speaking. "So how is she doing?"

"I mean, based off what she said to me, she ain't doing good at all, my nigga. Why did you fuck that girl over like that? I know it's three sides to every story, but, damn, my nigga, you fucked her over."

This dude was rocking one of those beards a lot of these niggas was wearing these day and kept rubbing his hands over it like he was thinking on something hard. My nose was turned up. Shit, I like my shit nice and clean, I wasn't with all that damn facial hair. Some women loved it, though. I guess Nicole did too, at some point. Hell, based off her reaction to him this morning, she still did.

"You know what? In hindsight, I can see how it may look that way, but please believe me when I say it was never intentional. Not at all. I probably could have been straight up with Nicole and told her what all went down with Tierrany. Honestly, I thought things with us were over with. There was a lot of my own personal baggage to what went down with Tierrany. Fucked-up shit that I blamed myself for. Hell, I still blame myself for it even though Tierrany and I have moved on from it."

"Well, Nicole said you were hiding an old girl-friend that you never really ended things with."

Kendrick's eyes bucked. "Is that *all* Nicole said happened?"

"Yeah. Pretty much, she talked about some crazy ex she had that tried to rape her. How you helped her, but she basically kept calling your wife . . . and please don't be upset, a 'graveyard bitch' who came and stole her life." I said, taking a sip, never removing my eyes off his face. I was trying to discern exactly who was telling the truth in the situation. Like I said, there's always his side, her side, and the truth. Even in my own situation with Mia, I knew the truth was somewhere in the middle.

"Maaannn! That's not even how it was . . ." Kendrick groaned. He then proceeded to tell me *his* version of the events that went down. I must say the nigga was caught between a rock and a hard place, but what was he supposed to do? He gave me way more information than Nicole had, and I completely understood why he made the choice he did. By Kendrick's own admission, things between him and Nicole had been perfect, but at the end of the day, those few months didn't compare to what he and his now wife had been through. I could honestly say I would have made the same choice. You got your ride or die, who has been with you from the start and literally almost died because of you, and your shorty died before he was even born. Nah, his loyalty was always going to be with that woman.

"I mean, I know I ain't got no business even thinking about Nicole. Please believe me when I

say I'm happy and blessed with my wife Tierrany,
but sometimes my thoughts wander to Nicole.
I wish she understood that I really do want her
to be happy. I want that more than anything.
Sometimes when I think that I might be the
reason she's bitter and can't trust the next good
man that comes into her life, it gets to me. Shit,
that sorry nigga Don Travious was with her for
years dogging her out, but I'm the one she's
going to blame for breaking her heart and doing
the most damage after only a few months. Ain't
that some fucked-up shit? So, my man, what are
you out here doing? Yo' ass don't even live here.
Don't play with her like that," Kendrick said,
frowning at me.

I stuffed a piece of crab cake in my mouth
while I decided how I was going to respond to
his accusation. If I responded at all. I didn't owe
this nigga no explanations. I glanced up from my
plate, and the nigga was still staring me down.
I wanted to laugh out loud. *Look at this nigga
right here,* I thought, chewing hard. *You done
fucked the girl every which way I can probably
imagine; she's sucked your dick, and you done
ate her pussy. Now you wanna play that big
brother role? Nah, you can't be her brother now.*
I grabbed my napkin and wiped my mouth.

"I mean, we're cool. No more, no less. I'm here for a month, maybe longer, but truth be told, this morning might be the last time I lay eyes on her. Period," I replied nonchalantly.

"This morning? So that means you fucked her last night, then?"

"What I did or did not do with Nicole last night is my business . . ." I replied smugly, ". . . but on the strength that I can clearly see you care about her well-being, and Nicole is obviously still hung up on you, I'll say this. Nothing happened between us that she didn't want to happen. Now, this conversation between us, my man . . . is over . . ." I said, pointing my fork between us. "This is the weirdest conversation I've ever had in my fuckin' life," I added before we looked at each other and both started laughing.

"Okay, man, I feel you. I'm just trying to look out for her. So what's your plan on running this club? You're all the way in New York. Shit, I don't trust no one with my money that far away. I mean, the people working there are pretty solid. So, hopefully, you're keeping them around and not totally cleaning house. If you did, I can feel you on that as well. I just know I have a few single mothers there. I'd hate to see them without a job," Kendrick said before digging into the food he'd neglected on his plate while he was interrogating me.

"Yeah, I saw most of them in action. Tiny is real cool. She waited on me all weekend. I've actually been in town since Thursday evening. I made it my business to check the place out every night before I signed on the dotted line today. My partner Dip is probably going to fly out here once we do a grand reopening."

Kendrick laughed out loud before taking a bite of his steak. The table was silent as we both enjoyed our meal before he spoke again.

"So, you were checking us out for real, huh?"

"Nigga, you damn right! All the zeros on that money our bank transferred over today I had to. I been all on the club's social media pages, Instagram, Twitter, all of it. I must say, you do a good job of managing all of that."

"Man, that's my wife doing all that. She's too scary right now to leave the baby, but she wanted to keep busy doing something during the day while she's at home. So she took over all that instead of me paying someone to do it for me. I damn sure wasn't going to keep up that. I move in silence, so I don't even be on social media like that. Me or my partner Antonio."

The minute he said that, I knew he was on some undercover shit. This nigga had probably been slangin' dope all over Virginia and the surrounding areas. Nowadays, the feds were watching everything, especially social media. Half of these dumb niggas out here posted their every move, making the job of locking them up even easier for law enforcement. So when he said he wasn't really on there, I knew something was up. Kendrick was a smart man.

I wasn't mad at him. Ain't no telling where my life would be had Mia and I not left Texas. When I met her, I was already fresh out of jail and ending my probation. Then add on everything that was going on with her end. Back then, I would have robbed and killed for her ass. Not that I ever told her, but there were a few times I did steal for her once the money we'd taken with us started to dwindle down. I quickly shook those thoughts off because the one topic that could still put me in a bad mood was Mia.

Nicole

Dammit! I thought, pulling into my parking space at work. I was frazzled as hell and out of sorts. It had been a long time since I'd been with a man who made my body feel this good. Kendrick, to be exact. I'd convinced myself no other man could make me feel that exquisite again. Jay had definitely proved me wrong. My spine was still tingling, and my pussy was throbbing at the thought of Jay.

I walked into my office, quickly shutting the door behind me. I was a nervous wreck. I hadn't been able to concentrate all day. Instead, I'd opted to throw videos in for the trainees all day long. Get it together, bitch! You had a one-night . . . or rather a two-night stand. It's over with. Move the hell on, I told myself. I'd been giving myself a pep talk the entire morning, and it hadn't helped at all. I couldn't get my mind off Jay. Every time I sat down, I found myself crossing and uncrossing my legs, trying to quell my growing desire for a man I didn't even know. What in the world was I doing letting that man fuck me like that?

Now that my year of celibacy had been shot to hell, I couldn't stop thinking about it. I glanced down at my breasts. My nipples were hard and pebbled. What in the entire fuck? I grabbed my cell phone and sent Cherell a text to come into my office so we could talk. Ten minutes later, there was a knock, and Cherell was waltzing through the door.

"This damn sure better be good because I was about to call Carlos and see if he wanted to hook up later on tonight," Cherell said, smoothing down her black pencil skirt.

"Are you still talking to that man?" I asked incredulously.

"You damn right!"

"You better be careful. Have you at least broken things off with Travis yet?"

Cherell cut her eyes at me and began playing with her nails. "Look, Travis has tickets to the Black and White Ball at the end of the month. All expenses paid, so I'm waiting until then, girl. You know I've been looking forward to that all year."

"Well, why don't you just break up with Travis and go with Carlos? Don't dog Travis out like this, Cherell. Come on now, you're better than that. What goes around does come around eventually," I said, cutting my eyes at her. I needed someone to vent to, but suddenly, I didn't know if I wanted Cherell to be that someone. Ever since the whole situation with Kendrick, I just couldn't stand any talk of deceit and infidelities. I wished I was surrounded by friends that I felt had the same moral compass as myself.

Granted, I knew no one was perfect, but, damn! Cheating was not a game, and people got hurt. Many of my friends at the time, Tondellya and Meka, mainly, felt like Kendrick didn't actually cheat on me. They thought I should have appreciated the fact he was honest with me the second Tierrany came back around and ended things with me, but fuck that. A lie by omission is still a lie. All the information he neglected to tell me so that I could decide if I wanted to hitch my wagon to his ass had been conveniently *not* told to me.

I'm honest enough with myself right now to know that had he told me, I still would have proceeded with dating him, but the decision still should have been mine to make.

"So, girl, what's going on? You got me down here, so spill it," Cherell said, sitting down in the chair in front of my desk and crossing her legs.

I cleared my throat, still trying to decide if I wanted to speak to her about Jay.

Fuck it.

"So, remember the guy who took me home from Table 51 on Friday?"

"Yaass, bitch! That brother was fine as hell. Did you give him some?" Cherell asked eagerly, leaning forward, awaiting my response.

My lips turned down immediately. Look at Cherell, wanting me to be a ho just like her ass! I ran my hands nervously through my hair.

"Well, we kinda ended up spending the rest of the weekend together."

"Why are you looking so crazy right now? Was the sex bad? Ugh! I hate when that happens—"

"No, the sex was amazing. It was so good. I have a hard time believing it felt as good as it did," I stammered.

"Huh? Girl, if you don't get off this virginal bullshit you be on, I swear to God, sometimes you sound crazy as hell. Why the sex can't be good?"

"Because I don't love him! I just met him that night . . ." I stuttered.

"And your point is what? Hell, that's basically how shit happened with you and Kendrick, and you swore to the gods that was true love."

I felt like Cherell had punched me in the gut.

"That's a low blow, Cherell. You know how I feel about Kendrick."

Cherell sighed loudly, looking me directly in the eye. "Actually, it's not, Nicole. It's the damn truth. Look, I'm not one of those 'friends' that's going to sugarcoat shit for you. Good sex doesn't equate to love, and being in love with someone damn sure doesn't mean the sex is going to be good. Trust me . . . I fuck with Travis's none fuckin' ass, and on paper, he's perfect. Sometimes it is what it fuckin' is. Period. Now, the question of the day is this . . . Do you wanna fuck his ass again?"

My pussy clenched at the mere question. Lord have mercy on me!

"I, I, umm—"

"I'll take that as a yes since you're sitting there stuttering and shit," Cherell snickered. "Call him up!"

"I can't. I put him out this morning and didn't even get his phone number. I was rude to him."

"Why?"

"Because! Why go through the motions when I slept with him on the first night? He is not going to take me serious now. I gave up all the goods, Cherell. So, instead of me sitting by the phone waiting on him to call me, I just thought it best to take charge and put him out before it even got to that," I said meekly. My whole argument for my bad behavior toward Jay this morning sounded weak to my own ears now.

What the hell had I been thinking?

"Besides, I think the only reason I slept with him at all was because I'd run into Kendrick that night. Cherell, how can just seeing that man even after all this time leave me feeling so messed up? It's like I see other women in relationships and being loved, and I feel like . . . Why can't I have that? Why is it taking me so long to get it right?" I asked, slumping back in my chair with a heavy heart.

I really hadn't intended on revealing that last part. Those were some of the thoughts that ran through my head on a daily basis. I didn't actually verbalize them because then, I really felt like a jealous-hearted loser . . . hating on the next woman for finding love and happiness. But I did wonder. I was educated, attractive, and had been told by both Don Travious and Kendrick what a good woman I was. But I still wasn't enough to keep them. To have their undivided love and attention. I wasn't enough.

"Nicole, why are you so hard on yourself? I seriously don't get it. From everything you've told me, you've had two relationships. You make it sound like you've had twenty boyfriends, and none of them were happy with you. I realize you may have had your hopes pinned on those two, but, baby, believe me when I say, you're being way too hard on yourself. Don Travious sounds like he was a clown-ass nigga. Be glad that didn't work out. As far as Kendrick, would you rather years went by? Be glad it was just a few months and move on from that." Cherell reached across my desk and handed me a Kleenex. I hadn't even realized tears were streaming down my face.

"Thank you . . ." I said, grabbing the tissue and dabbing my face. "I know you're right, Cherell. I think it's just the back-to-back disappointment. You know I messed with that white man right after Kendrick, thinking it was just black men were dogs, right? Girl, he was a dog too."

"Here's another suggestion. How about just doing you? Now your ass acting all tender and shit, but you need to just do you for a while. Date! Why the rush to make every man your husband?"

"Because I *want* to be married! I'm not going to lie about that to anyone. I come from a married household. My parents are still in love. I want to be married when I have children. It's what I want, and I'm not going to settle for anything less than that."

"I get it, boo. That doesn't mean every man you sleep with or date is the one! That's where you're fucking up at. In the end, the only one hurt is you because you've set these men up to be your everything, and they don't end up being shit. Take your time. I know you may think I'm this wild child out here fucking out both legs of my panties but don't get it twisted. My parents have been married for thirty years, and I want the same things you do.

"Now, I may be doing Travis a little dirty, but I'm not totally happy with him. I'ma end it, but do you really think I'm going to settle for thirty years of bad sex just because he has other things going for him? No way. I'm dipping my toes in the water to see what else is out here! Don't think these niggas ain't out here doing the same. Hell, I have no idea what Travis is doing when he's not with me."

Cherell had a point. I was going to think about everything she'd said, because I had to admit she had some very valid points.

"Okay, girl, let me get back to this class."

"Uh-huh, so are we going back to Table 51 to find this Jay nigga or what?" Cherell asked coyly, playing with her nails.

I bit my lip in concentration. "Do you think I should? Maybe I should just let it go. The sex was off the chain, but that man probably won't even look my way after how I acted up."

"Did he lay that dick on you good, though?"

I nodded my head vigorously.

"Then we're going back, bitch. Be ready after work on Friday."

Jeremiah—Friday

The week had been hectic as hell. Once we'd finalized the paperwork on Monday, I jumped into the club business headfirst. I'd been buried in paperwork for days going over every aspect of Table 51, checking the accounts with all the vendors and getting everything moved out of the previous owners' name. I'd also held a brief staff meeting with all of the employees. I wasn't too sure how that went exactly. The majority of the employees seemed to be shocked the place had been sold, and, of course, everyone was worried about their jobs. I did my best to alleviate their concerns and let them know that as long as they continued to be stellar employees, their jobs wouldn't be effected.

There were a million things to do, but it quickly became apparent to me that I may need to be here a bit longer than anticipated. I'd already spoken to a realtor about finding me a permanent spot. It just made more sense than renting a room. Even after the club was running smoothly and I was ready to go back to New York, I anticipated flying down here several times a month so it would be a good investment. There was a loud knock at my office door.

"Come in," I called out, easing my head up from the computer screen.

Tiny entered my office hesitantly.

"Hey, Tiny, what's going on?" I asked.

"Not too much. I just hadn't had the opportunity to really welcome you to Table 51 since finding out who you really are."

Oddly enough, I detected a slight attitude in her voice. I couldn't fathom why.

"Do you have an issue you need to discuss with me, Tiny?" I asked, leaning back in my chair and meeting her eyes.

"Well, I mean, why didn't you just say who you were last Friday when you first came in?" she asked.

"Tiny, all you needed to know was that I was a paying customer and to do your job. You did your job, and you did it well. That should be evident by the tip I left you, right? Anything else is irrelevant."

"You're right. I don't mean to sound ungrateful . . ."

"Well, you are."

"I'm sorry, Jay, or would you prefer Jeremiah?"

"Either. Tiny, do you know how to bartend?"

Tiny's whole demeanor brightened. "Actually, I tend bar. I tried to get in here, but there weren't any positions open."

"Well, we'll be opening up a new bar downstairs, so I'll talk to the manager today about you shadowing Javier and changing your position. We'll discuss it more in-depth later. Was there anything else you needed?"

Tiny was grinning from ear to ear. My girl needed to get that chipped tooth fixed fast. It was fuckin' up her whole look.

"Thank you so much, Jeremiah. Welcome to Table 51."

"Thank you," I said, smiling to myself as she scrambled from the chair and out of my office. My cell phone rang, and I saw it was Paige's worrisome ass.

"Whassup?"

"Hey, babe! How's it going?"

I stifled a sigh and proceeded to chat with her a little. There was no need for me to be an asshole to her, but being off the grid away from her and not taking her calls as much had definitely given me some much-needed clarity. I didn't even miss Paige's conversation—let alone anything else.

"So, Jeremiah, I was thinking, how about I come down there and visit you? I mean, you're down there by yourself, and my pussy is missing you something terrible. I know you needing some about now too."

"Oh, I'm straight," I answered smoothly.

There was complete silence on the other end of the line.

"So, what does that mean? You're straight."

"It means I don't go without things I need and want, including sex. Neither should you. If you wanna fuck, fuck."

"You haven't even been gone a week, and you slept with someone down there?" Paige screeched. I had to hold the phone away from my ear.

"I can't believe you would do something like this to me. After all this time, Jeremiah?" Paige asked, openly sobbing.

"Paige, how many times do I have to tell you, I'm not ya man?"

"Because you won't let yourself love me! I'm sorry my name isn't Mia—"

I promptly hung up on her dumb ass. Why the fuck would she bring Mia's name into the conversation? If she didn't have a chance before, she damn sure didn't now saying some shit like that to me. I flipped on the TV in my office, and my heart sank. There was Mia, live and direct on the screen being interviewed on *Entertainment Tonight*. I immediately switched that shit off. Let me get some damn food. This ho gon' bring up Mia's name now; watch all things Mia start popping up all over the damn place, I thought frowning.

Nicole

Friday was here in the blink of an eye, and I was nervous as hell. Cherell had already let me know Carlos, the guy she'd met last Friday, was going to meet her at Table 51 later on, so I made the decision to just drive myself. Hell, I didn't want to end up in anyone else's bed tonight just because I needed a ride home. I fidgeted in front of the mirror trying to decide on what to wear. I was showered, and my makeup and hair were done. I wanted to look cute but not overdone, like I was "trying." Shoot, I didn't know if Jay would even be there tonight, which was yet another reason my stomach was in knots.

Maybe my time with him was supposed to be just what it was. A brief encounter in my life. I sat on the edge of my bed placing my head in my hands. I should just stay my ass home, watch some Netflix, order some Chinese food, and relax. Yep, that's exactly what I'm going to do. I sent a quick text to Cherell and decided to lie down for a nap. All the pent-up anxiety inside me began to dissipate. *Cherell was right about one thing,* I thought, smiling to myself, *I need time to myself.*

Cherell

Unlike my girl Nicole, I did not mind making moves alone. I actually preferred it. I could do whatever the hell I wanted to do without a set of judgmental eyes clocking my every move. So I walked into Table 51 feeling good. Carlos was supposed to meet me here later on. I had invited him to meet up two hours after Nicole and I arrived to give us a little girl time beforehand, but when Nicole canceled, I kept my plans as is. It would give me time to scope out the place on my own and see who was in here tonight. Shoot, it might be someone cuter than Carlos up in here. Besides, Carlos was just someone I'd met. Please believe me when I say I take my own advice.

We kicked it the other night, but that didn't mean shit to me. Plus, I was still dealing with Travis for the time being anyway. I think Travis was picking up on the fact I wasn't happy. Now he was talking this marriage shit real heavy.

Dang! This is really the place to be, I thought, making my way around the club. Let me just find a small table near the dance floor and mind my own business.

I wasn't sitting five minutes before I spotted that fine-ass Jay that had Nicole tripping. From what I could tell, he was by himself. *This ho acting like she don't even know how to deal with a man! Her ass is lucky I don't run behind my friends' men,* I thought looking the brother over from head to toe.

Oooh, this bitch better be glad! This man know his ass is fine. Chocolate skin tone, nice and tall. Jay's hair looked freshly lined up, and he was grinning at someone behind the bar. I could see his set of pearly white teeth from across the room. That blazer was sitting just right across his broad shoulders. Hell, if his ass had smiled at me like that, I would have gave him the pussy on sight too. I knew I was having some terrible thoughts, but I was a sucker for a fine man, and that damn sure described Jay. Let me get my eyes off him and see who's in here I can actually have! A few minutes later, a waitress was at my table. I decided to take it easy tonight and just sip a glass of red wine for the time being.

"Hello, Cherell, how are you this evening?"

I glanced up to find none other than Jay gazing down at me.

"Hey, yourself, Jay. How are you doing? I see you're enjoying Table 51 as much as I am. Is this going to be your Friday night spot?" I asked.

"Do you mind if I sit?"

"Of course not," I said, waving him down to the seat.

Jay sat next to me overlooking the dance floor.

"Well, I guess this will be my new spot. I just bought the place. Well, my partner and I, that is," Jay said, rubbing his hand over his head. "So, you're going to find me in here basically every night for quite some time."

I almost choked on my spit. Not only was the nigga fine, he was paid too! Aww, hell! I may have to rethink my no-fucking-after-friends' policy. Nicole don't know what to do with all this man anyway.

"So, what's your honest opinion of the place? Tell me what you like and dislike about Table 51. I'd love to have your input," Jay asked.

For the next thirty minutes, we talked about his new club. It was a fun conversation, and I could tell from the way he relayed his vision to me that this was soon going to be one of the top spots in Richmond.

"Now, let me ask you something, Jay . . ." I said, cutting my eyes at him as I took a light sip of my wine, ". . . We're not going to address the elephant in the room?"

"Umm, as long as that elephant ain't named Nicole, we can address anything you like," Jay answered indignantly.

I burst out laughing.

"Well, it is, brotha man! Look, I know my friend can act crazy as all outdoors but give her a chance. She told me what went down with y'all and how she cut up, but please don't take it to heart and judge her for it. Give her a chance. Nicole was actually supposed to meet me here tonight. She wanted to see if you would come in tonight so y'all could talk, but I think her crazy self is too embarrassed about how she acted with you." I was hoping his impression of Nicole wasn't too bad because after talking to him, Jay really did seem to be a nice guy. I knew damn well I wasn't breaking girl code and trying to holla at his ass, so if they could make up, why not?

I just hoped like hell Nicole got out of this phase where she was judging everyone against Kendrick's ass. I'd seen him, and unless the nigga had some sparkling personality, I couldn't fathom what the big fucking deal was. Hell, in my eyes, Kendrick and Jay were neck and neck in the looks department.

"Give me her address and phone number," Jay said, pulling out his cell.

"For what? Oh, don't you worry, I'm bringing Nicole in here tomorrow," I said firmly.

"Okay. But I wanna holla at her tonight," Jay stated looking me dead in my face.

"Didn't you go home with her? You should already know where she lives."

Jay cut his eyes at me. "I didn't know where the hell I was going when I drove to that mutha-fucka! Nicole told me how to get there every step of the way. And I damn sure wasn't paying attention when she put me out. I barely made it out of that fucked-up subdivision, and the damn GPS on my rental was fucked up too! I had to turn that damn thing in for another one. So you gon' give me this girl's address or nah?" Jay asked impatiently. I hurried up and rattled it off to him. The last thing I wanted to do was piss off my new friend, and I just found out he was the owner of my new favorite club. Nicole could be on the outs if *she* wanted to, but I planned on being in the inner circle.

Okay, nigga! Shoot, I loved a take-charge man! I just hope Nicole has the same appreci-ation for them because I damn sure gave up all

her information. I thought about giving her a
heads-up but decided against it. That was part of
Nicole's problem anyway. Always thinking she
could control the situation and outcome. Nope,
let's see if Jay can show her something different.

"Okay, I see you, Cherell, so you and ol' boy
kept in contact since last week, I see," Jay said,
nodding his head in the direction of the club's
entrance.

Carlos was walking toward me grinning widely.
"You could say that," I said, suddenly shy. I
didn't have nearly enough drinks in my system
as the night I'd met him. When I have a few
shots, I'm fearless. Now I was squirming in my
seat like a schoolgirl. We'd talked on the phone
every day since that night. Sometimes more
than once.

"All right, I'm out. It was nice running into you
and don't be a stranger. You're one of the few
people I know in town. Matter of fact, let me get
your number too," Jay said.

I quickly rattled it off just as Carlos arrived at
the table. He and Jay exchanged a few words and
numbers. I swallowed my nerves and began my
evening with Carlos. My phone beeped several
times, but after checking and seeing it was just
Travis, I turned it off. I didn't want any distrac-
tions.

Nicole

I was busy stuffing Häagen-Dazs Rum Raisin ice cream down my throat, and I didn't feel any better. I hadn't even ordered my Chinese food yet, but I'd gotten hungry. Bitch, you should have just taken your ass on out. I'd tossed and turned so bad trying to take a nap I just gave up and started flipping channels. I reached for my cell phone and called my mama.

"Hey, baby, are you still coming to dinner on Sunday?" Mama asked upon picking up the phone. My mama never felt the need for pleasantries; she just got straight to the point.

"You know I am. Mama, can I ask you something?"

"All in my business, I see! Whatchu wanna know? Ooh, Nicole! I know God don't like ugly or gossip but let me tell you something first! Chile, why I run into that damn boy you used to go with, Don Travious! If he ain't the most pitiful sight I've seen in ages I don't know who is! If that boy don't have his doctor get himself some of that Magic Johnson medication quick, fast, and in a damn hurry! . . . Lord Jesus, I feel bad for his poor grandmother. Umph!"

Suddenly, my mama's voice lowered an octave.

"Now, baby, you're sure all your tests came back negative? I mean, you were living with that boy and all."

"I'm positive, Mama—"

"Positive!" Mama yelped through the phone.

"Oh Lord, Mama, I mean I'm *certain* I'm safe! Don Travious knows exactly who he got HIV from, and we were over and done when it happened."

"Okay, baby, you know I had to check. So whatchu wanna know and hurry up asking me questions. Me and your daddy have a meeting to go to," she stated, now sounding impatient with me. Two minutes before, she was scared for my life.

I glanced at the clock.

"What kinda meeting you and Daddy have to attend at ten at night?" I asked, dumbfounded. My parents rarely went out at night, so this came as a surprise to me.

Mama sucked her teeth loudly and cleared her throat. "Now, dammit, Nicole, yo' daddy and I have a meeting in the *bedroom!* You're a grown woman now. I shouldn't have to explain these things to you!"

My eyes bucked. What in the hell?

"Okay, gon' head to your meeting, then. We'll talk on Sunday. I love you. Bye."

"Bye, baby."

I ended our call and couldn't help but chuckle to myself. My parents were about the only couple I wasn't jealous of at this point. My cell phone suddenly rang, but I didn't recognize the number.

"Hello?" I answered hesitantly.

"Come outside and talk to me."

What in the world? The man sounded sexy as hell, but who the fuck was this playing on my damn phone?

"Who is this? I'd appreciate it if you would stop playing on my damn phone." Shit, I didn't have time for this mess. My day had been rough enough.

"Maaan, if you don't bring your mean ass outside . . . Come to the damn window," the voice said. I could hear his voice break as he started to laugh. Meanwhile, I set my melting ice cream on the kitchen counter and slowly crept over to my living-room window and peeked outside. It was already dark outside, but the streetlight illuminated Jay's face. Oh my God! What is *he* doing here?

"Umm, okay. I'll be right out," I said nervously.

"And don't have me out here waiting forever while you in there trying to get cute either. I've already seen you in every position," Jay said before hanging up on me.

Now, he didn't have to say *all* that. Damn! Lord, I ain't never let no man see me walking around in my head rag! Not even Don Travious, and we lived together. Once I'd decided to stay home, I'd scrubbed my face clean, wrapped my hair back up, and tied it down for the night. I peeked through the blinds again. Jay was leaning against his car looking at his cell phone. I took a deep sigh, shoved my feet into a pair of black flip-flops at the door, and walked out. I walked timidly down my front steps racking my brain with every step on how I should apologize for the way I'd acted toward him.

Jay glanced up at me and laughed in my face as he shoved his cell phone in his back pocket. Ugh! I could feel my cheeks heat with embarrassment.

"You said come right out! Now you're making fun of me?" I spat, folding my arms across my chest.

"Learn to take a fuckin' joke. And uncross your goddamn arms. I didn't come over here for all this attitude."

"Well, what *did* you come for? I damn sure didn't invite you." *Now, take that, asshole.* The second my mind processed what I'd just said I regretted it. Especially given the thoughtful way Jay was looking at me. He was staring at me like something had just clicked with him and that he was seeing me for the first time.

My mind was screaming for me to apologize immediately and make it right, but the words wouldn't come out.

"You know what, ma? I'ma go ahead and let you make it because it's clear to me, not having that man's love has turned you into a bitter bitch. And if I'm completely honest, I'm a bitter nigga my damn self. So, yeah, you're right. I don't have any business being here. As it stands, the simple fact that when I was fuckin' your angry ass Monday morning and you called me that nigga's name should have been enough for me to never wanna lay eyes on you again."

I groaned inside.

I could feel the tips of my ears heat with embarrassment. Yep, that's what I'd done Monday morning. Jay and I were having one last round of sex before he left for a meeting he had to attend, and I got caught up. He had me feeling so damn good, and I have to admit, in that moment, I wished it was Kendrick who was making me feel this way. Memories of mornings I'd spent just like that with Kendrick flooded my mind. Just as my orgasm hit, I moaned Kendrick's name. Loud. My eyes had flown open, but I quickly squeezed them shut, praying that I hadn't said it out loud. I had. Then an argument between us quickly ensued, and I just decided to cover it up by being mean and combative. After all, what other choice did I have?

Bitter bitch? Me? Was I?

I wanted to jump on him and scratch his eyes out. I looked around my yard for something to throw at his retreating SUV. Just that quick, he was gone. I'd run him off for the second time in week. I ran back into my house and picked up my cell phone and redialed his number. I called five times back-to-back and was sent to voice mail each time.

Jeremiah

By the time I went through the drive-thru at Popeye's Chicken and made it back to my suite I'd dodged fifteen phone calls from this crazy-ass Nicole. What the fuck did she keep calling me for? I placed my food on the table and jumped in the shower to wash the club off of me. I'd gotten out of there before it got really packed, but I'd also been there all day too. There was still a lot of work to be done. At the club back in New York, it was so well staffed, Dip and I usually strolled in about seven or eight at night and just stayed until closing. Now, being that I wanted my eyes on everything, I was damn near there from open to close all week. I planned on speaking to Dip about flying one of our managers out here to help with the relaunch of the club.

I must have been out of my fuckin' mind taking my ass over there. The pussy wasn't that good! *Nigga, stop lying; yes, it was,* I said to myself, laughing. I walked out of the bathroom drying my body off, rubbed myself down because I hated to be ashy, and slipped on some boxers. I sat down to eat, and my phone started buzzing again.

This girl is crazy.

"Please stop calling this muthafuckin' phone. Trust me when I say I won't be calling you or showing up at your house invited, or not, ever again. Why the fuck do you keep calling me?" I spat. Enough was enough.

"Jeremiah?"

I felt a painful clenching in the pit of my stomach, a dull ache of want I was pretty sure would never leave me at the recognition of Mia's voice.

"Hey, whassup?"

"Not too much. I'm home off tour finally and stopped in the club. Dip said you were out of town. How have you been?"

Now, what the hell was she doing at the club? Mia and I had an unspoken rule of sorts. Granted, it was implemented by myself, but I expected it to be adhered too. Mainly, stay out of my way. After all this time, Mia was under this impression that once things cooled down, we could morph into best of friends. I'd be like family. Basically, she wanted it all, and I just couldn't do it. Mia and I had never been "just friends." We skipped a few steps along the way, and I went straight into loving her and being her man. I took on responsibilities that weren't even mine, but I did it willingly because it benefited her.

"I'm good, Mia. How's Jacobi?"

"He's good. Growing up fast, and he still asks about you. His birthday is coming up—"

"I know exactly when his birthday is, Mia. Or did you forget I was the nigga cutting the cord the day he was born?"

"Of course I haven't forgotten, Jeremiah. Why the hell do you think I take so much shit off of you? It's because I know everything you've done for me. And I know I hurt you," Mia said, her voice thick with emotion.

"Look, why are you calling me? Don't you have a husband to tend to? How is married life?"

I don't know what made me ask the latter question. I damn sure didn't want to hear how happily married she was to Quinton.

"Well, I came by the club because Dip contacted me. He said you two just acquired a new club in Virginia and wanted to know if I'd be willing to perform there during your grand reopening. Which, I, of course, agreed to do. It's a shame he's the one who has to call and ask me these types of things. Jeremiah, you know damn well I'll do anything I can to put you in a better position. You're the reason my career is where it is today. And, yes, I do have a husband to tend to, and married life is different. Quinton is a lot to handle. Always has been, but when you're with the person you feel was created just for you, regardless of the circumstances, it's worth it."

"Created for you, huh? So I was just sloppy seconds for three years and didn't even know it. You were content to just lead me on for how long? Because had you never took your ass back to Texas to handle—you know what? You didn't take your ass back to handle any music business. You went there for him."

"No, I didn't, Jeremiah! You know why—"

"Mia, run that bullshit story by someone who might actually believe your ass. You went to Texas to handle unfinished business between you and that nigga. Period."

Damn, this shit felt like it was fresh. I gave this woman all of me, and she didn't give a fuck.

"Look, instead of us reopening old wounds—"

"Whatever, Mia. I have wounds. *I'm* the one whose heart got stomped on. You hooked back up with the love of your life and got married. Look, obviously, Dip wants you at the club opening, so if you're willing to do it, fine by me. I gotta go." I ended the call before Mia could say another word.

I couldn't stand people who acted like when they did something to you, you should just suck it up and get over it. I didn't operate that way. If Mia didn't know how to approach me in the manner that I needed to be approached in order to let shit go, then she needed to stop all her little weak, feeble attempts. Period. Wasn't no forgiving going on over this way.

I ain't gon' lie. I did require a small amount of groveling. A little begging and pleading wouldn't hurt either. The main thing I wanted her to do was acknowledge fully what the fuck she'd done to me. The lies she'd told me. Mia never was straight up with me about the relationship she'd carried on with Quinton under her mother's roof, and that I couldn't get past. All the fuckin' lies.

Sometimes, I even asked myself had she been upfront with me, would I have made the same decision and left with her. Hell, no, I wouldn't have. Ain't no damn way I would have involved myself with her, and she was lying up in the same house with a nigga she was fuckin'. All my choices were taken away from me in the matter.

The phone call almost made me lose my appetite . . . almost. I grabbed my food up and walked it over to the microwave, zapped it for a minute or so, and dug in. I was hungry as hell. My phone dinged, alerting me of a text message.

I rubbed my hands on a napkin. My eyes rolled back in my head when I saw it was from Nicole. What is it with this woman? I turned my phone completely off, finished eating, and took my black ass to sleep.

Nicole

"You did *what?*" Cherell seethed over her cup of coffee. It was just after 9:30 a.m., and I'd shown up on her doorstep with coffee and donuts in an attempt to gloss over the fact I'd brought my ass over uninvited at an ungodly hour on a Saturday morning. I couldn't stop myself. I had to vent to someone, and I'd nominated her for the job . . . regardless of whether she wanted it.

"I don't know what kind of ignorant-ass shit you're into, but if this is the way you acted during your relationship with Kendrick, you made it easy for him to go back to his ride or die. I need to ask Meka about your crazy ass!"

"Shut up, Cherell! He provokes me to talk crazy to him. I think he intentionally pushes my buttons," I whined. My hand was shaking like a leaf as I raised my mug to my lips. For some reason, Jay had taken me to the deep end last night. I felt crazed, just like I did when Kendrick first broke things off with me.

Cherell groaned loudly. "Exactly how many times did your stalking ass call him again?" she asked, reaching across her dining table to inspect the box of donuts I'd brought with me.

"About ten . . . maybe fifteen. Umm, and a few text messages," I mumbled low, my eyes downcast in embarrassment. It hit me then just how bat-shit crazy I sounded.

"Bitch, I don't know what to tell you! You're on your own from here on out! I did my best. I put you in a good position last night when I ran into him and we spoke. Played down your crazy ass to the point the man asked me for your number and address. I considered giving you a heads-up that he was coming, but I thought it was cute he wanted to surprise you. That brotha wasn't there five minutes, and you ran him off again? What is *wrong* with you, Nicole? For real. What's really going on?"

The perplexed look on Cherell's face let me know she'd set all games and snarkiness aside. She was really looking at me as if I had some mental problems. Sadly enough, I was wondering the same at this point. I'd excused my own behavior during the breakup with Kendrick as me being in love and just doing crazy things just because I was heartbroken and justifiably so (in my mind). But my rational mind knew that hearts were broken every day, every hour, and in that respect, I wasn't special. Most women weren't self-medicating with Xanax pills just to get through the day. Women who only dated a man a few short months weren't grieving as if they'd had a ten-year marriage with children involved. I should have been able to pop back from this rather quickly, and the hard fact is, I wasn't.

My hand raised to my face to quickly swipe away the tears slowly spilling down my cheeks as I shook my head.

"I don't know, Cherell. I don't want to be like this. I swear I don't. It's just when it comes to men, I don't have any confidence. I don't trust my heart or my head because I keep getting it wrong each and every time, and I don't know why. Three men and three mistakes in a row . . ." My voice broke. What was wrong with me? Was I *that* hard to love?

"Hold up. Are you counting Jay in those three mistakes?"

"Yes!"

"Hmm. Well, you can regret sleeping with him if you want too, but who is to blame for that? Quite honestly, I'm pretty sure *you* initiated that situation because you ran into Kendrick. *He's* the one who was used, regardless of whether he knows it." Cherell cut her eyes at me and took a bite out of her donut.

A flash of anger burned in my chest.

"Cherell, when the hell did you get to be so judgmental? I mean, it's not like your love life is the best. You're out here with a faithful man and cheating on him every chance you get with men you meet at bars . . ." I spewed. I think I was so mad because it was true. I hadn't even told her about me calling Jay by Kendrick's name, but it was as if she knew.

"*Excuse* me, bitch? That may be so, but you ain't heard me complain about shit but a limp dick. And even with that situation, I was unhappy with it, so I found a hard one to take its place. You don't see me walking around sulking about the shit! I also ain't the one lying in bed crying every day and popping pills to get over a nigga that plain and simple just didn't want me."

My eyes widened in shock. I never thought Cherell would be so cruel as to throw up what I'd told her in confidence.

Cherell picked up her cup of coffee and took a sip, peering at me through narrowed eyes.

I wanted to slap her face.

"Don't come for me unless I send for you. Friend or not. Especially when all I'm doing is trying to help your ass. Also, if you're trying to throw shade and call me a ho, you must be one too because I do believe you was fuckin' Jay at the same time I was lying up with Carlos. Also, let's not forget. Didn't you screw Kendrick the same night you met him? Like I said, don't come for me. Because while you were telling me all about this 'love story' you had with Kendrick the first day you met him, all my ears heard was you fucked the nigga on the first night. Maybe had you been as discerning as you like to think you are, your fragile ass wouldn't be sitting in my face this early in the damn morning."

My mouth snapped shut. She was right, even though I didn't want to acknowledge it.

"Let me ask you something and don't laugh, Cherell. Do you think I should maybe go talk to someone? A therapist, maybe?" I asked.

"If that's what you feel you need to do. I see my therapist every Friday. Faithfully."

"What?" I practically shouted. I was floored. Cherell walked a bit on the wild side, but she was one of the most "together" women I knew. Which was the main reason I'd naturally gravitated toward her upon the demise of my childhood friendships. Remaining friends with Tondellya was an absolute no for me. There were things I still couldn't reconcile within myself with her. Besides, Tondellya was now married to

Kendrick's best friend, Antonio. Being in any proximity with them would totally drive me insane. I hated that I hadn't been there when she had her first child. The truth of the matter is, my own misery wouldn't allow me to rejoice in her happiness. I hated myself for that every day.

Meka had a child now, so her life had calmed down slightly. With her new motherhood duties and baby-daddy drama, Meka's time wasn't as free as it used to be, which I understood.

"Why are you seeing a therapist, Cherell? You could have vented to me for free," I asked, shocked.

"Chile, please. You don't even have your shit together. What do I look like telling *you* my issues? I go and talk about some childhood shit I'm trying to work through. I find it helpful. Let me know if you want her number. She's a sister too," Cherell answered nonchalantly.

I was still in shock. Were black folks really seeing shrinks these days? The whole idea of it was still slightly taboo to me, even though it shouldn't be. I was a college-educated woman with a master's degree. My mind should be more evolved, I thought, reprimanding myself.

"You know what, Cherell? I think I *will* take her number. Text her information to me."

"Okay. Now, what are you wearing tonight?"

"Huh? I'm not going anywhere but under my covers tonight," I said, rolling my eyes. I grabbed another donut and stuffed it into my mouth. Calories be damned. At the rate I was going, I would be old, miserable, and alone anyway, so I might as well enjoy a few comforts such as food and drink. Hell, let me stop by the liquor store on the way home and grab a bottle to sip on tonight, I ruefully thought to myself.

"Uh-uh, bitch! My name and reputation is on the line now. We are going to Table 51 tonight, and if Jay is there, you are going to apologize to that man!"

I felt the color drain from my face. I knew at that very moment I was sitting there looking like a pale-faced black woman. I knew all the white powder all around my mouth from the donut I was eating wasn't making me look any better. I quickly choked down the food in my mouth.

"Apologize for *what?* He was rude as hell to me too!" I screamed.

"I'm going to let you sit there and think about the shit that just came out of your mouth just now while I look at you real stupid," Cherell said. She then proceeded to fold her arms across her chest, lean back in her seat, and cocked her head to the side staring at me.

My eyes darted guiltily around her place. My mind was racing with a million thoughts.

"Have you been redecorating? I see you've made some changes since the last time I visited. That red couch is gorgeous . . . Meka has one too. The last time we spoke, she was crying because her baby spilled milk all over it," I muttered lowly. I was too embarrassed! I didn't want to apologize to Jay. It was easier just to never go to Table 51 again. Just avoid his ass altogether.

"You really think I need to apologize?"

Cherell cocked her head to the other side.

"I'll be ready at nine," I said, resigning myself to yet another night of humiliation.

Jeremiah

I walked into Table 51 feeling fly, fresh, and free. I'd made up my mind to shake off anything negative. I'd gotten a rocky start by the time I actually did fall asleep. I lay there for hours mulling over the conversation with Mia in my mind before the stark realization hit me.

What the fuck was I doing losing sleep over another man's wife? My black ass should have been sleeping easy, knowing that I'd gotten out of that bullshit-ass relationship with Mia when I did. One thing I knew beyond a shadow of a doubt about myself was that I had integrity. It may have taken me some time to fully come into it, and, yes, I'd made some wrong turns along the way in my life, but I'd redeemed myself. But the one thing I can say is that in regards to relationships, I ain't never lied and played with anyone's heart. That's not the type of man I wanted to be. Life was too short to play those types of games.

I also thought about that damn crazy-ass Nicole.

Granted, if I saw her ass coming, I was running the other way, but she did help me see last night that I still wasn't where I wanted to be mentally. I wasn't trying to waste any more of my time thinking about what could have been with Mia and me. Yet, I still knew I needed to take some time to get my head where I wanted it to be. In the meantime, I was going to focus on getting this money where I needed it to be. My heart may not be full right now, but if it was any consolation, my bank account sure the fuck was.

"Hey, Boss man. I didn't think you were coming in today," Tiny said, grinning at me as I approached the bar.

"Of course. I just decided to take it easy today. How have things been so far?" I asked, gazing around. It was just after seven, but surprisingly, the place was half full with the early birds grabbing a bite to eat. The crowd was comprised of mostly couples, and people crowded the bar. I was glad to see that everything appeared to be flowing efficiently since I'd hired another bartender. Javier, the bartender who'd already been there, wasn't too thrilled when I said I was expanding the bar area. I guess he felt like I was taking money out of his pockets in regards to tips, but, hey, if he wasn't happy, he could walk.

Some niggas couldn't see the forest for the trees. I was assuring he made more money by providing faster service. The second bar, once it was completed, would bring in more of a crowd. I'd had them counting at the door, and while the club had good numbers, we weren't at capacity yet. I wanted Table 51 to damn near be standing room only. I wanted it to be the spot that had lines outside of people waiting to get in. That was my vision. It was gonna have to be theirs too, or they could start looking for another job.

Tiny came from behind the bar swaying her hips hard with each step. It was a wonder to me how she managed to work walking in high-ass shoes every night. I guess women got used to it. I recalled how Mia used to do everything in heels, training herself to always have them on, to sing and dance in them effortlessly. Shit, here I go thinking about her ass again.

"Jay, you want me to put you in an order of lemon-pepper wings and some fries? Or did you eat already?" Tiny asked, gazing up at me, her eyes a luxurious pool of chocolate brown. I hadn't even been thinking about food, but now that she mentioned it, I felt my stomach growl.

"Good looking out, Tiny. Shit, I didn't even realize I hadn't eaten until you mentioned it."

"Well, you know I'ma look out for you just like you did me," she grinned, walking past me toward the kitchen.

I smiled inwardly. I was glad my small gesture toward making her a bartender was appreciated. All week long, she'd been working extra hours behind the bar brushing up on her skills and learning how everything worked as far as ordering, working with various vendors, and maintaining everything the way I expected it to be.

Thirty minutes later, Tiny and I were enjoying a meal at the VIP table I'd adopted as my own.

"So, have you had a chance to hit any clubs besides here yet?" Tiny asked between bites of her fries.

"Nah. I didn't come here for all that. I already got caught up in some nonsense since I've been here."

"Really? With a woman?" Tiny asked nosily. I couldn't help but laugh. I swear to God, all women came equipped with a nosy gene. It didn't matter if you were just friends or fucking them.

"It was a li'l somebody I met here actually. It ain't nothing, though," I replied, concentrating on my food.

"Well, don't just be out here messing with just anyone because it's some real THOTS coming up in here. I mean, it's some classy ladies that come through too. You just have to be careful. Was the chick you met a THOT? And be honest too!" Tiny asked, cackling with laughter.

I laughed as well, trying to make up my mind. Was Nicole a THOT? Is that why her ass was so goddamn loony? Nah, crazy as hell maybe. Nah, scratch that probably. But she wasn't no ho. If she was a ho, I was too since I fucked on the first night. I couldn't stand when dudes tried to hold a woman to a certain standard but not themselves. So since I knew damn well I wasn't no ho and didn't dip my stick in every open hole, I wasn't going to call her one either. Plus, I kinda knew the backstory on her. Bitter bitch. Yeah, I'ma stick with that.

"She wasn't a THOT. Just wasn't my type."

"Humph! So what *is* your type? I mean, you know a few of the ladies here have been wondering," Tiny drawled out coyly.

I started laughing. I had to grab my napkin to cover my mouth.

"What's so funny?"

I took a quick sip of my water. It was too early in the evening for me to start drinking.

"I just find it funny how easily you claimed it was so many THOTS running around and to avoid them, but how you easily referred to you and some of the women all in my damn business as 'ladies.' Trust me, some of y'all THOTS too," I said, sniggering softly. I wasn't trying to offend ol' girl but still . . . Let's be real about the shit.

Tiny sat across from me pursing her lips tightly. I may have gone too far and offended her, but what was I supposed to do? Lie? I ran my napkin across my mouth and hands slowly.

"Don't get all sensitive on me now. I'm just keeping it real. To answer your question, though, ain't no need for any female working here to know what type of woman piques my interest. That is, unless she only wants to know so she can introduce me to her friend that *doesn't* work here. I don't shit where I eat. Ever."

"Never?"

"Ever."

Tiny folded her hands across her chest and cut her eyes at me. "Okay, damn. It's gon' be some mad bitches up in here. That's all I gotta say."

"Well, you just make sure you ain't one of them, because right now, I need a friend more than anything else," I said sincerely.

I could see the smile flirting at the corners of her mouth before it gave way to a full-blown grin.

"All right, Boss man. My break is over, so I'm getting back to work. I'll check in with you during my shift to see if you want a drink," Tiny said, rising from her seat and gathering our trash.

"I appreciate it. Don't worry about this stuff. I'll take care of it," I said, waving her off.

"Are you sure? Okay, I'll see you later," she said, walking out of the VIP. The little bit of dog that was in me couldn't help looking at her ass in her work skirt. Goddamn. I'd be lying if I said Tiny didn't have a nice body on her. Stevie Wonder could see that shit. If she didn't work for me, I might just overlook that chipped tooth. Or make sure the club's dental plan covered that shit so she could get it fixed. *You ain't shit, Jeremiah,* I thought clearing the table and throwing our trash away.

Two hours later, the club was officially in full swing. It was still early, but so many people had already come in, DJ Dre had already switched up the music and was going full swing. During the early hours, he mainly played more R&B type music, but the turnup was already in effect. I slowly walked the club checking out every section, making sure things were good. I felt like it always helped having myself or a manager watching over the club. Everyone performed their job better when they knew they were being watched by the boss. I even made it a point to visit several of the tables, introducing myself as one of the owners of the club. Hooked up some of the patrons with free drinks and a little conversation. I was pleased with what was happening at Table 51 and looked forward to implementing the few slight improvements Dip and I had planned.

The crowd was getting thick, I thought, maneuvering myself between tables when I heard someone call out my name. I glanced to my left and groaned, doing a poor job of masking the disdain I felt in my facial expression. *Suck it up, nigga, as long as her crazy ass leaves me alone and keeps buying these expensive-ass drinks, we're cool,* I thought, my eyes grazing over Nicole and landing on her friend Cherell. I gave Nicole a cordial head nod and smiled at Cherell.

"How are you tonight, Ms. Lady? Enjoying yourself?"

"Of course, I am. You see I've been in here three weekends in a row! Every time I come in here, you sittin' your ass up in here too!"

I busted out laughing. This woman was a fuckin' trip. Had she already started drinking? Cherell knew damn well I told her I owned the place. Where else did she expect me to be *but* here? She seemed cool as hell, though, from the few times I'd run into her. Too cool to be hanging around this nutcase friend of hers.

"Well, baby, anytime I'm around these parts, you'll find me right here. My partner and I just bought this place. So I can't give another club my money," I said, reminding her again, in case she'd forgotten.

Nicole

I turned my head and rolled my eyes. *Baby?* This man probably up in here fucking and calling every woman he meets baby. And *owns* the place? I don't recall him telling *me* that. Then again, both times being around him it's not like I gave him the opportunity.

I sat there growing more aggravated by the second. Was he really going to stand there and ignore me?

"Ooww!" I yelped loudly, my hand gravitating toward my shin where Cherell had just kicked me under the table. Damn, was I bleeding? I looked up to find her beady, evil eyes pinned on me. I caught the slight head nod toward Jay she was giving me. I inhaled deeply, trying to work up the courage to speak to him. Jay was in the midst of speaking to a waitress who was looking at him as if she wanted to rip his clothes off. *Really,* bitch? That's your damn boss, and even I can see you licking and biting your lips!

"Get your black ass up and ask to speak to him privately! Shoot, and his fine ass owns the club too? Look, don't fuck this up for us!" Cherell gritted underneath her breath.

Us? What us?

My mouth felt dry as hell. I started to speak, and my voice cracked, so I took several swallows to coat my throat. Now the waitress was just here skinning and grinning in Jay's face, and here we are customers, with no drink in front of us.

"Well, Cherell, I hope you enjoy your night. Your drinks are on me tonight. I already told the waitress," Jeremiah said, grinning at Cherell sexily. *Is this nigga flirting with my friend right in front of my damn face?* I thought, anger easily rising inside of me. I quickly quelled it.

"Excuse me, Jay? Do you think we could speak privately for a few minutes?" I managed to croak out. Where was that damn waitress at? I damn sure picked up on the fact he said *Cherell's* drinks were on the house. *Not* mine.

The pause grew as he debated on speaking with me. I could see him at war with himself on whether to tell me to go fuck myself or allot me a few minutes of his time. As each second passed, I felt more humiliated. I shouldn't have even tried.

"Follow me," Jay said, turning on his heel and walking away without another look at me. I scrambled out of the booth and ambled after him as best I could. I feared losing him in the crowd. Jay walked to the rear of the club until we were walking down a long hall I'd never noticed before. He paused in front of a door, pulling a key out of his pocket, and opened the door, ushering me inside.

Jay closed the door behind us and walked over to lean on what I assumed was his disheveled desk. There wasn't much to the office; no personal effects, pictures, or anything. I could see a private bathroom and a television.

"Look, can I help you with something or you just wanna stand here being nosy? I have a club to run. I ain't got time for this shit," Jay spat, looking at me with nothing but sheer annoyance across his face. I could tell by his entire demeanor and the energy he was giving out he wanted nothing to do with me.

I raised my hand to the back of my neck and nervously rubbed. It was an annoying habit of mine. I'm sure I looked like an idiot. Jay's phone rang, and he reached into his suit pocket and pulled it out.

"Jeremiah speaking, how can I help you?" he asked, throwing up a finger toward me to pause my speech, even though I'd yet to utter a word. Jeremiah. Good Lord, even his full name was sexy as hell, and if we made it out of this conversation with any sort of understanding at all, even if it was just speaking in passing, Jay would never flow from my lips at all. It would always be Jeremiah.

I took the intrusion of his phone call as a sneaky opportunity to look at him. The suit he was wearing was definitely custom made, and the canary yellow of his dress shirt comple- mented the charcoal grey of his suit. He looked amazing. I wondered who he was talking too when I heard him laugh and his thick, long fingers raised to his mouth to conceal a smile.

Who was making him smile? Why did I care?

I rocked nervously back and forth on each leg waiting for him to end his call, gathering the nerve to get my apology toward him out. In all honesty, I was starting to get a little upset. Who was he on the phone with? And why was he being so rude? I shook off the negative thoughts I was having and tried thinking positively.

"Sorry about that."

The sound of his voice broke me out of the little motivational speech going on inside my head.

"I'm sorry, Jeremiah. I mean Jay. You didn't give me permission to call you Jeremiah," I stammered. "I just wanted to apologize to you for my behavior last night—"

"Oh, you don't have an apology for the Monday morning you threw me out of your house or for calling me another nigga's name. Shit, I'd been fuckin' you two days, and you didn't know the difference? Sounds like you're forgetting a day to me," Jeremiah said, suddenly all ears now. I hung my head low, embarrassed as hell. My mind was swirling about how I'd shown my ass so much . . . literally in such a short amount of time.

I raised my head, a shy smile spreading across my face. "I'm sorry for everything. I know at this point you may find that hard to believe, but the person you met the other week is not who I am. What I've shown you isn't the real me. I'm a much nicer, calmer person than what I've displayed to you. Quite frankly, than what I've shown to the majority of people in the last year. It was important for me to let you know that," I said in a rush.

We stood there looking at each other for a moment. I was waiting on him to say he accepted my apology.

"Well?"

"Well, what?" Jeremiah asked brusquely.

My heart sank, and I quickly tried to shake it off. The entire point was just to apologize. I'd behaved awful toward him on more than one occasion, so Jeremiah had every right not to accept my apology.

"Oh! My bad. Apology accepted. You showed your ass, but on the real, we all go through it. In all honesty, I haven't been myself the last year either," Jeremiah said, walking over to me and extending his hand.

Damn!

I knew he didn't mean any harm, but he was extending a handshake to me, and just a week ago he'd been inside me. *I've got to do better than this, Nicole,* I thought to myself. I can't blame anyone for me feeling like this but myself. This pussy of mine is on lock—along with my mouth!

I held my hand out and grabbed his for a shake. His hand felt incredible. Strong yet soft. I immediately recalled these very hands caressing every inch of my body. A shock of electricity ran up my spine.

"Are you okay?"

My eyes flew open. Oh my God. Am I really standing in front of this man who probably can't stand the sight of me anymore, damn near having an orgasm? What in the entire fuck!

"So, umm, you own this place? I guess we didn't discuss our jobs the other week," I rambled, trying to cover my embarrassment.

"I have a partner, but, yes, I'm an owner. What is it that you do, Nicole?"

Jeremiah

I wanted to kick myself. Why the hell did I ask this crazy girl what the hell she did for a living? I don't give a damn. She's fine, but she's crazy as fuck. The pussy's good, but she's a nutcase. Unstable as hell. I accepted her apology, but that's it. She gon' have to sit all this crazy on another nigga's doorstep because I ain't got time for it.

She does look good, though, I thought, easing my eyes, hopefully, inconspicuously, up and down the length of her body.

"I'm a trainer at Health Care Solutions," Nicole answered, glancing up at me looking nervous. She looked scared as hell!

I don't know what she thought I was going to do to her in here. I was the calm, and she was the storm, in case she hadn't noticed by now.

"Hmm, I don't exactly know what that job entails, but do you enjoy it?" I asked just to make conversation, my mind quickly wandering to how my club was doing, but I let it go. I'd only owned it a week. It had functioned fine without me all that time, so I was pretty sure I could give this crazy girl a few minutes of my time since she'd made a point to extend an apology to me. I did get the feeling it was sincere, so I'd roll with it.

Nicole began to laugh. I liked the sound of it.

"Honestly, I don't. But they pay me well enough that I've gotten over it enough to walk in every day. I have a master's degree in Human Services, so it's definitely not what I went to school for," she said, shaking her head.

"Well, you should certainly make use of that degree and do something your heart leads you to do. That way, you never feel like you're working a day in your life," I answered, sitting down in the chair in front of my desk and pointing her toward the empty seat next to me.

"Is that what you've done? Your heart led you to want to run a club?"

"Ehh, running a club would elude to the fact I'm no more than a manager. I own clubs. In two states. No, I didn't dream of wanting to do this, but the opportunities owning clubs have presented to me have satisfied everything I dreamed of as a child," I answered soberly. I was trying to discern if she was trying to be funny or not.

"Interesting . . . What exactly does that mean, Jeremiah?" Nicole asked curiously, crossing her long, sexy, toned legs. I ain't gon' lie, she definitely had my attention in that regard . . . but she was still crazy.

"That means as a little boy I dreamed about eating every day, without worrying about where my next meal was coming from. I wanted to see other places than where I was born. I wanted not to move around from one shitty housing project to the next. I've always wanted a nice home. Honestly, in my mind, it's just regular shit everyone should want for themselves. But I didn't necessarily have those things as a child. My brother and I struggled as kids, and sometimes we suffered. I just don't ever want to feel that again. So 'running' a club affords me those small luxuries."

Nicole was listening to me so intently she was nodding her head gently, almost as if she was lulling the conversation out of me. Maybe she had, because I damn sure hadn't intended on revealing any of that about myself.

"I understand."

"Do you?"

"I mean, my childhood experience was the polar opposite of yours, but, yes, Jeremiah, I understand."

"Cool. I appreciate you taking the time to extend an apology tonight. You didn't have to, but you did, and I admire that."

The smile on her face almost made me feel like maybe I needed a little crazy in my life. Was crazy that bad? Nah, fuck that. Lies go right along with crazy, and I'd damn sure had my fair share of that.

"Okay, so I don't usually do this . . . Matter of fact, I've never done this. But, umm, well, Jeremiah, can I take you out? Like on a date," Nicole stammered.

I was caught off guard battling whether I even wanted to be bothered. The only thing this woman and I actually did agree on was fuckin'; when it came to conversation, we didn't get along. Why she wanted to beat a dead horse was beyond me. Yet, here she was, sitting in front of me looking fine as frog's hair and asking me out on a date. Why? So she could get me out in public and cuss me out again? I didn't know what to do.

So, naturally, I just went ahead and told her insane-ass . . . yes.

Jeremiah

What in the hell am I doing? I thought to myself as I walked to the lobby of the hotel I was still staying in. Finding a place I was interested in purchasing was taking a bit longer than expected, even with the help of a realtor. Nicole and I had communicated several times during the week, and our conversations had gone surprisingly well. No episodes or outbursts on her part, so I was feeling a bit more confident about going out with her tonight, but I can't lie, I was still a bit wary. I was wondering to myself what would be the next thing to set her off. I was also skeptical about having her drive us tonight. If she got to tripping and I had to dip on her ass, I was going to be stuck. I still wasn't that familiar with Richmond being that the only places I really knew how to navigate were how to get to my hotel, the club, and any eateries in-between.

I hadn't made much time for sightseeing. I walked through the sliding doors and found

Nicole standing in front of a black Mercedes, waving at me. I couldn't help smile as I walked toward her. Nicole was a beautiful woman, no doubt. Her hair was cut in a chin-length bob that was wavy, smooth, toffee-brown skin, and her makeup was tastefully done. I didn't care at all about women wearing makeup. What I didn't like is a woman who walked out of the house looking like she was about to participate in a drag queen competition. Squared off, unnatural-looking eyebrows—I don't like that shit. Tasteful, that's what turned my head.

Nicole was wearing a long black-and-white maxidress paired with some jeweled sandals which showcased her bright red toenails. A flash of her legs wrapped around my body and her soft feet grazing my back flashed across my mind. Her toes were bright pink that night. Goddamn, nigga, pull it together!

"Hi! I'm on time, right?" Nicole beamed. She seemed to be really excited about this date. I had no idea where we were going tonight, and she'd refused to give me any hints. Nicole insisted she'd never asked a man out before, so she was determined to give me the kind of date she'd want from a man. I tried to assure her I wasn't that hard to please. Be on time, a nice meal and some good conversation, and I was good to go.

I walked over, pulled her close, and gave her a tight hug in greeting. "You look beautiful."

"Thank you, so do you. I mean, you look handsome," Nicole said, laughing as she opened the door and ushered me inside of her car and we pulled off.

Nicole turned on some music, and I groaned internally at her choice. Mia. Really? I had to physically restrain myself from reaching out and changing it.

"Ohh, I love me some Mia! This is my girl. Don't mind me, Jeremiah. I know I can't sing, but I wish I could. I sing in the car every time I'm driving," Nicole said, singing a few lines of Mia's latest song flooding the radio. "I know you've heard of Mia, right?" she asked, turning to me shimmying her shoulders and snapping her fingers as she maneuvered through the thick flow of early evening traffic. I wanted to jump out of her ride into oncoming traffic. Jesus, take me now!

"Yeah, I've heard of her. Not really my thing," I muttered. Yeah, I was salty.

"Boy, you crazy! This girl is the *truth!* Do you *hear* me? Oh my God, I think she writes all her lyrics about her husband with his fine ass. I can only pray to be blessed with a love like the one she has with her husband. His name is Quinton.

Anyway, let me stop. I'm over here fan-girling right now. Just know, the minute Mia hits the area for a concert, my ass will be there sitting front and center," Nicole crowed excitedly.

I was just playing before, but, nah, Jesus, take the wheel right now, or this date is going to go downhill fast.

"Okay, then," I replied dryly.

"Hang with me, Jeremiah, and Mia's music is going to grow on you," Nicole said, glancing over at me with a wide smile pasted on her face before she quickly put her eyes back on the road and switched lanes.

Shit, if that's what you think, you've got me all the way fucked up. This might be our first and *last date,* I thought to myself, temper flaring. A love like Mia and Quinton? To each his own, but I still maintain that muthafucka was a damn pervert and needed to be in jail. I know what the fuck I saw through that window!

My mood was already in the toilet due to Nicole unknowingly running her damn mouth.

Seconds later we pulled up to a beach.

"Come on, we're having dinner on the pier, but our reservations aren't for another hour. It's just a short walk, but I want to take you to this spot I like watching the sun go down. Are you okay? Do you not like seafood? You aren't allergic, are you?" Nicole asked, panicking.

Damn, let me snap the fuck out of it. It ain't like she knows I have history with Mia. She's just making polite conversation.

"Oh no, I love seafood. Come show me your spot," I said, reaching for the door, ready to escape the vehicle. I took a few gulps of fresh air trying to quickly clear my head while I walked to her side and took her hand. Nicole looked surprised.

"Lead the way, Queen," I said, giving her my most sincere smile. Nicole pulled me along and proceeded to talk. Once she got started, it was full speed ahead, and surprisingly, I didn't mind it at all. Nicole told me it was her favorite spot because her dad used to bring her here as a child to spend quality time together while she was growing up. That when she needed to think, she came here for walks and immediately felt better.

"I'm just happy this place hasn't been ruined for me. Honestly, I've come here so many times in the last year it ain't even funny, but this place never seems to change. People change, come and go, but this beach and the beautiful sunset are always consistent. I've needed that the last year," Nicole said thoughtfully.

"Well, I'm glad you had a place to come. It sounds like you've been through some things in the past year," I said gently. I was pretty confident I knew exactly what she was referring to, but I definitely wasn't going to let her know I was privy to all of her personal business. Hell, her relationship drama, from what I'd been told by Kendrick, is what had set her off in the first place. I could see nothing good coming from me revealing the fact that I knew what happened in her last relationships with the rapist nigga and Kendrick.

"Yeah, it was pretty rough for me. That's life, though, I guess. I'm still a work in progress. But let's not discuss that. Isn't that breaking a major dating rule anyway?"

"What's that?" I asked. We'd just arrived at the end of the pier and were leaning over the railing. Damn, the water splashing and watching the waves did have a kind of relaxing vibe to it.

"You know what it is. You're not supposed to discuss your exes with people. It sends the wrong message," Nicole replied.

"Bullshit. Honestly, I don't know who created that rule. I can see not bringing up exes in the middle of sex with someone new . . ." I said, looking over at her real quick, ". . . or comparing. But when are you supposed to discuss them? I kinda feel like there's a time and place for everything; it's all about discussing things at the right time. But eventually, it has to happen. How else are you going to learn about each other?" I asked, glancing over at her. I can't even lie, if we were in a romance novel, this whole scenario would have been on point. The glow from the lowering sun was hitting the side of her face just right, and the wind was blowing through her hair just right. Not so hard that her head was looking a hot mess, just all sexy like. I started laughing because it was funny to me.

"What's so funny?"

"Nothing . . ." I said, shaking my head, ". . . You look pretty, though. Let me get a picture," I said, pulling my cell phone out of my jeans. After taking several shots of her on the pier and a little more conversation, we made our way to the restaurant.

There was a nice crowd in the place, which was a good sign to me. It smelled good as hell. Our waitress seated us, and we placed our orders. After that, it was a blur of conversation, food, and drinks. Nicole was funny. She had a crazy sense of humor and seemed to like some quirky things I found hilarious.

"Stop laughing! See, this is why I don't tell black folks. They don't get it!"

"I mean, you just don't look like you read science fiction and postapocalyptic shit."

"Don't play, Jeremiah! You mean to tell me you don't watch *The Walking Dead?*"

"Nah, I ain't never seen that shit before," I said, dipping a chunk of lobster into some butter and taking a bite.

"Really? Never? Oh, we're doing a *Walking Dead* marathon one night. You're living in the dark ages, and I feel it's my duty to put you on. Besides, you're losing points with me. First, you don't listen to Mia, and you don't even watch my favorite show? What can I do with you?"

I bit my lip trying to stop myself from busting out laughing at the table before my eyes met hers.

"I must not have left much of an impression on you if you really don't think I can do anything to entertain you other than watch TV and listen to someone lyric on their facade of a relationship. Matter of fact, I know I didn't since you calling me by another man's name."

Nicole dropped her fork in her plate and frowned at me. "Jeremiah, please stop bringing that up. I thought you forgave me for that? It's embarrassing enough without you bringing it up every chance you get. Stop it. I know exactly who I was there with. That was just a slip."

"I'm just making sure you know who the hell you're here with! I ain't never had no foul shit like that happen to me. I'm just making sure. What's my name? Let me make sure you remember," I asked arrogantly.

"I know your damn name . . . *Jeremiah!*" Nicole said, trying to stifle a laugh.

"Say Jeremiah D'Sean Wilson ten times. You better put some respect on my damn name, girl!" I said, popping a shrimp in my mouth.

Nicole fell out laughing, slapping my arm. Little did she know I was dead-ass serious! She quickly composed herself since we'd snagged the attention of a few tables surrounding us.

Then Nicole and I sat in silence eating our food.

"You left a very lasting impression on me. It's the reason after all my craziness we're sitting here right now. I'm just hoping you'll impress me again," Nicole said softly.

"I can leave a lasting impression on you over and over again if you let me."

Nicole

I anxiously crossed my legs under the table. The minute those words left Jeremiah's mouth, my panties were soaking wet. I couldn't take my eyes off of him. I wanted him so badly, but I'd come to the slow realization that I wasn't a casual sex girl. Granted, he was the only man I could honestly say I'd ever had casual sex with, but look at me now. On a date with him, and I couldn't deny the fact I was interested in him. Initially, I'd wanted to blame my having sex with him on the hit-and-run meeting I had with Kendrick and his wife, but the reality is, the minute he came to my defense and the way he'd done it so effortlessly, saving me from an embarrassing situation, made a mark on my heart that I couldn't deny if I wanted to. The same thing happened the day I met Kendrick, and, no, I wasn't comparing these two men, but I had to admit to myself that it was a quality I liked in a man. I liked feeling protected and cared for. What was so wrong with that?

"Nicole, do you want to get out of here?"

My eyes were in my plate, too nervous to look at him. I didn't think I could get any wetter, but I did. My mind skated to the conversation I had with Cherell. Other women did this all the time. Not to mention the fact I *wanted* this man.

"I do," I said, nodding my head slowly. I really do.

An hour later, Jeremiah and I were back in his hotel room.

Paige

My flight into Virginia was horrible! I only prayed it wasn't an indication of how Jeremiah would react to the fact I was showing up on his doorstep unannounced. Oh, the fuck well. This nigga should have answered his phone and spoken to me, but this conversation was going to be had!

It had been four weeks since Jeremiah had left New York, and I was not happy to discover that he was extending his trip yet *another* month, according to him. It was like pulling damn teeth to get him to reveal that information to me. Not to mention the sporadic way he was taking my phone calls. My situation had gone downhill fast.

I must have spoken the lie about being put out of my apartment into existence because as sure as I'm gorgeous, that ho had put me out. Talking about I wasn't pulling my weight in regards to the rent and utilities. That I wasn't paying my bills, yet, I was showing up with new weaves, shoes, and outfits. Well, umm, yeah. How the fuck did she think I was gonna get a nigga to lace me with some cash if I wasn't looking up to par?

I, of course, wasn't going to reveal to Jeremiah why I had to leave my apartment, so I thought I could appeal to his sense of compassion by telling him that my roommate had gotten violent with me. I even lied and said I had a restraining order on her ass. Little did I know, Jeremiah evidently didn't have a sense of compassion! During the conversation I kind of hemmed and hawed around, waiting for him to offer for me to stay at his place since it was empty as hell. When he didn't, I straight up asked if I could crash with him for a while until I got on my feet—only to be turned down again.

I still couldn't figure out where I went wrong with him. I'd fucked him everywhere possible. Given this Negro access to every orifice on my body, and he still wasn't mine? I know at this point I probably should have given up, but all his rejection did was make me want to go harder to make him mine. Besides, all month long I'd been tracking his new club on Instagram, and it was easy to see this nigga's club was about to blow up yet again. Here it was Wednesday night, and I had this cab pulling up to Table 51. I hope like hell there was only one club in the area with this name because coming all the way from the airport, I saw my fare was up to $98.63. I flipped stingily through the exactly $600 I had in my wallet. Damn. I should have just called and told him I was at the airport so I could save this little bit of change. I briefly considered if I could ditch this damn cabdriver but quickly realized that wouldn't work since I had two heavy pieces of luggage in his trunk.

I begrudgingly handed him over an even $100 and exited the cab and watched as he lifted my luggage out of the trunk and set them at my feet.

"Hold on! Aren't you going to carry these in for me?" I asked incredulously.

"Lady, this ain't no valet service. But if you wanna give me fifty bucks more, I can carry them in for you," was his response.

"This is very unprofessional of you, and I will be filing a complaint with your supervisor," I spat.

"The number's on the cab, bitch," the man shouted as he hopped back into his cab and sped off.

Another bout of misgivings about my decision to come here washed over me as I lugged my bags to the inside of the club. Why is this place so packed already? It's just after five.

"Hello, welcome to Table 51. I'm Tiny. Can I help you with something?" a snaggletoothed waitress asked me, curiously looking at the bags surrounding me. My purse was heavy as hell on my shoulder, so I set it on top of the pile to give my shoulder some relief.

"Actually, you can. I'm here to surprise my boyfriend, Jeremiah. Can you please tell him Paige is here? Thanks, boo."

"No boo here, but you can call me Tiny . . . as I already stated. So you say you're boss man's girlfriend, huh? Well, he's not here for the night yet. You might do better just calling him," this big-booty ho had the nerve to say to me. I was picking up on a funny vibe from her already! She must be over here trying to fuck Jeremiah, ol' busted mouth bitch! I could tell by the catty way she was looking at me. By the way she was staring me down, I could tell her ass was intimidated by me. Many weaker bitches were, so that wasn't anything new to me.

"Honey, I didn't fly all the way from New York not to surprise my man. I'll just wait here for him. So if you could just get these bags to his office for me, I'll occupy myself at the bar until he arrives. What time does your boss usually come in?"

This Tiny lady folded her arms across her chest cutting her eyes at me. "You know what, lady? I don't disclose my boss's comings and goings with our patrons. As you can see, our establishment is open. So, if you'd like to come in . . . and purchase a drink, you're more than welcome. As for your bags, take your time carrying them to your table because this is not a valet service," Tiny said before turning her back on me.

My shoulders slumped. I was exhausted! The hospitality in Virginia was definitely lacking. I threw my shoulders back and marched through the club scouting a table that would at least let me hide my bags. People were nosily watching me since it took two trips before I was settled. Once I was finally able to rest myself, I grabbed the menu on the table. I was starving. I flagged down another waitress and placed an order for some wings and a drink. Jeremiah know damn well these drinks are too damn high. I looked toward the bar and saw Tiny talking with another woman and laughing as they looked over my way. Surely these hoes weren't talking about me? As soon as I see Jeremiah, I'ma have this bitch Tiny's job.

These Virginia hoes gon' find out I'm the wrong bitch to fuck with, I thought, greedily digging into the food that had just been set in front of me.

Two hours later and Jeremiah still hadn't showed. My eyes were getting heavy, I was so damn sleepy at this point. I folded my arms in front of me and lay my head down. *Let me just close my eyes real fast and gather my wits*, I thought to myself.

"Uh-uh! Excuse me, miss, we do not allow squatting in here. I'ma have to ask you to leave. We're starting to get packed up in here and need the table. You been over here stone-cold sleeping for the last hour, and I let you make it with that, but you crossing the damn line!" I heard loudly above my head.

My hand swiped away at the drool coming from the corner of my mouth. Oh my God! It was officially packed in this damn club, and Tiny's loud voice had drawn stares my way despite the loud thump of the music. I was feeling a little defeated at this point. I glanced at my cell phone. It was 8:30 p.m. Where the hell was Jeremiah? Maybe he wasn't working as hard as he claimed to be.

"Look, I'll order another drink, okay? Bring me a top-shelf blended margarita," I asked, embarrassed as hell about my current predicament.

"Okay. But you need to do something about these damn bags too! I let it slide when we weren't crowded, but I can't have folks walking

all around your shit! This is a damn fire hazard.
So I suggest you find somewhere to put your
stuff before I put this drink order in for you."

"I asked you when I got here to put them in
Jeremiah's office!"

"Lady, I don't know you! That office is locked,
and even if it wasn't, I wouldn't let you put your
shit in there. Jeremiah and I are cool, and I
damn sure ain't heard the first word about a
girlfriend named Paige!" Tiny said, sucking her
teeth at me.

Fuck this shit. I'd been here for hours now,
and Jeremiah hadn't shown. I was just going to
find me a cheap room for the night and get me
some damn rest. I'd just come back tomorrow
once I was relaxed, showered, and at my best.
I know one thing, for sure. I wanted this bitch
Tiny's head on a platter.

"I'm leaving. Rest assured I will be speaking
with Jeremiah about how shabby you treated me
from the second I walked through the door," I
sneered.

"You do that, honey," Tiny said without so
much as a flinch as she watched me struggle to
my feet and drag bags one by one through the
crowd and to the entrance of the club. Would
you believe in a club full of men, not one of these
niggas offered to help me with my bags?

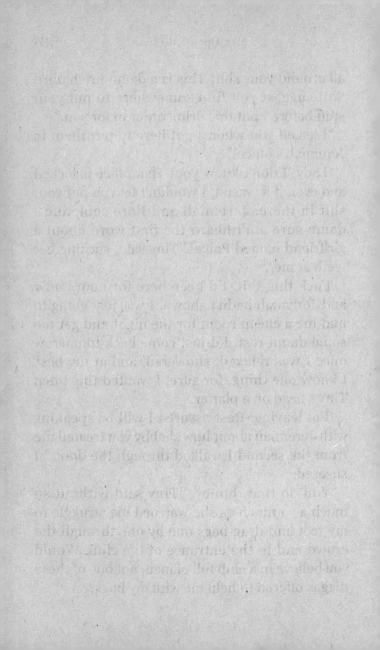

Jeremiah

"Thank you so much, Jeremiah! Oh my God, they're beautiful," Nicole gushed over the phone.

I could picture the smile on her face vividly in my mind as I pulled into the parking lot of the club. I'd been hanging with her tough since our first date so much that I was neglecting some of my duties at the club. Nothing too terrible. I just hadn't been practically living there like I'd once been. I went in early and left early as well. Another change was I'd moved into my place a few days ago. I didn't even come in yesterday, deciding to take some time to kinda get my place together a bit. Afterward, I'd gone and chilled with Nicole for a couple of hours. I didn't know what was going on with us. I didn't know what to call what we were doing, so I just decided to not label it at all. What for? We were both healing from breakups that had left us with a few battle scars, and I won't speak for her, but I knew I wasn't ready for more than what we were doing right now.

We had some laughs, great conversation, and sometimes we didn't need to speak at all. After the night we'd gone to my hotel with every intention to have sex, we changed our minds. Well, Nicole did. She said she wasn't ready, and I understood that. We made the decision not to have sex again until it felt right for both of us. Instead, we'd fallen into an easy friendship of sorts. It did include a little kissing and hugging, but that was about it. I wasn't pressed for no pussy at the moment anyway, so it was no big deal. I did have to admit she'd turned me all the way out . . . on that goddamn *Walking Dead*.

I couldn't believe that shit. Then she was trying to ration the damn shows on Netflix, only letting us watch two at a time. I was good, though. Instead of jumping ahead when I was by myself, I left it alone and let it be our thing.

"How did you know I like orchids?"

"It wasn't hard to figure out, Nicole. I have used your bathroom. You have all those damn purple orchid pictures . . . *and* the shower curtain," I said, laughing as I opened up the car door.

"Hmm, keep noticing things I like, Jeremiah, and I just might think you like me. Are you still coming over for dinner tonight?"

"Yep. I'll be there. Have a good day, okay?" I said before ending the call. I walked into the club and the morning cleaning crew was there making sure the club was in tip-top shape. The new bar on the other side of the club was complete, and I saw Tiny and Javier over there lining the shelves with liquor. I didn't expect to have it open tonight but by Friday night, definitely. I'd had a heavy curtain installed to close it off in the event I didn't want it open on any particular night.

Tiny spotted me and started walking toward me with her hands on her round hips. She wasn't in uniform yet and had on a pair of jeans that looked painted on. Goddamn! I had to remind myself she was my homegirl, but it was getting hard to do. Shit, I'ma have to stop spending all my free time kickin' it with Nicole so hard since we're just friends. Hell, it's been a few weeks since I've had any type of sex. I mean, it ain't like I'm some type of savage, but a man does have needs. If Nicole ain't ready to meet them, someone else will.

"You decided to come to work today, I see, huh?" Tiny said coyly.

"Yeah, I had some shit going on. You know I told you I was moving into my place. Speaking of that, didn't you tell me you were going to take me around to pick out some furniture? And don't take me to the bargain basement furni-

ture store either. I want some good quality shit,"
I said, cutting my eyes playfully at her. "Come
take a break and holla at me real quick," I said,
turning to walk to my office. I heard Tiny call out
to Javier she'd be back and a few minutes later,
we were in my office.

"So, everything was good last night over here?"
I asked, waking up my computer to run numbers
from the bar.

Tiny sucked her teeth. "Look, Jay, we cool
and all, but you need to decide what you want
me to do. Be the second bartender or the night
manager. Shoot, you running me ragged keeping
track of things up in here!"

"Come on now, Tiny. You know I appreciate
all you do. But I can't put a permanent manager
in place until Dip gets here. Charles already
mad we ain't keeping him in that spot. We make
those decisions together, and there's a lot of shit
involved due to the fact neither of us live here.
That job is going to be a lot of responsibility,
but you'll be the first one to know when we start
looking. But on God, you gon' need more experience than pouring drinks, making conversation,
and a fat ass. Straight up."

"Ohhh, you think my ass is fat, Jay?" Tiny said,
swaying her hips back and forth and glancing
behind her like she didn't already know she was
hauling a trunk back there.

"And that comment wasn't meant to sexually harass yo' ass either! I'm just keeping it real shit!"

Tiny burst out laughing.

"Jay, you know your ass crazy. Now let me tell you about the nigga who did bring some damn drama to the club last night! You should have been here for it."

I didn't even know what had gone down, and I was already going from zero to ten. I didn't want a muthafucka around to think they were going to walk into Table 51 causing drama. I'd pulled the police report from Table 51 for the last year, and the calls made were minor issues, and I wanted it to stay that way too.

"Who was it? I bet it Javier's ass! You know I been had my eye on that nigga! He's been giving me a funny vibe from the day I walked in this bitch. Then last week, he was arguing in the parking lot with his ol' lady. I'm have to pull him to the side."

"Uh-uh! Slow ya' roll, potna! The nigga who brought drama to the club last night was *you!*" Tiny said, pointing at me.

A look of confusion clouded my face.

"First off, not that you had to tell me or anything, but I thought we were cool. I told you about my ol' man Darron. How come you didn't tell me about your girlfriend Paige? She came in here last night looking homeless as hell! I ain't saying she ain't cute with that head full of Malaysian flowing down her back. But homegirl showed up with two big-ass suitcases in the damn club! Who does that? Talking about she was gon' surprise you."

"Paige? Tiny, what the hell are you talking about? Here? In Virginia?"

"Umm, yes."

Tiny proceeded to run down the entire incident with Paige from the minute she trudged in with her bags until the second she left. I was floored. Then I was pissed. Paige was gonna make me strangle her donkey-brain ass.

I stood up pacing my office floor. Exactly what the fuck did she think was going to happen by showing up unannounced in Richmond? I knew I should have cut her ass off completely the second I saw her trying to get clingy. You know what? I'm not even tripping on no Paige shit. Her ass better have some fuckin' relatives here in Virginia she came to see because if she brought her ass all the way here for me, her feelings are going to be hurt.

Stalking ass. The other week she'd made yet another attempt to move into my New York place, and yet again, I had to tell her no. Why the hell would she bring her ass here?

There was a knock at my office door, and I snatched it open. One of my workers told me that Paige was here to see me.

"Ya little girlfriend is back wit' her luggage, I bet. Again. You gon' have to check this bitch because this don't make no damn sense! And I find it hard to believe you call yourself dragging two Louis Vuitton bags behind you, but you don't have money for at least a rental car? Bitch out here trying to play bougie with me. Know damn well she probably showered in a Motel 6. Look, Jay, don't have me cuss ya girl out," Tiny said, rolling her eyes at me, walking off, still talking shit.

I followed right behind her ready to talk some shit of my own. I didn't see her in the main club area.

"Tiny, where is she?"

"At the main entrance. The worker told her she couldn't bring all that mess in here today. I let her make it yesterday, but this ain't no damn storage facility," Tiny shouted.

A few heads turned trying to see what the commotion was all about. Damn! The last thing I wanted was my employees being privy to any drama going on with me. It was bad enough I'd lost all professionalism with Tiny, but in my head, she didn't count since I met her before she really knew who I was. Tiny was officially my homegirl, even though I checked out her ass every now and then.

I made it out to the main entrance of the club that was basically reserved for counting and stamping people as they entered the club. Dip and I had also upgraded the security cameras, so the second you entered, you were on camera in case some shit went down and the surveillance footage was needed.

"Oh my God, Jeremiah, I was just trying to contact you. One of your employees has really been giving me hell about coming in here. I hope all the people working here aren't like this," Paige screeched.

I threw my hand up, and Paige's mouth snapped shut as she fidgeted with her skirt, smoothing out nonexistent wrinkles from the short-ass dress she was wearing. I decided it was best not to cause a scene. For now. I stepped forward and picked up her two bags.

"Follow me, Paige."

I marched through the club toward my office with Paige running her damn mouth the entire way. What the hell was she even talking about? The second I crossed the threshold of my office door, I threw the bags to the floor and whipped around.

"Paige, what are you doing in Richmond?"

"Well, I-I came for you, Jeremiah . . . I mean, when you said you were going to be here longer, I thought I would come to you. I know you're a busy man . . ." Paige said softly, easing her way toward me and planting her hands on my chest, ". . . I've missed you, Jeremiah. Haven't you missed me?" she asked, dragging her hands down my chest until they landed on my crotch.

"Actually, Paige, I ain't been thinking about your ass. Now, look, it's a free country. You can hop your ass on a plane and fly wherever the fuck you want to. But my question is, why are you at my place of business with your luggage in tow?"

"I can't believe this. Why do you treat me so cold? You act like I've done something bad to you. I've given you *all* of me," Paige pouted, a pool of crocodile tears gathering in her eyes.

"Cut that crying shit out! I have told you time and time again that we are *not* together. I don't owe you shit. I'm not responsible for your fuckin' feelings! You got the game all the way fucked up, Paige. This is getting to be too much for me. Now, you lead me to believe you could open your legs and give that pussy to me like a big girl. Now, here you are acting like you're catching feelings."

"*Act?* I'm *in love* with you, Jeremiah. You may have said out of your mouth you didn't want to be with me, but the way you kept sliding that big dick of yours inside me at every opportunity was telling me a different story! So how was I supposed to believe you really didn't want me when you kept sleeping with me?" Paige shouted, then burst into tears. She sat down in my office chair burying her face in her hands sobbing loudly.

Goddamn.

The last comment kinda got to me. She had me on that point. I knew better than to take a woman's word for it that she could just have casual sex. I knew there were some women who could have sex-only relationships, but they were few and far between, in my opinion. The same went for men.

Hell, even when a man don't really want you, if you're giving him the pussy exclusively on a regular basis . . . We consider your pussy our pussy—until we meet the female we want on all levels. So, add in some conversation and laughs after the fuck sessions, and it was a wrap. Feelings were involved no matter how much you've tried to warn the other person not to catch them for you.

I ran my hands over my head exhaling loudly and sat on the edge of my desk.

"Look, stop all that damn crying. I don't wanna hear that shit."

Paige's cries grew louder.

"Okay, you say you came to see me, so we may as well make the most of the visit since you brought your ass down here," I said, irritated as hell. I knew I sounded like an asshole, but, damn, being honest evidently just didn't resonate with her.

"Really?" Paige whimpered, gazing up at me. I handed her a Kleenex so she could wipe her snotty-ass face.

"Yes. Let's get you checked into your hotel, and we'll get some lunch, but after that, you're on your own for the day. I'm here working, so I don't have any extra time to give. Hey . . . Why do you have your bags with you anyway? Shouldn't you already have a room? Why didn't you just leave them there?"

Tiny said she was here last night with all her shit. Why was she still carrying it with her?

"Well, I thought it would be fun if I stayed with you. I didn't come to stay in a hotel. I'm here to be with you," Paige sniffled.

"Paige, how long are you here for?"

"How long are you going to be here?"

"How long I'ma be here ain't the issue! If you must know, Virginia is officially my second place of residence. So don't concern yourself with what kinda moves I'm making," I barked, rising to my feet. Paige had more nerve than a toothache right now.

"Okay. Well, I'll just be honest . . ."

"Please do," I groaned.

"I don't really have much extra money on me. About $450 now. After the cab ride here, and that bitch made me leave here yesterday without seeing you, so I got a cheap room for the night . . . and I was starving, so I bought a meal from McDonald's last night and this morning."

If this pitiful-ass ho didn't get out of my face with this bullshit!

It was clear to me there was more to this story. The thing is, I didn't want to hear it because I really didn't give a fuck! It had nothing to do with me. I threw my head back quickly mulling over what I was gonna do with this woman.

"Okay, this is what we're going to do. It's Thursday, so you'll stay with me through the weekend, Paige. Monday, you need to be on a plane headed home. Now, if for some reason you want to stay here, you're a grown-ass woman. You can stay here if you want to. But what you *can't* do is stay with me. Let me be clear. Monday . . . You will be leaving my home. Under no circumstances will your stay with me be extended."

Paige nodded her head in agreement.

"Thank you so much, Jeremiah. I just wanted to see you and spend some time. I've been having a really hard time lately. I tried talking to you about it before on the phone. I don't know what I ever did to make you treat me so harshly, but I'm sorry about it. I just really like you and have always considered us friends. I mean, we've been together for months."

"Paige, I keep telling you to stop saying we're together. We've *never* been together. We have sex. That's all it's ever been for me," I said firmly.

"Only because that's all you ever let me be."

Nicole

I stared at my cell phone for at least the tenth time today. Nothing from Jeremiah. I was a bit bewildered by his lack of communication the last two days. All my insecurities started floating around in my head once again. They'd given me a little peace the last few weeks, but now it was back full force. Just that quick. Granted, we'd gotten off to a very rocky start, but since I'd apologized, and we'd gone on our date, things had been good between us. We sent each other funny texts throughout the day, impromptu calls during the day just to say hello, and Thursday, he'd even sent me a beautiful bouquet of flowers to my job. I was shocked by that because all I did was mention quickly the company I worked for, and he'd remembered. I'd invited him over for dinner Thursday night and even left work early that day to prepare for the evening, only to have him call and say something had come up and he wasn't going to make it.

I was trying to keep everything in perspective and not be upset by it, but I wasn't going to lie. I was disappointed when he canceled. Cherell chalked it up to him being busy with the club and suggested we just go to Table 51 and have drinks and casually "bump" into him, but hell, no. I was not going to get into the habit of doing that. First of all, I'd never been the type to sit in a club all weekend, every weekend anyway. Club hopping occasionally was more than enough for me. I liked doing various activities. Sometimes I like to take drives, go to the movies, concerts. Clubbing was Cherell's thing, not mine.

Not that I was knocking it. It just wasn't my style. Beside, how stalkerish was that anyway? I already felt like one from the way I dealt with Kendrick.

So here I sat on a Saturday night, twiddling my thumbs alone. My cell phone rang, and I picked up for Cherell.

"Hey, girl, what are you doing? Getting ready to hit the club?"

"Surprisingly, no. Girl, even Jesus rested. I'm burnt out. I had my outfit laid out and everything, but I just wanna chill tonight. So I decided to call your homebody ass and see if you wanted to grab dinner and drinks."

I had to laugh. Even when she was relaxi.
Cherell was on the move. *Why not?* I thought.

"Let's go. You know I want some seafood, so
let's go to Croakers Spot."

"Oohh, girl, that sounds good! Let me get my
inner fat girl on today. A bitch like me might
even roll out in some yoga pants! I'll be there
to pick you up in thirty minutes," Cherell said
before ending the call.

I wasn't leaving the house in sweats, but I did
hop into the shower real quick and threw on
a pair of tastefully ripped skinny jeans and an
off-the-shoulder, fitted, cropped top along with
my favorite pair of Red Bottoms. A light dusting
of bronzer and a swipe of red lipstick and I was
ready to go.

An hour later, Cherell and I were sipping
drinks and anxiously awaiting our food. I was
starving, the place smelled so damn good.
Croakers Spot was packed. We chatted easily
as we waited. Cherell was catching me up on
what had been going on with the dude Carlos
she'd been kicking it with since our first night
at Table 51. Honestly, I really was listening with
half an ear due to the fact Cherell was a cheater,
and I didn't condone that shit at all. But from
what I did hear, it sounded to me like my girl
was catching some serious feelings about this

guy and didn't want to admit it. Hell, she could lie to me if she wanted to, but she couldn't lie to herself.

I was just in the middle of laughing at something Cherell was saying when I glanced up—and my eyes locked with Jeremiah's. My heart clenched in my chest, and I quickly looked away. He wasn't alone. There was some video-vixen-looking woman clinging to him. My arm immediately raised to my neck, and I began to rub it.

"What's wrong, girl? You look like you've seen a ghost," Cherell asked, slightly turning in her seat to see what had caught my attention. "Oh. Girl, don't even sweat that shit."

"I'm not," I said adamantly. I had no logical reason to be upset at seeing Jeremiah with another woman. I laughed inside. I could lie to Cherell, but I couldn't lie to myself. My feelings *were* hurt. I know we were just chilling, but it just felt like a kick in the gut to me that Jeremiah just didn't want to hang with me. Maybe I'd been taking up too much of his free time, and he wanted to spread his wings and get to know other people. I couldn't be mad at that.

But I was.

"Shit . . ." I muttered under my breath, ". . . I'll be back, girl. Let me go to the bathroom real quick before our food gets here," I said, quickly rising from my seat and maneuvering myself between the many tables on my way out of the eating area. On the way there, I took a detour and went outside. I didn't need to use the restroom at all, but I could use some fresh air. This is some bullshit. Why me? Why do I always meet these men who don't mean me any good? I don't even ask for much. I don't want to date around and ho myself out! All I want is *one* man. Is that too much to ask for, God? You didn't even make *one* man just for me? To love me, think the world of me, and never want to hurt me? You just left me out, I see. I guess this love shit is meant for other women. Not me. I wanted to wrap my hands around Jeremiah's throat and just squeeze I was so angry.

I'm going to really have to talk to someone about this shit. I hate feeling like this. I'm going to bite the bullet and ask Cherell for her therapist's number. I threw my head back and closed my eyes, inhaling deeply to relax myself.

"It's not what you think."

I jumped at the deep voice coming from behind me and whipped around to find Jeremiah standing so close to me we were damn near rubbing noses. I attempted to take a step back only to have him grab my waist and pull me in even closer.

"I don't want to think anything about it, Jeremiah," I sighed, feeling defeated.

"But are you? Believe me when I say *it's not what you think*. Her name is Paige. I know her from back home and calling her a friend is a huge stretch," he whispered. "Don't be mad with me. Shit has just been a little hectic on my end."

I couldn't help it, but my temper flared.

"It's not too hectic if you're out on dinner dates. And you brought her to the place *I* took you?" I spat turning my head from him. I didn't want him looking at me with those sexy deep-set brown eyes. Jeremiah turned my face back to him and forced me to face him.

"Nicole, I don't lie. I wouldn't do that to you. I don't have any reason to. If I say something, trust that it's just as I said it to be. Have you missed me?" Before I had the chance to answer, his soft, full lips were on mine, and his tongue was exploring every inch of my mouth with confident ease. Each lick, nip, and suck he made was leaving me weak with wanting him and creating a slow burn that was coursing through every inch of my body. I grabbed his arms, holding on to him possessively. Jeremiah broke our kiss, and his mouth found my neck. I felt like dragging him to the side of the restaurant and letting him have his way with me right then and there.

"I missed you. How long are you gon' be out with Cherell tonight?"

My body was in flames seconds before, but I felt like cold water had just been doused on me.

"*Really*, Jeremiah? She gets the date, and I get offered what? A booty call? As if it ain't bad enough I even let you kiss me just now—"

"You didn't have a choice in the matter."

"What? Yes, the hell I did!"

"Oh, don't get me wrong. You had a choice, but you didn't want it. Because instead of pushing me away or slapping my face for even making a move, you wanted my tongue down your mouth just as much as I wanted it to be there. And just like I'm standing here with my dick hard as Chinese arithmetic, I know if I took my hand and put it inside of those tight-ass jeans you out here wearing, your pussy is shower wet," he stated.

I wanted to argue with him. Dispute his allegations, but it would have been useless because every word out of his mouth was true. My mouth snapped open and shut trying to form a nasty retort.

"Well, I don't appreciate you speaking to me so vulgar! In public too!" I replied lamely. I couldn't think of anything else to say. Jeremiah began to laugh at me, which only served to piss me off further. Why did all the men I dealt with take me as a fucking joke? Jeremiah grabbed my arms, and placed them around his neck, pulling me into him by taking a firm hold of my ass.

"Let me tell you something, Nicole. If you think that's vulgar, you ain't heard shit yet. If I'm fucking you, making love to you, worry when I *don't* tell you how I wanna be inside you so bad I can barely stand it right now. Concern yourself when I *don't* tell you for the last month I been thinking about sliding into that tight pussy again and having your juices running down my muthafuckin' face. If you fuckin' with me, Nicole, worry when I ain't saying shit. The shit I say ain't vulgar. It's just me letting you know how much I want your ass. Do you feel me?"

"I understand," I said, burying my face in his shoulder. I was church mouse quiet all of a sudden.

"That ain't what I asked you. I said, do you *feel* me?" Jeremiah asked again, pulling me even closer to him, if that was at all possible. It dawned on me that he was referring to the long, hard dick poking me in the chest. Hell, yes, I felt this nigga! I thought, damn near salivating at the mouth I wanted him so bad.

"Okay, good . . ." Jeremiah said, placing some much-needed space between us, ". . . So can I see you tonight? Wrap this eating shit up, and I'll do the same. I've missed you."

"Bae? There you are! The waitress has been by twice to take our order. I can't hold her off any longer, boo!" A sweet, syrupy . . . fake voice called out. I cut my eyes toward the door, and Jeremiah's date was headed straight for us.

"Oh, let me meet your little friend, Jeremiah. Hi, I'm Paige," she said, draping herself on Jeremiah and smiling sweetly at me.

I stood there feeling like an idiot despite what had just transpired between us. Those were just pretty, sexy words coming from his mouth. Actions spoke louder than words, and Jeremiah's *action* was that he was on a date . . . with another woman! My mind flashed to a pair of wolverine claws extending from my hand and slashing across this bitch's face. *Little friend,* my ass.

Instead, I pasted a grin on my face as fake as the one she was wearing. "Nice to meet you. I'm Nicole."

"Well, girl, it is so nice meeting you. Jeremiah means so much to me, and we've been friends forever. I missed him so much I had to come down and check out his new club and make sure he was okay."

"Well, I hope you enjoy Richmond during your stay. It was nice running into you, Jeremiah. I'll see you around," I said before quickly walking off. I couldn't do the fake shit, and I was not going to stand in this woman's face trying to make polite conversation.

When I walked into the restaurant, I did need to visit the bathroom to get myself together. I walked into a stall, quickly relived myself, and when I walked out to wash my hands . . . there stood Jeremiah's friend, Paige. I gave her a curt head nod and proceeded to the sink to wash my hands.

"Look, I don't know what you think you got going with Jeremiah, but please believe me when I say it's a wrap. That is *my* man, *my* dick, and I have invested *too much time* into that man for me to let any bitch think she's going to insert herself into my relationship. Back the fuck off. I'm telling you right now," Paige stated in a thick New York accent that miraculously hadn't been present moments before outside.

I was in shock. This entire scene took me back to my days with Don Travious, when I used to have various women he was cheating on me with feeling like they could approach me about my man. Uh-uh. I was *not* trying to stroll back down memory lane.

"You know what, Paige . . ." I started, trying to steady my voice before I went full-blown crazy on her ass, ". . . If you have an issue with Jeremiah, I suggest you take that up with him. He is not my man, so the last thing I'm about to do is stand in a public bathroom arguing over a man that doesn't belong to me . . . and from the looks of things, you either," I spat, giving my hands a final once-over with the rough paper towel and walking out of the restroom steaming mad. I was livid.

When I reached the table, Cherell was surrounded by crab legs and was going to town.

"Girl, the food been here for the last ten minutes. I tried to wait on you, but my ass was hungry. Oh, and hurry up and eat. Carlos sent me a text, and I'm going over to his place when we're done," Cherell managed to get out between dipping her crab legs into melted butter and stuffing her fat face. I rolled my eyes.

"You know what? I'm going to get my food to go. My appetite is totally gone. I'll just finish my drink while you eat."

"You ain't said nothing but a word," Cherell said, grabbing her ear of corn.

Could this night get any fucking worse? I'm gonna wait until Monday at work, get the number to Cherell's therapist, and then set up an appointment. I know one thing . . . Jeremiah is a bad idea all around. This man ain't no damn good. Ain't no way in hell that woman would be cornering me in the bathroom if they aren't fucking. They either are currently fucking or have before. *Greedy-ass nigga just trying to fuck everything moving, ol' dirty-dick bastard,* I thought folding my arms across my chest. I looked to my left, and Jeremiah was looking dead in my face. I frowned deeply and cut my eyes at him before turning away. Bastard-ass, muthafuckin' bastard! I sat there and hurled every insult I could think of at him. In my head.

"Hurry up and eat that food, Cherell. I feel sick all off a sudden. I think this mojito is messing with my stomach tonight," I lied.

"Really? Mine too. My stomach is a bit upset now that I think about it."

As mad as I was, I had to contain a howl of laughter. *No, Cherell, your stomach is hurting because you ordered enough food for three people and have demolished it all in a matter of minutes.* A waitress walked past, and I flagged her down for a to-go box. This night was an official wrap for me. The only place I wanted to be was up under my comforter asleep.

Jeremiah

I sat around the table from Paige seething. I couldn't do this shit not one more night. Paige had worked my nerves from the second I'd decided to let her stay through the weekend. Thursday, I'd quickly wrapped up a few things at the club; then we went by my place to drop her luggage off. While I was at work, I debated on if I should just drop her ass off at a hotel and pay for it through Monday. The minute I presented the idea to her, she started that goddamn crying shit up again, talking about she came all this way for me not to be stuck in a hotel. She kept at it for a good twenty minutes about how bad I was treating her that I fell for the okeydokey. At the end of the day, Paige had never actually done anything to me. Yeah, she worked my damn nerves, but aside from her thinking I was going to eventually cave and be in a relationship with her, she wasn't that bad.

But it got worse.

When we walked into my new place, Paige seemed to be awestruck. I'll confess I got a good deal on the place. After presenting me with a few spots that weren't to my liking, my realtor finally let me know there was an opening for townhomes over in the Fall and Sky Subdivision. It was a little pricier than what I'd wanted to kick out, but the area was prime real estate. Two bedrooms, 1,693 square feet. I figured if something went down with the club or I just wanted to sell it sometime down the line, I'd get a pretty penny for it as long as the economy stayed somewhat stable.

Paige stepped inside my home and immediately started decorating my damn house. I mean, she walked every room down to the laundry room telling me how she would fix it up. I had to quickly let her ass know that when she bought herself a home, I was sure she'd enjoy decorating it. I was trying to be nice about it, but it seemed to fall on deaf ears.

The day I moved in, which was only practically days before, I'd had a bedroom set. I wasn't worried about any of my other bedrooms yet, and I damn sure wasn't expecting to be entertaining guests. So I left her in the house while I ran to Walmart. When I walked back in with the air bed and set it up in the spare bedroom for her ass, Paige had the nerve to look offended. Not only did she look offended, something told her little pea brain self that she was in a position to actually voice her displeasure.

I ain't never wanted to hit a woman before. But that night? Paige had one foot out the door and the other on a banana peel fuckin' around with me.

I was already irritated because the very night she showed up, I had dinner plans with Nicole that she caused me to cancel. I had already arranged the day before to have flowers sent to her job to start her day off right, and I could damn near see her smiling through the phone when she'd called, gushing over how beautiful they were. Nicole had extended me an invitation for dinner that night, and for the first time in well over a year, I was actually looking forward to being with a woman. Not on no I-need-to-get-my-dick-wet shit either.

I really wanted to just be with her. Since the night we'd gone out, Nicole was slowly but surely growing on me with her li'l geeky, crazy, pretty ass.

Around two in the morning that Friday I was awakened by Paige trying to suck my dick. Paige got a good two licks in before I realized what was going on and cussed her ass clean out. I ain't never tripped out and turned no head down in my entire life, but I just knew Paige was trouble. The simple fact she was here uninvited let me know beyond a shadow of a doubt I couldn't fuck up by lacing her with none of this dope dick again. Nicole wasn't even a factor in my decision.

At the end of the day, Nicole and I were just cool. All we did is hang out and talk, but there had been no discussion on where our new friendship was headed. Which was crazy as hell since we'd already fucked once. We were hustling backward, but that was okay with me. I needed to check her out, and I didn't feel like she was ready for anything more anyway. I'd even hooked up with Kendrick and his partner Antonio for lunch twice. They were some cool-ass niggas, and I'd told them I would definitely be extending some invitations to them . . . and their wives for the grand reopening happening in the next two weeks. They were impressed when I let them know the R& B singer Mia would be performing and that she was also bringing along a special guest. I had no idea who, since I was leaving all Mia dealings in Dip's hands. In fact, that nigga was going to be flying in next week.

Friday, I'd taken Paige's ass to the mall because she insisted she needed to see if she could find a few outfits to wear to Table 51 over

the weekend. When I asked her why she was trying to spend her last bit of change when she had
two large suitcases full of clothes, Paige claimed
she couldn't show up with the owner of the club
wearing "old rags." I just shook my damn head.
But when we got to the mall and were standing at the checkout counter at Macy's, she had
to pick her goddamn face off the ground after I
cussed her the hell out. What had given Paige
the impression that *I* was going to be paying for
her shit?

I was mad I was allowing her to put me in
position to be out in public clowning black
queens in front of white folks in the first place,
but Paige was pushing my damn limits. Paige
was so mad about how I'd talked to her in the
store that she was quiet the entire ride home.
I was happy as hell about it too. I considered
cussing her raggedy ass out twice a day until
I put her on whatever plane, train, or bus she
planned on taking her annoying ass back to New
York on.

Friday was okay, but only because she knew
I was taking her to the club that night. Paige
was in her element when she was turning up,
so she was right at home. The night was almost
bearable . . . until she felt like she could go back
and forth with Tiny. I had to quickly squash

that shit. I cussed Paige out and then had to go
smooth my girl Tiny's ruffled feathers.

"You don't like your food? Mine is delicious! I
want you to bring me here again before I leave,
boo!" Paige crowed, smacking her greasy-ass
lips. Paige was fine, but my stomach roiled in
disgust at the sight of her. I'd spent damn near
$500 on groceries the few days since she'd been
here. For some reason, I got the feeling Paige
was throwing shit in the cart she knew damn
well she didn't buy when she was spending her
own damn money. All kinda fancy cheeses and
shit! Where they do that at?

"So who was that chick you were talking to
outside? Ya li'l piece of Virginia pussy? Okay. I
see you. I get it. You're a man, and I know how
you like to get down, Jeremiah. That's part of
the reason I came down here anyway. So you can
dig up in this good-good," Paige purred, finally
rubbing a napkin across her butter-stained
mouth. "I love fucking you, Jeremiah. So, I
figured I'd bring this pussy all the way to you
before I ever let another nigga get in between
these thighs."

"Well, you might wanna rethink that shit,
Paige. Check, please!" I called out to our waitress.

Monday couldn't get here fast enough.

Nicole

I'd been home for the last two hours and still couldn't get settled. I couldn't get Jeremiah out of my mind, and it was driving me crazy. How did I let a man I barely know get in my head this way and just stick? I rose up, turning my pillow over to the cool side. I lay there blinking in the dark. I couldn't sleep for shit and considered taking a Xanax. I'd been so good about not taking them lately. It seemed like ever since Jeremiah and I began speaking regularly, I didn't automatically reach for them the second I opened my eyes.

I don't even know Jeremiah, and he's got me feeling so disjointed. I wanted to scream. I reached over and turned on the lamp on my nightstand and leaned down to grab my laptop from the floor. I'm about to Google this nigga. I'll bet if I find his Instagram, I'll see if that's his girlfriend. Check this nigga's Facebook and see what his relationship status is. Because if you sit around waiting on a man to lay his cards out on the table for you to see, your ass will be waiting, I thought bitterly. I hadn't thought about Kendrick as much the last few weeks either. I mean, I still thought of him daily, but it was a little less. Hell, I can admit for the last year, Kendrick was on my brain from the second my eyes opened until the minute they closed, and many nights the nigga was running in my dreams as well. But as of late, it was a little less. No pills, I smiled and laughed more. Even that damn Khalid Carson in my training class had the nerve to comment on the change in my demeanor.

The first thing I decided to do was look for him on Instagram. The first spot I went was Table 51, and my screen filled with pictures of people partying. Jeremiah was in quite a few of the newer pics, but I continued to scroll until a face I didn't think I was capable of ever forgetting caught my eye. Kendrick.

I clicked on it to read the caption but didn't see anything that stood out. I hit the back button and continued looking. Why are there so many pictures of Kendrick and Antonio on this page? I wondered. My heart cinched in my chest when I stumbled upon pics of Tierrany and Tondellya. They seemed to be the best of friends now. I couldn't help but feel a wash of sadness looking at Tondellya. She had always been beautiful; her bright green eyes seemed all the more vivid now that I could see she was truly happy. I stared at a picture of her laughing and gazing up at Antonio for damn near ten minutes.

How could I have been so selfish as to ask her to walk away from all this happiness just because I was miserable? What kind of friend was I? Especially knowing firsthand how Tondellya grew up, always craving love and wanting a family of her own. My girl had found it, and I questioned her loyalty to me just because shit wasn't working out on my end. I clicked off and threw my phone on the bed.

I was still curious why Kendrick was in all those pictures, but who knew? I guess that was his spot. I shouldn't be surprised, though. After all, I ran into him there as well. My phone dinged with a text alert, and I grabbed it.

If you're awake come to the door.

My heartbeat quickened. Are you fucking kidding me? I jumped out of bed. *The nerve of this asshole thinking he can just show his face . . . and at this hour of the morning too!* I thought angrily, glancing at the time on my phone. Oh shit, it's only 10:30 p.m. I walked out of my bedroom to the front door. I didn't even bother turning on any lights or covering myself because

I was not letting Jeremiah set foot in here. He was just too confusing to me, and it was clear to me, I had a whole lot of things to deal with before I contemplated allowing another man into my life.

I dialed his number, and he picked up immediately.

"Why are you at my house, Jeremiah? I did not invite you here. Go home."

"I can't. I need to see you. Let me see you, and I'll go home. Just for a few minutes."

Good Lord! I was on the other side of the door beginning to melt. He sounded so good. Then I got hot and cold thinking about his black ass out on a date earlier tonight with another woman after ditching his plans with me on Thursday.

"I can't. It's late."

"It's only 10:35, girl."

"I have work in the morning," I said quickly.

"Tomorrow is Sunday. Since when do you work on Sunday?"

Shit!

"I'm really tired. I'm in bed."

I could hear Jeremiah suck his teeth loudly.

"Maaan, come on now! Baby, please stop playing these games with me. I can hear your ass clear as day on the other side of this door. You can hang up your damn phone and start talking instead of playing on the damn phone."

Ugh! I got mad and flipped on the light only to inspect this cheap-ass, thin front door of mine. I'm going to Lowes tomorrow and put in an order for a nice thick door! All of a sudden I heard a rapid beat from the other side of the door. Jeremiah had started acting like it was his personal drum set. I cracked the door open with the chain intact.

"Jeremiah, please go home. I can't do this with you. It's too much. I have a lot of baggage of my own to deal with, and honestly, I don't have the strength to go through another heartbreak. I can't deal with any lies, I just can't," I said, my voice breaking. I tried to close the door back, but it was met with resistance. I looked down, and Jeremiah's foot was in the crack of my door.

"Okay, I'll leave but lean closer."

"No! What, Jeremiah?" I cried impatiently. As soon as this nigga left, I was popping a Xanax.

"Gimme a kiss."

"I ain't letting you in here, I already told your ass."

"You don't have to let me in. Kiss me real quick."

This man had as much of his face through the door crack as he could get. I hung my head laughing at his ass and stood on my tippy-toes and pressed my lips firmly against his through my chained door. We both stood there, silent with our lips planted together before Jeremiah broke our kiss.

"Nicole, are you still in love with Kendrick?"

I stumbled back, shocked that he would even *ask* me that and was rendered speechless because I honestly didn't know how to answer him. After all of this time, there was a part of me that wanted to just say no. But a greater part of me couldn't honestly say I was really over him. Then as of late, I'd been wondering if what I felt was love at all. The more thought I gave my situation, the more convinced I was that what I was wallowing in wasn't heartbreak but rejection. I'd poured my all into both relationships I'd ever been in. Spent years trying to be everything I thought Don Travious wanted in a woman, only to always keep falling short in his eyes. I knew my friends will say that, oh, he was a dog, Don Travious wasn't ever going to be faithful to any woman, so don't take it personal, but I don't believe that. I'm of the belief that when you find the person that you truly love, you'll get yourself together. The love you have for that person should be so strong that you could never see yourself doing anything that would intentionally hurt that person or cause them any type of pain.

Because hurting them would be like hurting yourself.

So call me a foolish romantic, but that's the way I feel. I just wish the feeling was reciprocated.

So, after all the time and effort I put into that relationship to know that he wasn't getting right because I just wasn't the one for him cut me to the core. It chipped away at my self-esteem in ways I'd never spoken out loud about. Even to my best friends at the time.

With Kendrick, it was slightly different. I fell hard and quick for him, and my feelings were so real. Meeting him made me feel like everything I'd ever wanted was right within my grasp. It was right there dangling in front of my face like a carrot in front of a horse, and I wanted it so bad. Then to have everything come crashing down around me once again was devastating to me. A double dagger to my heart because when Tierrany appeared on the scene and Kendrick wasted no time cutting me loose, it was clear to me, even though I've fought hard to accept it. I still had to be honest. The way I wanted a man to love me, wanted Kendrick to love me, would never happen because that type of love, the love that made you feel as if you'd go crazy if you didn't have it, the kind of love that made you not want to spend a second apart, Kendrick just didn't feel for me.

It's not like it wasn't in him as a man. It was. Kendrick just felt that way about Tierrany and not me. I don't think a good month passed before he married her. When I heard the news, I was a complete wreck. I didn't think it was possible to be broken down any worse than I already was. But, yeah, it's damn sure possible.

That was the bitterest pill to swallow. Even now, over a year later, I could taste the bile rising in my throat at the thought of it.

Tierrany had shut down on Kendrick. Hadn't spoken a word to him in three years, but when she made the decision she wanted him again, the love he had for her was so strong that no one would stand in the way of him being with her. Not even me, despite all the love he knew I had for him. I was merely a roadblock to his one true love, and he quickly moved me out of the way to be with her. Ain't this some shit? We women spend all our time talking about snagging a man and making him fall in love with us, cooking meals and laying some good sex on him, when in reality, it's all very simple. When he decides you're the one, you just are. You don't have to do a thing for that man's love but just be you.

I knew I looked crazy standing there looking at him through the door, tears streaming down my face.

"Nicole, can you please just let me in so we can talk?" Jeremiah pleaded. I unlocked the door completely and widened the door to allow him inside. My head was swirling with so many thoughts I didn't even care about how I must look to him at the moment. I really didn't give a damn. This was me, head rag and all.

"I guess there's no need for you to answer my question, huh?" Jeremiah asked, leaning against the front door, observing me falling apart in front of him.

"I don't mean to do this in front of you, Jeremiah, it's just that I . . ." I began to stammer, ". . . I don't know if I can honestly answer that. I know that we'll never be together again. I've given up hope on that, but as you saw for yourself the day you met me, it doesn't mean that I don't want what I know I can't have. I wish I could have Kendrick walk into a room and me not want him. Or not obsess about the fact I feel I could have had everything with this man, but that's how I've felt this entire time," I blubbered through my tears.

"Then I met you. Completely by accident, and I'm not going to lie, I do know the sex was amazing, but I did it because I couldn't be with the man I wanted to be with that night. But I think about you, and you run me a little crazy, and I tried to avoid you, but you won't leave my mind either, and I don't know why."

"Can I have something to drink?"

"Jeremiah, drinks are what led to all this confusion I'm having right now as it is! I don't want any alcohol involved in this conversation," I said, exasperated. Before he'd knocked on my door, I was ready to pop a Xanax, but now, all I wanted was clarity.

"Damn, Nicole. A nigga can't get a drink of water out of you? I ain't said shit about no liquor," Jeremiah said, frowning his handsome face up at me.

My shoulders sagged, and I turned toward the kitchen embarrassed I'd overreacted. Yet again. Jeremiah followed closely behind me. He took a seat at my kitchen island, and I excused myself for a few minutes. I needed to splash some water on my face and gather my wits. I also took a second to take the damn rag off my head and run my fingers through my hair real quick.

Jeremiah looked up from his glass when I walked back into the kitchen.

"Whatchu got to eat in here? I'm hungry as hell."

"What? Did you *really* bring your tail over here to eat this time of night? Why that bitch you took on a date tonight didn't feed you?" I asked hotly, hands firmly planted on my hips.

Jeremiah began to laugh at me.

"Anyone ever tell you, you have a bad temper? I think ya *is* crazy. You may wanna work on that before you get into your next relationship," he said, raising his eyebrows at me.

"Well, I didn't used to have a bad temper. It's niggas like you that changed me!" I snapped.

"Don't lump me with the other men you been with. I ain't like these other niggas. Besides, I've tried to learn a few things along the way myself, and the one thing I know is this. There are people that will fuck you over and leave your heart in the dirt. But rare is the time you were blindsided and didn't see the shit coming. No end of a relationship just comes out of nowhere. There are always signs, but we all eat lies when our hearts are hungry," he said.

His last words left me rooted where I stood as I digested them. In that moment, no truer words had ever been spoken to me. During my time with Don Travious, my heart had been hungry for his love. By the time I met Kendrick, I was literally starving to be loved. So much so that I'd ignored every sign.

I'd poured my heart out to Kendrick and told him I was in love with him. Had he ever said it back? Not even once. How fucking oblivious could I have been? It was a sobering revelation to me.

I sighed, walking to my refrigerator and pulling out my three to-go boxes from earlier. I'd laughed at Cherell eating so much food, but when I'd placed my order, I was just as greedy as she, so I had plenty of food to throw in the microwave. I heated up the food, plated it, and refilled our water glasses before pulling up a seat next to him at the island and digging in. Not a word was spoken as we both settled into a steady rhythm of filling our bellies.

Jeremiah

We all eat lies when our hearts are hungry. I recalled reading that quote once somewhere, and it resonated within me. I'd never forgotten it. When things went bad with Mia, I remembered it. I also vowed to never let my soul starve again.

I concentrated on eating my food. Meanwhile, I was going over exactly what I wanted to say to Nicole. I was kinda kicking myself for coming over in the first place, because at the end of the day, I wasn't ready for no deep shit. I felt like a broken record telling myself that shit over and over, but I was trying to stop myself from feeling something for this wacky-ass woman! Neither my heart nor my head was ready for that, but this crazy girl was pulling me in. I didn't know how or why since it ain't like all of my encounters with her had been the best, but lately, beyond the physical, which I was very attracted to, I'd seen a side to her I really liked, no matter how much I was trying to downplay it to myself.

I sent her the damn flowers because I'd wanted to make her smile. I was calling her because her voice made my heart beat a little faster and her laugh made me smile.

When I was around her, I didn't think about Mia at all. Though I can't lie, once I was alone again, I compared her to Mia. Not in the aspect of her not being as good, but, damn. Nicole was quite clear she was still in love with Kendrick. The very last thing I ever wanted to go through again was falling head over heels with a woman who was still carrying around love in her heart for someone else. Shit, the nigga seemed cool to me and appeared to be in love with his wife. But what if they shit fell apart and he realized what a good woman he had in Nicole? Hit her up on some "for old times' sake" shit? The way she was breaking down and reminiscing about the nigga, she'd be right out the door.

Nah, one time and one time only. I wasn't playing second fiddle to another man ever again. Just like I'd told Nicole, there were signs shit was going on with Mia and Quinton and I ain't just talking about the one I saw through the window either.

There were so many times I'd wanted to see Mia, but her Mama Terri would be tripping. Quinton wasn't that much older than us at the time, and he and my brother Cedric were good friends. I talked to Mia about asking Quinton to help us see each other a little more. Cover for her sometimes if she was at my house, or say he'd given her permission to leave the house and she'd refused. Once I even surprised her and showed up at the house with Cedric, and Mia was jumping around the house like a scared house cat. I tried to pull her in for a hug, hold her hand, give her ass a kiss, and she was ducking and dodging me at every turn. Those were the signs right in my damn face, but I ignored them because I didn't want to acknowledge the true meaning behind her actions.

"So, are you going to tell me why you're here tonight, Jeremiah? You've eaten. Your ass shouldn't be thirsty, so explain."

I shook my head. This crazy girl right here . . . I'm surprised any nigga got shit past her—period— the way she's interrogating me! But then again, I guess I'm now the man who has to pay for the mistakes of every other man. Little did she know I was a good guy. Even with my interactions with Paige and any other woman I'd dealt with since my breakup. I'd told no lies. A woman may not have liked what I was saying to her, but I felt like I at least deserved some respect as a man because no lies were told.

"Nicole, it's simple. I'm here because I want to be. I told you earlier tonight I wanted to see you—"

"*To fuck!* That's it. That's all you want from me," she spat.

I had to restrain myself from going smooth the fuck off on her ass. Where the fuck did she get the idea that I was some type of desperate pussy-hound?

"Has something about the way I've presented myself to you since the day we met led you to believe I was some desperate-ass nigga? Let me tell your black ass something. The way you've acted, I could take your ass or leave you, but for some reason crazy as it is, there's something about your ass I'm genuinely attracted to. I'm doing my damnedest to see past all your insane behavior, but keep pushing me, Nicole. This ain't that serious. You think you been through some shit? Well, so the fuck have I. Just like you ain't with the bullshit, neither am I. I can fuck anyone I want to, Nicole. I ain't pressed for no goddamn pussy. Not even yours. I already had it the first night I met your ass—in case you forgot."

I didn't necessarily mean to cuss her ass out the way I did, but I was tired of some of these women mistaking my kindness for a weakness. I was straight up about my shit on a daily basis, but sometimes the women I dealt with tried to push their boundaries with me, and I wouldn't hesitate to let her know she was barking up the wrong tree.

"I'm sorry, Jeremiah—"

"Don't be sorry, Nicole, just watch your fuckin' mouth. Aside from the fact it's rude as fuck, you don't know what the hell you're even talking about. You don't know me like that to feel so comfortable trying to assassinate my character as a man. Especially given the fact I've been decent to you from day one. I rescued you from an embarrassing situation, and sometimes, I wish I'd let your ass twist in the wind. I should have let your dumb ass stand there looking stupid as hell in front of that man and the woman he chose over you."

"Jeremiah, stop it. I said I was sorry . . ." Nicole started crying yet again.

"God bless! Stop saying that shit all the time. Every time I look up, you're saying sorry for some shit that shouldn't have been said from the muthafuckin' jump. It's like you enjoy starting shit with me. Look, just because you didn't stand up for yourself with those other niggas, don't think you gon' take all that shit out on me. I ain't here for it."

"Well, what *are* you here for, Jeremiah? Because I keep asking you, and I'm not getting a straight answer from you. So tell me, what *are* you here for?"

"I'm here for you, Nicole. I'm only here for you."

There wasn't shit else I could say tonight. Nicole was exhausting to me. Mentally exhausting. Maybe I did need to just take my ass home and slide into the easy pussy I had waiting for me. I didn't want it, but it was easy. There was no work involved. I could just bide my time until a love walked into my life that was easy. Getting to know someone shouldn't be this fuckin' hard. My head was throbbing, so I raised my elbows to the counter, closed my eyes, and rubbed my temples. Thankfully, Nicole shut her damn mouth.

"I'm sor—"

I cut my eyes at her quickly, stopping her midsentence.

Nicole bit her bottom lip trying to prevent herself from saying anything else. I closed my eyes and continued rubbing when I felt her arms wrap around me from the back and her hands replaced my own. I gave in to the slow, rhythmic motion of her soft hands.

"Thank you."

"I've had an occasional migraine myself. Do you get them too?"

"Nah. You just gettin' on my damn nerves," I said. Nicole mushed me in my head while I doubled over in laughter. I guided her around me until she was standing in front of me trying to look mad as I caressed her soft hands. She was doing a poor job of it. Nicole knew damn well her ass was annoying.

"Look, I'm here because I wanted you to know I was sorry I had to cancel dinner with you. Please believe me when I say I was looking forward to it."

"Who is she to you? Why is she here if there's nothing going on between you?" Nicole asked, looking me in my eyes, trying to detect a lie.

"Paige and I were friends. I say *were* because after this stunt she pulled coming here I can't deal with her. I've known her at this point . . . umm, five months. It's purely sexual between us. We've eaten a meal or two together during that time, but that's about it. She's been pressuring me for a relationship the entire time. And I've been honest with her about the fact I'm not looking for that. In fact, before I came here, she brought it up again, and I told her that it wasn't happening. I never even told her the name of the club down here! She just showed up at the club with her luggage. You know how I left work early Wednesday and came over here and kicked it with you? Tiny said she just showed up at the club that day. I promise you she's outta here on Monday. Then she had the nerve to show up broke!" I said, praying she just took what I said because if she kept questioning my truth, I didn't know how much more I could deal with.

"Okay. I have other questions too, Jeremiah. Don't think I don't notice how you always let me go on and on about myself like a fool, but you only reveal a little about yourself."

I couldn't help but smirk a little at the comment. I'd deduced Nicole was too self-involved to even notice I was being intentionally evasive.

"I'll tell you anything you want to know, but let me warn you. I'm what you'd call a . . . semi-open book."

Nicole snatched her hands from me and placed them on her hips.

"What exactly is that, Jeremiah? Look, don't start making shit up on the fly just because you don't want to talk. That's not being fair to me. You are very pushy and aggressive when you wanna ask me something and be expecting an answer. Just like you barging in here tonight. So I suggest you open your book all the way up just like you make me do."

"Look, I'ma answer you but just don't pressure me. If I'm ready to start talking about something, I will. I'm just not ready. You act like I made you tell me something," I gritted out.

"Okay, you're here from New York, so what does that mean? What if we take this step toward getting to know each other, and then you have to leave? I have to ask because even though Lord knows it would make my life easier if I could be the casual girl, I'm just not."

"Don't I know it, ol' high-strung ass. Well, let's see. You know this is the second club Dip and I own together. I also told you I just bought my place here, so at the moment, I guess I live at both places. If my life leads me in a direction that I feel like this is where I need to be more, that's what I'll do. Regardless, I'm always going to need to travel back and forth for business."

"So, you mean you may spend two weeks here and two there?"

"If I need to. Otherwise, I wouldn't let anything keep me away from you too long. Why? You ain't gon' have a hard time keeping ya legs closed two weeks for me, are you?"

I felt a quick mush in my head again.

"Boy, please. They been closed since the last time you were between them. And I'm a very loyal woman, even though I've been burned before. So tell me what happened with your ex. I don't want to be the only one unpacking all my baggage."

I rose up and walked back to her living room. This was going to take awhile. I proceeded to tell Nicole everything that transpired between Mia and me that I had firsthand knowledge of. I mainly stuck to the points that hurt me the most. The lies and the deception, working my ass off to provide for a family that I was stripped of. Hell, easy street came for Mia and me damn near three years after we moved to New York. Before that, I took care of everything. I told her as much as I could without ever revealing her name.

Regardless of how I felt about how badly Mia had treated me, I would always protect her, even if it was just her reputation. Over a year later, the media was still talking about the whole incident. I was still being contacted by certain publications to tell my side of the story. I'd even been offered a book deal for a tell-all. I'd refused them all. The entire incident wasn't a game to me. It was my life and had damn near destroyed me.

"So she won't let you see the little boy anymore?" Nicole asked softly.

"Nah, I can see him. But can you understand how confusing that is? He's four now, but at the time he was three. I just felt like it was best to ease out of his life slowly and let his father step in fully. Obviously, she never stopped loving his dad, and it ain't like the dad turned his back on him. He never knew he had a son. I just felt like if it was me, I wouldn't want another man stepping on my toes. So even though I can't stand his ass, I gave him the respect I'd want given if it was my child. Also, it just plain hurt to know the family I'd prayed for just wasn't going to happen anymore. I gave up everything I knew to be with this girl. I mean, don't get me wrong, it ain't like my life was all sweet in the first place, but I left it all behind for her. I was still a kid my own damn self, but I provided for us and made sure shit was straight for all of us. I ain't know shit about living in no damn New York City. I just knew I wasn't going to let her down."

Out of nowhere Nicole leaned over and hugged me.

"You're a good man."

I felt drained after the entire conversation— hell, the entire night.

"A'ight, Nicole, I'ma head out. It's been a long night so I'ma let you get some sleep."

"You don't have to leave, Jeremiah . . . I mean, unless you want to, that is," Nicole said, glancing up at me shyly. Her hand was on her neck doing that rubbing thing I noticed she did whenever she was nervous or upset. I wondered if she even knew she did that.

"Nicole, I've worked too hard over the years to ever sleep on a couch, and if I lie in the bed with you tonight, neither of us are going to just sleep. Straight up," I said as honestly as I could.

"I wasn't asking you to stay so I could sleep, Jeremiah. Straight up," Nicole said, looking at me, a smile playing at the corners of her mouth.

Paige

It was after two in the morning, and Jeremiah had yet to walk his black ass into the house. Oh, the disrespect was too real up in this bitch! I lay on this shitty-ass air bed Jeremiah was making me sleep on and was getting hotter by the second thinking about how shabby I was being treated. I was humiliated the other night when he'd turned down my blow job. There I was, pussy slicker than okra, and this nigga had the nerve to say no? I'd already licked the tip and everything! I just didn't get it. Then his ass gon' be outside the restaurant while he was with me . . . hugged up and kissing some little Holly Hobbie-looking bitch! Oh yes, I was observing them for a minute before I walked up on they asses and broke that shit up.

My cell phone dinged again. I was so over all these text messages I was getting from my ex-roommate, so I ignored it. Then my phone started to ring. Ugh! I grabbed it and smiled. It was my girl Chantal calling.

"Girl, you lucky I'm in the kitchen getting a snack! I just put Jeremiah's ass to sleep," I sniggered into the phone, lying. Chantal was my bestie, but the last thing I wanted was her all in my damn business. As it stood, I'd lied to her and our other friend Desiree and told them Jeremiah had sent for me to come down here.

"Humph! Well, you better fuck his ass so good he move your ass down there permanently! Girl, Janell is hunting your ass down for real! Why this ho roll up on me at the club tonight like I owed her ass rent money?" Chantal quizzed.

My mouth turned down at the sound of Janell's name. Fuck her. If she couldn't show a little bit of patience about me giving her that li'l two grand, she could kiss my entire asshole. I tried to explain to her that Jeremiah was going to hook me up with the money and that I was probably going to be able to pay ahead, but she acted like she couldn't wait. Janell acted like she actually *needed* that bill money from me. Her grandmother owned the apartment we were staying in. Yes, she'd been covering all the household bills for a few months, but things were tight on my end. To be frank, I didn't like feeling like I was under a microscope every time I walked in the door.

Don't let me come in the house with a shopping bag or any takeout 'cause she was all in my ass questioning how I had money for all that but not for my bills. Don't even get me started on my weave and nails. What kind of friend was she? I guess she wanted me to be out here looking bad. Never that!

"Look, girl, Janell is tripping. I told her I would square that all away once I got back home! She knows damn well I explained how Jeremiah needed me down here for his club opening next week."

"Well, I know one thing. I sure don't appreciate being approached about *your* late bills. Janell was all loud about the shit too, like *I* owed her ass. Anyway, how is Virginia? Ooh, I wish Dez and I could get down there for the opening because Jeremiah and Dip's spot damn sure be lit up here! Girl, why I see on Instagram that Mia is going to be performing at the opening? You *know* that's my bitch! Why you ain't tell me? You know what? I'm talking to Desiree tomorrow about a road trip down there for the opening. We ain't hit the road in a minute, so why not? I'm excited! I'll call you as soon as we work out the details and tell you when we're on the way. Bye, girl, I'll holla at you tomorrow."

With that, she was gone, and I was screwed.

How the hell am I going to manage to stay here another week? I trifled through my purse trying to see how much money I had. I didn't have much to start with in the first damn place, but then Jeremiah left me hanging at the mall the other day. I felt stupid as hell at the counter. I didn't even have much with me, but I'd thought for sure Jeremiah would be nice and catch that li'l $250 price tag for me. Nope. In addition to him not paying, the nigga went smooth off on me right in front of everyone. So to save face, I had to play it off and reach in my wallet and pay. I refused to look like a broke bitch and leave the shit in the store. That would have proved to him I was a liar. It killed me to hand that bit of change over. I had a little less than two hundred dollars left. Thank God Jeremiah went grocery shopping, or I'd be really looking crazy. Shit, I know damn well my cards were maxed out too.

I jumped up and began pacing the room. Think, bitch, think!

Okay, Jeremiah claims I need to be out of his house on Monday. Maybe if I tell him my friends are coming down from New York to support the opening of his new club, that will soften him up a little, and I can at least stay with him until the weekend. If these hoes are coming, they'll be here on Friday, and I can just crash with them, I thought quickly.

Bitch, you know you quick on your goddamn feet! I thought, giving myself a virtual pat on the back. Now, I just needed to extend my invitation in his home. This visit didn't go as planned at all for me. We hadn't even fucked. Where this nigga at? I shot him a quick text asking if he was okay and letting him know I was worried about him.

A half an hour later he'd never responded back. I threw myself back on the air mattress and decided to get some sleep.

The smell of coffee and bacon tickled my nose, leading me to crack my eyes open. Damn, what time was it? I guess I'd finally knocked out after tossing and turning seemingly forever. I grabbed my cell phone to check the time. 7:30 a.m. I wonder when he came in the house. He must be in a good mood, the nigga in here making breakfast for us too? I grinned and hopped up to wash my face and brush my teeth. I decided to keep on the short, flimsy nightshirt I had on. I was naked underneath, and my ass cheeks slightly hung out. Before I hit the kitchen, I stopped in the hall and rubbed my breasts so that my nipples poked out.

"Good morning," I said, walking in rubbing my hands through my hair like I was still sleepy. Shit, I was wide awake. Jeremiah was standing in the kitchen shirtless with a pair of silk pajama

pants hung low on his rippled waist. Lord have
mercy, if this man don't break down and give me
some dick I'ma go crazy. I may have a few ulte-
rior motives but don't get it twisted. I wanted
this man! It ain't like I was out here fuckin' other
niggas either. I was selective with who I let in
this pussy. Jeremiah just wasn't falling in line
the way I wanted him to, and I knew the reason
why. He didn't have my ass fooled. That girl
from last night wasn't the one who was in my
way. Mia's ass was.

That was the only bitch who was my real
competition. Why the fuck was she gonna be
doing the club opening? The spot in New York
had been blessed with all kinds of artists from
the day it opened. That's why the club was so
hot, because in addition to the impromptu mini
concerts, celebrities coming in and shutting shit
down happened on the regular. Everyone from
Chris Brown to Drake came through and shut it
down on any given night. So why the hell did he
reach out to Mia to come perform? It's because
he wanna see her. That's a married woman, and
he's still sniffing around her like a sad puppy
dog. Well, I'm about to slap this sad puppy on
the nose and get his ass in line!

"Morning," Jeremiah responded, plating up
himself a heaping amount of food. He'd gone

all out. Bacon, eggs, grits, and toast. "I didn't think you'd be up this early. I think there's one slice of bacon and a little bit of eggs left," he said, walking past me with his steaming hot plate of food.

I was pissed. I felt like swiping his shit to the floor and tearing this entire kitchen apart.

"Jeremiah, when did you get to be so rude? Cruel even?"

His head jerked back. "Huh? What the hell are you talking about, Paige?" he said, taking a seat at his island and never missing a beat once he commenced to stuffing his fine-ass face.

"I'm a guest in your home, Jeremiah! Here you talking about it's a little left? You should have made sure there was enough for me too when you cooked. I would never treat you so poorly. Honestly, I don't know what this is all about. Then you didn't even come home last night. You just left me here in a city I know nothing about. I'm here because of you. I came here to support you, and look how you're doing me. At the very least, I thought we were friends. I just don't understand your behavior toward me. I don't deserve this," I said. A genuine tear had the nerve to slide down my cheek.

I really didn't get it. I'd never seen this side of him before. Granted, our times outside of the bedroom were few and far between, but how could I have been so wrong about him? Had I known he was such an asshole, I would have dedicated all these months to a nigga that I could have made some progress with!

Jeremiah dismissed me with a wave of his hand. I was livid.

"I'ma get with you in a minute, but I'm hungry as hell right now. I ain't letting my food get cold talking about this nonsense with you."

Fifteen minutes later, I was seated next to him quietly eating the extra eggs and bacon I'd cooked when Jeremiah drained his glass of orange juice, wiped his mouth, and turned to look at me. *Here we go,* I thought. I already regretted my outburst, but I didn't think I was out of line to say what I had.

"You know what? I sat here debating on if I should even address the bullshit you stood in my face and said. I mean, after all, you're out of here tomorrow, so why bother—"

"We can just move on from that," I interrupted in an attempt to change the direction of the conversation.

"But fuck that. Fuck you too, Paige. Let me remind you of something. I *didn't* invite you here. I've barely spoken to you since I got here. *Intentionally* avoided your phone calls. So why in the hell you'd hop your ass on a plane and come here I'll never know. So don't act like I got you down here and have treated you poorly. I didn't ask you to be here, and I don't wanna be staring in your mouth right now. But I'm trying to make the best of the situation since your broke ass is here. You so worried about the fact I didn't come home last night. That ain't none of your goddamn business. And you damn sure ain't getting no breakfast, lunch, dinner, or dick from me. Stay in your muthafuckin' lane, Paige, before I have to drop your ass at the airport right now," he said, snatching his plate up and walking back in the kitchen.

"I just didn't know you were like this, Jeremiah," I said, choking back tears.

"You knew what I wanted you to know, Paige. You know how my dick works. That's all you've ever needed to know. But the entire time you couldn't be satisfied with that. Don't sit there looking stupid, like I'm telling you some new shit and hurting your fuckin' feelings. I told you from the jump I wasn't interested in a relationship with you or any other woman at the moment. When a man tells you that, believe him. What, you think you know me more than I know my goddamn self? If you're feeling any type of way about me saying this to you, you ain't got nobody to blame for it but yourself, Paige."

With that, Jeremiah walked out of the kitchen leaving me stewing in a mix of regret, shame, and another feeling I couldn't quite put my finger on, though I had the slight feeling it kind of felt like revenge.

Nicole

Last night had been amazing! Granted, it started off crazy enough, but by the end of the night, or should I say before Jeremiah crept out of here early this morning, there was no doubt in my mind I wanted him. The only thing I needed to concentrate on, because I knew myself, was jumping heart-first into the situation. History had shown me that I definitely had the tendency to put the cart before the horse. If I continued along that road, I was going to get hurt. *Relax, Nicole*, I thought, chiding myself. *Have a good time and don't become consumed.*

The reality of our situation was that both of us were fucked up. There wasn't any nicer way to put it. We'd both been fucked over before. Badly. He more so than I. I still felt slightly stupid about my behavior over Kendrick after investing only a few months of my time. Yes, my feelings were true, but the reality was, it was mere months.

Jeremiah had been with his ex for years. Had
taken on the role of being a father to a baby
he knew from the start wasn't his. Lesser men
would have left her ass. I don't know what kind
of woman this was who blinded him to make all
these sacrifices, but she was trash! A liar, cheater,
and the ultimate user. That's what it sounded
like to me. Ol' girl was straight using Jeremiah.
She knew damn well her ass was knocked up by
that other man. I'll bet he did know about that
damn baby. She probably told the baby-daddy
about the pregnancy, and he told her to kick
rocks! I rolled out of bed, stood, and stretched.

My body was sore, but it felt so good I wasn't
complaining. The first time we'd had sex, I
wouldn't say I was drunk, but I was definitely
feeling good. Running dead into Kendrick that
night—with the woman who'd taken him from
me—was a blow to my entire being. So the
alcohol helped me stay sane that night. I knew
the sex with Jeremiah that night was damn
good but didn't shit compare to being completely aware and cognizant of how my body
was feeling. Every inch of my skin responded
to his touch. As a lover, Jeremiah was incred-
ibly attentive, staring into my eyes and talking
me through every orgasm. My God, this man
had mastered the art of dirty talk. I didn't real-

ize I liked it so much. I hated to see him leave this morning, but he headed out early. He said he needed to go on home since he technically did have a houseguest. We were meeting later tonight at Table 51. I was going to call Cherell in a bit to see if she wanted to join me. I knew it would come as a shock to her because since I'd met her, Cherell was always the one dragging me out of the house, admittedly kicking and screaming most of the time. I was looking forward to being around people for a change. My head snapped up. I think I'll make a few phone calls today too.

Table 51—Sunday Night

"Yaass, bitch! I'm so glad you called me today, I don't know what to say!" Meka crowed loudly from the front seat, pulling down my car mirror to check her face. I was actually out with my girls tonight. What was left of them, at least. Meka and Cherell. We'd just pulled into the parking lot of Table 51.

"Bitch, when I tell you being a mama is rough, you better believe it. This child of mine runs me ragged. The only reason I'm free tonight is because my mama knew I was about to lose it and offered to take his li'l bad ass off my hands for the weekend. His sorry-ass daddy damn sure don't do shit! Fine as I am and I haven't even been able to hit the streets to find me a new man. Okay, so you mean we're all walking up in here single? You already know how I roll. I need to scan the room and see who's up in here for me. Shoot, Meka Johnson is coming out retirement."

I glanced up into the rearview mirror, and my eyes met with Cherell's. She was sticking her finger down her throat making a gagging face. I bit the inside of my lip to prevent myself from busting out laughing. Lord, this was going to be a mess! Tonight was the first time Cherell and Meka had been introduced, and I quickly realized they were two peas in the same pod. Cherell was slightly better in her delivery, but they were both man-eaters to the core. So one of two things could happen. They would end up being the best of friends, or they'd hate each other and become competitive.

I don't know how I always ended up with friends so crazy. Tondellya and I matched more in personality. I felt a quick pang of sadness. Damn, how are Meka and I here without Tondellya?

"Well, what are y'all bitches waiting on? Let's get up in here. Shit, these shoes are for looks only. I damn sure don't want to be standing all night. This place is packed. Niggas don't have to be at a job in the morning or what?" Meka said, climbing out of the car.

Once we walked in, my eyes began scanning the crowd for Jeremiah. We'd spoken quickly that afternoon and confirmed that I would be stopping in tonight. I knew he was working, but he promised to spend a little time with me when he could, and I was okay with that. Actually, I'd coached myself all day on playing it cool and casual. I felt like an idiot having to do it, but, hey, fake it till you make it.

"Where ya boo at?" Cherell asked as we took a seat in a nearby booth.

"He's not my boo . . . We're friends, Cherell," I said, blushing.

"Uh-uh . . . Who is this boo? Why am I *just now* getting wind of a potential boo? Damn, there's some eye-candy up in here tonight. It's nice in here. Tondellya invited me here a few times, but I could never make it. Shit, Tondellya over there living good! A nanny and all that shit so she can still go out! We ain't all got it like that. I need a damn drink," Meka said, twisting in her seat, searching the crowd for a waitress.

Lord have mercy! Had Meka always been this damn loud? Yeah, she had been. It just seemed amplified since it had been so long since we'd actually gotten together.

"Hello, ladies."

My eyes looked up from the cell phone in my hand to find Jeremiah standing there towering over us. Our eyes locked, and I couldn't stop the silly grin from slowly spreading across my face.

"How are you this evening, Cherell?" Jeremiah asked.

"Fabulous as always."

Jeremiah turned to Meka. "Hello, I'm Jeremiah. Welcome to Table 51," he said, addressing her.

I can't even lie, I felt the claws coming out just observing the way Meka's thirsty behind was obviously drooling over him. I mean, damn! Show some couth. A little sophistication.

"Hello, yourself, Jeremiah. I'm Meka. It seems like you know everyone at the table except the most important person. Me," she purred.

I saw a flash of something I didn't quite recognize in his eyes.

Jeremiah chuckled lightly.

"Nah, I think I know the most important person sitting here. How are you tonight, Nicole? Come talk to me real quick," he said.

Meka's mouth dropped as she watched me ease out of the booth, take Jeremiah's hand, and walk away.

"Who in the hell is that?" he asked once we were in his private office.

I squeezed my eyes shut, laughing. "That's my childhood friend Meka. She takes a little getting used to, but she's harmless."

"Damn, I thought Cherell was a character, but I think Meka might have her beat, and that's just after one meeting. Come here," he said, pulling me into him. I was positive he could hear my heart beating through my chest.

"Did you enjoy yourself last night?"

"You know I did, Jeremiah."

"Okay, cool. I'm just checking, because if you didn't, I'm willing to go back in until I make it right."

"Can you come over tonight?" I asked shyly.

I hadn't even planned on inviting him over but being in his presence only made me want him more. I think he was just messing with me asking if I enjoyed myself. You goddamn right I did is what I wanted to say, but I didn't want to make it seem like I was *that* desperate for some dick. Jeremiah leaned down, placing his mouth on mine. I melted into the intoxicating taste of his mouth. Hennessey laced with a hint of cinnamon. My legs began to quake slightly, and I grew wet under the ministrations of his hands palming my ass. My hand naturally gravitated toward his hard dick. Even through the expensive fabric of his pants, the thick length of him left me wanting more.

I deepened our kiss. I needed to feel him. I looked into his eyes, growing more turned on by the fact I could tell by the look in *his* eyes how much he wanted me. It had been so long since a man had looked at me that way I felt brazen. I *wanted* to please him. Jeremiah licked and sucked on my bottom lip. I reached out to touch him. I didn't think his dick could get any harder, but it damn sure felt like it was. I made the decision right then and there—I wanted him in my mouth.

"Can I taste you, Jeremiah?" I asked as my hands grazed the waistband of his pants. My heart was beating so fast waiting for permission. I should have just done it, but part of me wanted to know that he really wanted me. If he said yes, I'd know my desire for him was mutual. I wanted his big head to tell me yes, not the smaller one I wanted to wrap my lips around.

"You don't have to ask. It's all yours."

I took a deep breath and relaxed my body. Jeremiah walked us over to the love seat in his office and sat down with me standing in front of him. I pulled my dress up above my waist and straddled his lap, rubbing my hands over his chest and landing at his tie. I slowly rubbed the length of his tie, feeling the expensive silk between my fingers. The things I could do with this tie, I thought. Jeremiah reached out, rubbing his hands over my breasts. My pussy clenched, and I let out a moan, leaning in to kiss him again, slowly gyrating my hips on his manhood. Jeremiah pulled my hips closer to him and bucked underneath me. *Oh my fucking God,*

I thought, *I'm going to come right now! This man is going to make me come just doing this.*

"Oh shit, Jeremiah! You're going to make me come!" I moaned loudly.

"Well, come on, then. Whatchu waiting for?" he said, grabbing me by the nape of my neck and attacking it with his tongue, rocking me hard against him. The friction from the steady rubbing of his fabric against my clit was sending me into a frenzy. Then it happened—my mouth opened into a silent scream before a loud moan escaped, my eyes squeezed shut, and I saw stars. Seconds later, my body relaxed, and I could feel Jeremiah's hands slowly caressing my back.

"Are you all right, baby?"

"Uh-huh," I nodded, relaxing my head into the crook of his neck. *Shit, that's not how that was supposed to go,* I thought slightly embarrassed. *How did I go from wanting to taste him to humping his leg like a dog in heat?* I quickly shook that off because I wasn't done by a long shot.

I stood up and removed every stitch of clothing I had on. Jeremiah couldn't take his eyes off of me, and his hand grabbed his dick.

"Goddamn, girl, look how you got me over here," he said, glancing down at himself and back up to me.

I reached down and helped him ease his pants and boxers down around his ankles. Then I quickly eased back up, unbuttoning his shirt, running my hand up and down his chest. I could feel his heart beat. Slowly I dropped to my knees. Licking my lips getting them moist enough to slide back and forth on his dick, the sight of it made my mouth open wider in anticipation. The taste of his velvety smooth length easing down my throat had me dripping wet. A moan slipped from between my lips as I felt him pull out of my mouth and graze my lips with the bulbous head of his pipe. Jeremiah eased it down my throat inch by inch, slowly bobbing my head up and down until the juices started to flow. The wetter my mouth got, the harder it was for me to contain my speed. I went faster, and I could feel his legs shake, causing my nipples to get so hard they hurt. I was enjoying his dick in my mouth.

I reached up and placed one hand on my own nipples, pinching them. The slight nip of pain caused a tingle down my body as my other hand slid up and down his dick. I glanced up to see Jeremiah's head thrown back, but he looked down and caught me gazing at him. He grabbed the sides of my head firmly, and his hips moved lightly, leaving him with full control as he fucked my mouth. Then he yanked me up, quickly positioning me over his dick. I felt him slide inside me, sending a chill up and down my spine. He rested his hands on my ass and rocked inside of me, causing my ass to slap his thighs every time he slid himself completely inside of me. Every stroke was deeper. Harder. I could feel my juices dripping down his dick. My head was spinning at the pure pleasure I was receiving. I felt like any second I would explode.

The only sound in the room was our bodies connecting and grunts and groans of pleasure. At one point, I couldn't tell who was making what sound. All I knew was I felt incredible, Jeremiah felt amazing, and we fit together like a beautiful puzzle. I tried not to yell out, but the pleasure I was receiving was so amazing I couldn't contain myself, calling out his name every time he dug into me. I felt his speed pick up, the tension between us building to a fever pitch. Jeremiah's breathing became labored. He was no longer taking it easy as he pounded my pussy roughly. He ran his hands over my breasts and bent his head, taking a nipple in his mouth. My entire body spasmed as I exploded once again. The only thing I could remember at that point is me begging him not to stop. Seconds later, I felt his hot seed spill into me, and we both collapsed onto the couch breathing heavily.

We lay there in silence until a voice came over Jeremiah's walkie-talkie.

"Shit, I forgot my ass is working tonight," he sighed, easing himself up. "Look, I still need to see you later. This wasn't enough."

All I could do was smile and nod. My legs felt like Jell-O, and I needed a damn nap now!

Jeremiah quickly cleaned himself up and left me in the privacy of his office to finish washing myself up. Tiny rang his cell claiming there was an emergency at the bar and he was needed, so I told him I could manage getting back to the table on my own. I certainly didn't want to rush back out with a freshly fucked look on my face, so I took my time washing up, applying some fresh lipstick, and giving my bob a sexy tousle. I pushed the lock on Jeremiah's office door and walked out, making my way down the empty hall when someone suddenly popped out in front of me.

It was Jeremiah's unexpected houseguest, Paige. I simply smiled, said hello, and kept walking when I felt a pull on my arm.

"Don't touch me," I said, yanking my arm out of her grasp.

"I guess you think throwing that piece of good girl pussy on Jeremiah is going to keep him, don't you? Tuh! Think again, bitch!" Paige spat glaring at me.

"You know what, Paige? Whatever issues you have with Jeremiah, I suggest you take it up with him. You don't know me, bitch, and the best thing I can tell you to do is not put your damn hands on me again either," I said, trying to walk away when she stepped in front of me.

"I know you're disrespectful as hell. Why you would be cocking your legs up to a man you know has another woman at his place is beyond me. What? Is Jeremiah telling you he ain't fucking me? Because he's a goddamn liar! But I'm cutting his ass off. I just didn't want you to be walking around confident and under the impression you ran me off, bitch. *I'm* the one who cuts niggas off. I will leave you with a little bit of advice, though," Paige said, folding her arms across her chest and rearing her head back to look at me smugly.

"What's that, Paige?" I asked. Not that I gave a damn about what this evidently bitter-ass bitch had to say.

"Take notes . . . Ummm, what's your name again? Nicole?"

"Don't play with me, bitch. Just like you recognized me in the sea of women in here tonight after just one time meeting me, you know my damn name."

"Touché, bitch, touché," Paige said, laughing.

"I don't have time for this shit," I said, starting to walk off.

"Please don't go falling in love with Jeremiah. He is a bitter and emotionally crippled man. No matter how good you are to him, how much pussy you throw his way, or are just there for him, period, he is *never* going to love you. Ever. So don't waste your time. You standing there looking all conservative and shit, and I know damn well you ain't got nothing on me in the looks and body department. But you know who you're never going to compare to? His ex-girlfriend Mia."

I just stood there looking at her blankly. I may not have known Jeremiah long, but I felt like he was truthful about everything he'd revealed to me about his painful breakup. I didn't know what Paige was trying to prove, but she wasn't telling me a thing Jeremiah hadn't told me himself.

"You so fucking dumb. I can tell by the stupid look on your face you don't even know who the hell I'm talking about. Jeremiah's ex-girlfriend is the R&B superstar Mia. The only bitch with the keys to that nigga's heart is her. Why the fuck do you think she's coming all the way here next weekend for a little measly club opening? Mia sells out Madison Square Garden, boo.

So you might be thinking you have one up on me, but you damn sure don't have shit on her. Very few women intimidate me in the looks department, and she's probably one of three. I ain't even gon' mention the fact she's rich and talented. What do you do again?" Paige said, cackling with laughter as she walked off, leaving me in a stupor.

I stood there with my mind in a fog before I made myself snap out of it and walk back out to the main area of the club, coaching my feet along the way.

"Took your ass long enough! I thought y'all might be in here somewhere fucking. Ya boy been back out here and sent us a bottle of Dom!" Meka whisper-yelled excitedly. I reached for an empty glass on the table and the bottle. I needed a drink. Hell, I needed three or four. My mind began playing like a video. Jeremiah turning down her music in my car, not liking it too much, and the blatant lie of not telling me who she was.

Yes, we'd spoken about his ex last night, but he'd clearly only revealed the parts of his story he wanted to, and I'd been okay with that. But now knowing who his ex was, could there be other reasons he wasn't as forthcoming? I hadn't even paid attention to the fact he'd only addressed her as his ex. Was I creating smoke

where there was no fire? Or was there? Ugh! I
was so confused. Did I really have a reason to be
upset? I sat there stewing in confusion.

I hadn't even noticed Cherell was gone.

"Where did Cherell go?" I asked, skimming
the crowd. Maybe she was on the dance floor.
It was too crowded for me to catch her if she
was. Jeremiah had created a buzz around town
by implementing a theme at the club on various nights of the week. Sunday was now called
"Sunday Steppers." The grown and sexy crowd
loved it. This was the second Sunday doing it,
and looking at all the couples tearing up the
dance floor with their intricate moves was fun.
All the matching outfits, it was a definite change
of vibe from the Thursday through Saturday
crowd who came in here to turn up. The kitchen
also deviated from the appetizers they usually
served to a full-blown meal they served by the
plate. It was nice and as packed as the place was,
word was definitely getting around. Jeremiah
told me that once his friend Dip arrived, more
than likely Wednesday nights would be Dance-
Hall Reggae night. Dip was Jamaican and
insisted on representing his culture I was told.

I turned my head to find Jeremiah's eyes
glued to me. I gave a halfhearted smile. I don't
know why I couldn't help feeling lied to, and

for me, a lie of omission was still a goddamn lie. Why was it so hard for men to be honest? I asked myself, a small ember of anger flared inside of me. Mia's coming here next week? He's going to be around her? This is just too much. I may still have some hang-ups concerning Kendrick, but I'm not around him! This means he still talks to her. The flame inside me rose a little higher. I'll bet he still sees that little boy. Talking about it's too damn hard. Hah! It must not be! He's still communicating with the mama. These niggas kill me with the lie upon lies!

I tried.

I attempted to stay calm and not blow up because it could all be for nothing, but, no, I felt like he should have given me full mutha-fuckin' disclosure.

Jeremiah

Thank you, Jesus! I thought, pulling off from the airport where I'd just dumped Paige and her bags! Monday couldn't have come sooner because this girl had plucked my last nerve. After the conversation . . . if you could call it that since I just let her know how I felt about some shit, Paige had the nerve to still ask if she could stay another week. Talking about could she just crash for a few days since her girls were coming down for the grand reopening on Saturday.

I didn't give a damn.

My hospitality had been pushed to the limit, and I wasn't extending it any further. To no-god-damn-body. Shit, as it was, I was taking the day off from the club because I was going to be having deliveries made to my place all day long. I didn't really have time to fix my spot up, so I'd called in a favor to my homegirl in New York who'd helped me do my place there. She knew my style, and she'd picked me out some nice

pieces of furniture. At least the place wouldn't
be so empty, and I could have it semi-ready for
when Dip got here Wednesday. He'd be staying
with me for a while. Even though I'd been here
a month, I was barely holding it together, even
though on the outside, I made it look easy.

We had to hire a club manager among many
other things. I was supposed to see Nicole last
night, but at the last minute, she claimed she
wasn't feeling well, so those plans fell through. I
asked her if she still wanted me to come through
and stay with her, but she said she just wanted
to get some sleep. I sent her a text earlier this
morning asking how she was, and she said
fine. She said she was running late for work
and would text me later. I made the decision
to surprise her at work with lunch. Which was
yet another reason I was in a hurry to get rid of
Paige. She was throwing a monkey wrench in my
plans for the day.

I thought about sending her ass to the airport
in a cab, but I didn't want to be rude. I walked
into Nicole's favorite spot, Croakers Post, and
picked up the to-go order I'd called in. Twenty
minutes later, I was standing at the security desk
of Nicole's job waiting on her to come down and
get me.

When Nicole rounded the corner and saw me, I saw the surprise written across her face.

"What are you doing here, Jeremiah?"

"Didn't you say you take lunch at noon? I brought a little something to eat."

Nicole looked sexy as hell in her little work outfit. Black fitted pencil skirt . . . I knew what type it was from Mia. She's all into fashion, talking about pencil skirts emphasized your hips and booty. They damn sure did, the way it was cupping Nicole's ass, and she had on a sleeveless, fuchsia-colored top that had these flouncy looking ruffles going down the front. She was bad. Looking all professional and shit.

"I did." Nicole got me a visitor's badge and led me through the building to her office. Damn! There were some men I saw working, but the employees, for the most part, were women, and it seemed like all eyes were on me as we walked past. Once we entered her office, Nicole turned to look at me.

"You know I don't really play around when it comes to work, Jeremiah. You really should have called before you just showed up."

Damn. That wasn't exactly the reaction I was hoping for when I decided to pop in. Maybe she was busy at work. I should have considered that.

"I apologize. I didn't mean to take you away from anything. I just know you mentioned taking lunch around this time. If I'm interrupting, I can leave. I know you have a lot on your plate."

Nicole sighed loudly.

"I mean, you're here already, so we may as well eat," she replied snidely, waving me over to a round table situated in the corner of her office.

Okay. Maybe I should drop this food off and get the hell out of here, I thought apprehensively, taking a seat and starting to unpack the food and utensils.

We sat silently eating.

"Did I remember your favorite foods?" I asked, silently proud because I knew I had! This was her spot, and I'd recalled the first time she took me there her telling me so. In addition to the night we ran into each other there, we'd eaten the takeout together at her house later that night. Besides, it was so quiet in her room I was starting to feel awkward.

"Not really. But it's okay. I'll eat it anyways since you tried."

I finished chewing the food in my mouth, biting back a retort. Instead, I took a sip of my iced tea.

"You look pretty today. I meant to tell you that when I saw you downstairs."

Nicole put down her water.

"As opposed to any other day you've seen me, huh? I'm sure you've seen much prettier, Jeremiah," Nicole said ruefully.

I eased a napkin over my mouth before setting it down on the table. "Do you have a problem with me today, Nicole? If you do, I'd appreciate you addressing it like an adult instead of sitting here making all these little snide comments and having an attitude about some shit that only you're aware of," I said. I wasn't about to sit here and play these games with her. Why did women do this shit? Say why you're mad so we can fix the shit. Instead, you wanna sit here with an attitude.

"Are you still in love with your ex, Jeremiah?"

I was stunned by the question. We'd just discussed this the other night, and I thought we were both clear on where we stood in regard to our exes. Why was she bringing this up again now?

"Why are you bringing all this up, Nicole?"

"Why can't you answer the damn question? Just answer me," she demanded.

"Or what?" I said, gearing up to tear into her ass.

Nicole sat there blinking at me gripping her fork.

"Answer you or what, Nicole? You already know I have love for my ex. Just like you do. That's already been established, so why are we talking about this today?"

"You have love for her? What a joke! Nigga, you still want her, or you wouldn't be bringing her around!" Nicole seethed, throwing her fork on the table and jumping from the table, pacing her office floor.

"I can't believe I was so stupid I gave you the benefit of the doubt, and still you lied right in my face, Jeremiah. Right in my damn face. You're the diabolical type of liar I really can't stand. A person that will lie for no reason at all. Just to be lying because you don't know how to tell the damn truth! I can't believe I was so stupid! Again," Nicole spat before bursting into tears.

I was taken aback. What in the entire hell was Nicole even talking about? I didn't want to see her cry, but the irrational behavior she was displaying right now had me fucked up.

"Nicole, baby, I would never intentionally do anything to hurt you, but apparently I did, so please tell me what it is so that I can clear it up," I implored. I was so confused.

"Why didn't you tell me your ex-girlfriend was Mia? How could you conveniently leave out *that* part of the story? You basically told me everything else, so why would you leave out that?" she spat, pointing her finger in my face.

I slowly shook my head. You have *got* to be fucking kidding me.

This cannot be life. I opened up my mouth to speak but just as quickly shut it, stood up, and walked my black ass out. I was not about to stand here and argue with this crazy girl at her job—or anywhere else—over something as dumb as her not knowing who my ex-girlfriend was. I jumped in my car and took off. I was over trying to make something out of nothing with this nutty-ass chick.

Nicole

"Cherell, come to my office," I sobbed into the speakerphone on my desk. I couldn't stop the tears coursing down my face. How could Jeremiah just act like he'd done nothing? As if he hadn't wronged me in any way. I wasn't crazy. He should have said something! Adding to the way I felt is that last night after I'd told him not to come over, I arrived home and undressed, then proceeded to pour over the Internet Googling everything I possibly could about him. Hell, Jeremiah, Mia, Terri, and the infamous Quinton.

I was floored.

Unbeknownst to me, Jeremiah was a low-key celebrity! I read interview after interview of Mia praising Jeremiah for giving her the push she needed to do music. They had layouts in magazines, and every blog and tabloid had candid pictures of them along with little Jacobi. I loved Mia's music and listened to her on satellite radio while I was driving, that's how I mainly

found her music. But over the last year, I damn
sure hadn't been reading blogs and magazines.
I was depressed, and outside of work, spent all
my free time sleeping and watching Netflix. I
couldn't believe how much celebrity gossip I'd
missed.

I pulled up the Web site for his club in New
York . . . dozens of pictures of him with visiting
celebrities. I barely got a wink of sleep pouring
over every YouTube video and article I could
find about all of their asses, and I had to admit,
it was some juicy shit! Mia's mama was crazy
as hell. I clicked back and forth between two
different videos like a madwoman. One of her
talking about Quinton, another about Jeremiah.
And the one thing that was clear as hell to me is
this. Mia had been deeply in love with both of
these men. What if she wanted Jeremiah back?
Paige was right. I couldn't compete with Mia.
Jeremiah loved her, and they had history.

Cherell burst into my office.

"Bitch, what are you in here crying about?
Oooh, whatchu over here eating?" she asked
nosily, walking to the table.

"Jeremiah's ex-girlfriend is Mia."

"Who? She live in Richmond?" she asked, popping a shrimp into her mouth.

"Cherell! The *singer* Mia! *That's* his ex-girlfriend."

Cherell's eyes bucked. "Nah, bitch! 'Ballad Of a Bad Bitch' Mia? Married to that fine-ass nigga Quinton? With the crazy mama in jail for kidnapping her baby Mia?"

"Yes!"

"Damn! You know when all that shit went down, I was all on the blogs reading about that craziness, girl! It was everywhere, but it died down quick because all ol' girl would say in interviews is 'no comment.' You know, I *knew* Jeremiah was connected to some shit, but I had no idea. Matter of fact, I saw the flyer that said Mia was going to be at the club soon. Damn! Well, you knew the nigga had some money. Those townhomes he bought go for over half a million dollars. What's the problem, and where you get all this damn food?" Cherell spouted off, acting like it was no big deal.

I couldn't believe she was being so cavalier!

"*Excuse* me? Don't you think he should have *told* me who the hell his ex-girlfriend was? I think that was a *major* detail to leave out, don't you?"

Cherell screwed her face up. "Umm, no. He ain't gotta tell you shit about his last relationship, let alone her name if he don't want to."

"Are you kidding me? Don't you think that's weird? Deceptive even? We both sat and talked.

I was honest with him about everything that had gone on in my last relationship. I thought he was doing the same. Yet, there he was lying in my face the entire time. That wasn't just his *ex*-girlfriend. Jeremiah *proposed* to her!"

"Deceptive? Nicole, if you don't sit your crazy ass down somewhere . . . First off, this is why it's a bad idea to talk about your exes in the first damn place as far as I'm concerned. Unless something goes on that directly involves you . . . Why is that your business? It's *not!* Anything that went on in their relationship has nothing to do with you, unless he was whupping her ass and now he's wrapping his hands around your insecure throat. You might need to know about *that*. But he was perfectly within bounds not to tell you her name," Cherell said, shaking her head at me like I was the biggest fool she's ever seen. She was looking at me with so much disdain I began to wonder if I was being unreasonable.

"I just think it's important—"

"Why? Because for the last year you've run your mouth about Kendrick to anyone willing to listen? Some people are private, and how dumb do you sound? Being that Mia is a celebrity and with all his connections to her, I can definitely see him not being forthcoming with you about it. Honestly, Nicole, you're my girl and all, but as fine as that man is, I don't see why he bothers with you at all. Has anyone ever told you you're too much damn work? And especially for a nigga that ain't known you but a month."

I felt like I'd been punched in the stomach. It was hard enough feeling like I was hard to love by the opposite sex, but hearing my close friend say it was sobering, to say the least. I actually had heard it before. From Jeremiah. I guess from the forlorn look on my face Cherell could tell she'd hit a bit below the belt.

"Look, I didn't mean that exactly how it came out. You're my girl, and I love you, but I have to be honest. You're very high-strung, and I can't figure out where that comes from, Nicole. It worries me, and this is coming from a person who knows she has her own personal baggage. I ain't saying Jeremiah is the one, but who knows? He could be, but you'll never know because you keep looking for reasons to make him seem like a no-good man. If you ask me, Kendrick wasn't bad to you either. Don Travious don't even count! That was some high school shit that should have ended there. Something my therapist told me is this, if all your relationships aren't working out with different men, you need to look at what they all have in common, and that is *you*."

I'd heard that phrase before as well, but I never thought it was something that applied to me. I was good, I was loyal and faithful to a fault, and I expected to be treated the same by people I invested my time and emotions into. It got me nowhere.

Cherell sighed. "Just ease up, Nicole. You ain't special, boo. I mean you are, but you ain't, if you know what I'm saying. You keep taking everything as a personal attack on you when we all get fucked over sometimes, no matter how hard you've vetted that person and tried to protect yourself from being hurt. It happens to the best of us. Men too. Now you done talked all this shit to this man and called him a liar—and for what?

"Does that make it any better for you, because let me tell you what I think. I can't even imagine being in love with a man in the public's eye and being totally humiliated in front of the world the way he was. The details the public knows about what all went down with Mia were bad enough. So I can't even imagine the details we don't even know about. So why would he be so eager to tell anyone all that when, since it's happened, he's been the one who got dogged the fuck out, and Mia married ol' boy and is living life happily ever after?"

Ugh! Why did Cherell have the ability to break things down in a way that I could actually receive it? Now I really *did* feel like shit. But I did have one more thing on my mind.

"Cherell, do I need a makeover?"

"No, why? You look cute, girl; booty poppin' in that skirt," she said, giving me a once-over.

"You know that chick Paige is the one who told me about Mia, right? That ho ran up on me in the hall last night. She kept saying I didn't have a chance with Jeremiah because Mia was so pretty and a star. Making it seem like I could never be anything to him—"

"I *know* you didn't take that bitch serious, Nicole? I don't know why you didn't point that bitch out last night. I damn sure would have set her straight," Cherell said, clapping her hands, "Shoot, it's been a minute since I've had to lay hands on a bitch, and I need to do it one more some before I settle down, get married, and have me two pretty babies," she said, sucking her teeth.

"Dang. You have that all planned out, don't you?" I said, laughing. "The last time she called me Holly Hobbie! And I remember the one time I did get into it with Kendrick's wife . . ."

"Oh, you mean the day you rolled up in his house like a damn ninja?"

"Yes," I said, embarrassed at her accurate description of my behavior. ". . . His wife said something about me being 'mammy made' too! That's two people talking about me like that. Why are they saying that to me? Be honest. I can take it," I asked sincerely. I was really confused. I won't lie and say I've been keeping up with the latest fashions, but I damn sure didn't think I looked bad! When Tierrany had said it to me, yes, I'm sure I was looking crazy at the time. After all, I'd been on a stakeout in front of Kendrick's house on no sleep and drinking coffee. So I could see it. But where was this Paige tramp coming from with her comments? Her ass cheeks were hanging from the bottom of her dress both times I'd seen her. I damn sure wasn't going to start dressing like *that*.

"Nicole, please, you look fine. A bitch like me is always down to spend, so we can shop and do lunch anytime, but to answer your question, no, you are not out here looking busted. If you were, I wouldn't hang with your ass. Period. Shit, I have a reputation to protect," Cherell said, walking to the door.

"I'm going to take it this crisis is over?" she asked at the door.

I nodded my head, resigned to the fact I'd fucked up with Jeremiah, yet again.

Cherell snapped her fingers and walked quickly over to my desk, grabbed my notepad, and began to scribble.

"Here," she said, pushing it to me, ". . . before I forget. The number to my therapist. No pressure, but in case you need to talk to someone who can dig a little deeper than I can, boo."

Meanwhile, in Manhattan—Mia

It had been a long day and I ain't even going to lie, Lord knows I love my little boy, but I'd never been so happy to see someone go to bed before! I needed to bottle up and sell his energy. I'd make millions. I could stop singing, touring, and everything else that came along with this lifestyle. I stepped into the walk-in closet and stood there overwhelmed, looking at all the clothes. I was headed to Virginia tomorrow night for Jeremiah's club opening. Jeremiah himself still hadn't communicated with me in regards to me showing up, but in the last year, I'd come to accept that. In turn, Jeremiah would just need to accept the fact that if I was needed, I'd come through whether it was Dip calling or if he broke down and did it himself.

I walked around the closet trying to see what would fit the occasion. I didn't feel the need to go all-out; after all, it was an intimate club performance, but I still had a reputation to uphold, so regardless, I needed to "slay," as my girl Beyoncé would say.

"Mia!"

"I'm in the closet!" I called out to my husband Quinton. I gave a slight eye roll. I know he better not come in here talking shit, because I'm not in the mood to go round for round about this again.

"Whatchu doing?" he asked, stepping inside and taking a seat on the leopard print chaise lounge situated inside the closet. Yep, it was *that* big. The damn closet was larger than Jeremiah's and my first apartment when we moved to New York.

I glanced over at Quinton, and my heart skipped a beat. Damn, how did that still happen? After all these years, it still caught me off guard how devastatingly handsome my husband was. It didn't help he was shirtless and in his boxer shorts. Quinton's body was amazing. He'd always been naturally good-looking, but his personal trainer had definitely brought everything out times ten.

"I'm trying to figure out what I'm taking with me to Virginia."

Quinton sucked his teeth loudly, grumbling under his breath. "I thought we'd talked about this, Mia . . ."

"We did. You stated your opinion, and it doesn't need to be rehashed again, Quinton. I know exactly where you stand." My head began to throb slightly. When Quinton was upset about something, he was like a lion with a fresh piece of meat in his mouth. He wouldn't let go.

"Oh, so you just don't give a fuck about what I feel? *That's* how we doing it now, Mia? *That's* what this marriage is about now?"

"Oh my God, Quinton! Stop creating drama where there is none! I'm leaving for two days. I'm going to perform at the club one night, and then I'm coming back home to enjoy the rest of my downtime with you and Jacobi. What are you getting mad about?"

"I'm mad because why does it seem like you not letting this nigga go? We've been married almost two years now, and any time you think you can interject yourself into Jeremiah's life, you do it. Why?"

"Really, Quinton? Spell 'interject.'"

"Don't think I can't! Shit, I'm a college-educated man. And don't try to throw me off. You know damn well I'm right. I'll bet Jeremiah ain't even the one who asked you! *Did* he? Tell the truth, shame the devil, Mia."

"I already told you it was Dip that called me. So what?"

"I just think it's time for you to let that shit go. You act like you owe that nigga something, and you don't."

The dress I was holding in my hands fell to the floor as my hands gravitated toward my hips, and my eyes narrowed.

"*Excuse* me? I owe Jeremiah *everything*. I owe him my *life*."

"Oh, here we go with this shit again! You don't owe that man shit! If anything, he's still owed a few ass whuppings for keeping my son from me for three years. Keeping you away from me too."

Here goes Quinton with the bullshit again. Before I blew up and said something I really didn't mean, I reached down, picked up the dress, and continued flipping through my closet trying to compose myself. I loved my husband to death, but at times he still didn't get it. Quinton refused to believe that Jeremiah and I packing up and running away from Texas was all *my* idea. At the time, I was running away from my mother *and* him. Quinton, in his mind, chose to leave himself out of the equation. Refusing to believe there was ever a time in life that I didn't want him. Yes, his ego was just *that* big.

"Oh, you ain't got nothing to say to that, huh?"

"Quinton, you already know I'm going. So why are you trying to intentionally start a fight with me? Why, baby?"

"Because I don't like feeling like I'm sharing my wife with another man. *That's* why. Shit, it's like you have this loyalty, an allegiance to Jeremiah that you won't let go for some reason." Quinton had a disturbed expression on his face. He looked hurt, but what could I do? He was my husband, but even to save his feelings I wasn't going to lie to him. We'd already had too many lies between us in the past.

"I am loyal to Jeremiah, Quinton—"

"See! You ain't even trying to deny it!"

"Why should I? I've never denied the way I feel about him to you or anyone. I never will. I loved him in the past, and I love him now. Just in a different way."

"That's fucked up, Mia. How do you think that makes me feel to hear my own wife say she's in love with another man? I want that nigga out! Outta your mind and out of your heart, do you hear me?" he yelled, jumping to his feet.

"You're crazy as hell if you think I'm about to stand for this shit. What kinda man do you think I am?"

I didn't know what to say to him in this moment because one thing I'd come to know about Quinton was that loving him wasn't easy. Don't get me wrong. I'd literally gone through hell and high water to love him. Even though my mother was horrible, I'd betrayed her to be with him, I'd hurt Jeremiah for him, even broke my own child's heart by breaking the bond he had with the only father he'd ever known to be with Quinton—not to mention public opinion. I knew what some people said about me. The tabloids *still* wrote about it.

I'd made so many strides in my career, three Grammy Awards, two American Music Awards, and a plethora of other accolades, and yet, *that* story still topped some of my accomplishments.

Quinton paced in front of me like an angry bull. "You always running after this nigga. I'm tired of this shit. Muthafuckin' tired, you hear me? This man still in love with you, and you fuckin' know that shit. So why you, a married-ass woman, would put yourself in the position of being around him is beyond me," he raged on.

"Quinton, Jeremiah doesn't even speak to me. These arrangements were all made with Dip," I tried to explain.

"All the more reason you need to sit your ass down somewhere! He doesn't even have the common decency to ask you himself. Are you even getting *paid* to do this?"

"Dip looked out for me in the past too. Dip is the one who put a roof over our head and looked out for us when Jeremiah and I moved here—"

"I damn sure don't wanna hear that story again," he cut in.

"Well, end this dumb-ass conversation then. Stop fuckin' talking because at the end of the day, Quinton, guess who's going to be on a plane headed to Virginia tomorrow? Me, that's who," I gritted out. I'd had enough of all this damn whining from him.

"You fucked up. You know that? You don't respect me or this marriage at all, do you? You always doing some shit to hurt me because you know I ain't going nowhere. You know that shit. So you throw this nigga Jeremiah up in my face any time you feel like it. You don't owe that man shit. He don't even fuck with Jacobi no more, but you act like he's fuckin' God. The nigga fucked your sister and everything," Quinton raged on. He was on autopilot, saying anything that came to his head to make me hate Jeremiah.

"*Really*, Quinton? Do you *really* wanna take it there? Since you wanna go there and throw shit in my face, how many times have *you* fucked my mama? You're trying to hold Jeremiah up for judgment behind *that*. Are we *really* the people who should be throwing stones behind some shit like that?" I asked angrily. I was pissed. How dare he try to throw stones! He and I, more than anyone, knew that life happens. I'd been deeply hurt by what took place between Jeremiah and my sister, but I knew one thing as well. It only happened because Jeremiah was drunk. I knew my sister Tanya had been the aggressor in the situation. I also knew had Jeremiah been sober, it would have never happened. I was positive about that.

"That's different! The situation between us doesn't compare to what *he* did."

I took a few deep breaths trying to compose myself. Regardless of whether Quinton and I were mad at each other, I was still going to make the club appearance, but I didn't want it to be this way. I needed to find a way to make my husband feel secure. We'd been through the fire together, and I needed him to know that my choice had been made a long time ago. I'd chosen him.

"Baby, what is this all about? In a year we've seen Jeremiah about four times. That was just dropping Jacobi off so that he could see Jeremiah. I've never been alone with him. Please tell me what it is about Jeremiah that has you feeling this way?"

I put the clothes in my hand down and walked over to him, wrapping my arms around his waist and looked up, gazing into his eyes. Quinton avoided looking at me, but when he did, I could see the tears in his eyes. I reached up to wipe them away.

"Baby, tell me, please."

"I just-I don't want you around that nigga . . ."

My heart tightened in my chest. "You don't-you don't think I'd cheat on you, do you?" I was stunned. If this is where my husband's head was at, I definitely couldn't leave with him feeling this way. The love I felt for Jeremiah would always be there, but it was nothing compared to the love I felt for Quinton Jones. We'd gone through so much together, and I knew as well as I knew my own name, we were in this marriage to the grave.

Quinton grabbed the sides of my head tilting it back as he gazed into my eyes intently. "Nah, I know you love me. I know you wouldn't do no shit like that."

"So tell me. You know we can say anything to each other, Quinton. You know what—"

"I don't know, Mia. I just feel like if there was ever a man that could take you from me, it's that nigga. You think I don't know the only reason we're here . . ." Quinton held up our hands displaying the gorgeous matching wedding rings adorning our fingers, ". . . is because that man couldn't forgive you for a few lies? Every day when I look at you and Jacobi, I thank God Jeremiah didn't have no forgiveness in his heart for you at the time. Then just as fast, I ask God not to ever let him get any either. I know that sounds fucked up on my part, but, hey, my name is Quinton Jones, and sometimes I say and do some fucked-up shit. I just don't want no man to be able to think he can walk in and take what's mine. And if any man could, it's Jeremiah. I know it, and so do you. Even if you don't want to admit it. You two have unfinished business because of him. Then I have to listen to you talking about what a good guy he is and how you so sorry he got hurt. He's a man; he'll get over it."

"Did you get over loving me?" I asked, smiling in an attempt to lighten the mood.

"Don't get cocky. That's different. We were meant to be. I said that the first time I laid eyes on you walking out of Sam Houston High School that day. You were mine and didn't even know it."

"Well, how come you're not just as confident that nothing or no one could ever tear us apart, Quinton? That's how you should look at things. I'm confident that way when it comes to you!

How many beautiful celebrities have we been around? Too many to count and I don't feel like any of them could take you from me."

"Yeah, that's because you already know the lengths I went through to be with you. You ain't never had to do shit for me but be you. Totally different, babe."

Back in Virginia—Jeremiah

There was a loud knock at my office door that caused me to frown. Who the hell was knocking so damn loud?—

Hell, who was knocking at all? I wasn't in the mood to be bothered.

"Come in!" I called out to the intruder. Hell, I should have told everyone I didn't want to be interrupted. Emergencies only. I had enough on my plate as it was without fielding nonsense. Two waitresses came in earlier asking about the uniforms and could they change the colors of the skirts they wore since it was a new club. Basic shit I didn't feel like dealing with. My nerves were bad enough as it is. Mia was due to fly in tomorrow, which had me feeling discombobulated, and Nicole was acting her usual shade of crazy.

I was trying to wipe her completely out of my mind, though. I'd had enough of her bullshit to last me five years. And she wasn't even my woman! I couldn't lie, though, it didn't stop me from thinking about her any less, which only caused me to be madder. I mean, the nerve of her to bring up Mia like I *owed* her some kind of explanation.

The door flew open and in walked Dip.

"Man, what's your ass doing here already?" I asked, my eyes flying to my watch. "I thought you weren't due in till after six?"

"Yeah, I was, but ya boy caught an earlier flight. Got me an Uber to carry my ass on over here. She was fine too. Got her number," Dip said, looking around the office.

"Well, I'm damn sure glad you're here. Let me walk you around the place and introduce you to the staff that's here right now. I know they're curious."

"I know they are. Who the fuck is the nosy chick out there with the chipped tooth?" Dip asked, cuttin' his eyes at me.

"Aww, man, that's the homegirl Tiny. She's cool as fuck. If you asked for me, I know she was asking you 101 questions like mama bear," I said, laughing. Tiny had somehow taken on the role as my little sister since we'd had our talk a few weeks ago.

"Well, Tiny better not come at me with an attitude anymore before her ass be without a job," Dip said, sucking his teeth.

"How her name Tiny anyway with that big ass and all those titties?" Dip asked aloud.

I threw my head back. This nigga didn't have a lick of sense.

"Nigga, I have no idea but don't make it your mission to find out," I said, pinning my eyes on him as we walked out of my office. Dip started laughing. He had a tendency to mix business with pleasure once in a while. In New York, we'd had to let two of our best waitresses go due to them actually coming to blows over him at the club. Luckily, everything was on camera because both of those trollops tried to get lawyers and sue us for being let go. After viewing the footage and the recordings Dip had of them threatening the false allegations, the case was thrown out of court. Dip then sued them for the court costs incurred.

Needless to say, from that point on, I kept an eye out on him, reminding him that we had too many women coming into the club on a daily basis for him to try getting with the women on our payroll. I gave Dip an extensive tour of the club as well as the property outside.

"This was a good investment. We made a good choice," Dip said, smiling.

"That we did, my nigga," I said, walking toward the club.

"So you know Mia comes in tomorrow. You good with that?"

I stopped dead in my tracks and turned to face him. "Well, I ain't got much choice but to be good. We gon' have to have a talk about that too, Dip."

Dip stuffed his hands down the pocket of his loose jeans and squared his shoulders. "Nigga, you got something to say, speak your piece."

"Well, nigga, since you asked, stop calling Mia every time we got some shit going on! We could have had just as good of a club opening without her here. She just adds on stress to an already crazy situation."

"Nah, my nigga . . . *You* add the muthafuckin' stress. Mia and I ain't stressed. That shit's on you. We good, potna."

I looked at Dip and shook my head, laughing. Was this nigga *really* trying to flex? "You gotta problem, Dip?"

"Matter of fuckin' fact, I do. Look, I told your ass a long time ago I was in this shit to win. That means any leverage I have with anyone to get to the next level I'm using. Any connections I got, I'm taking advantage of. One of those connections just happens to be Mia. Look, I know you loved the girl and felt like you got fucked over, but, shit, it is what it is. Life happens. It's time for you to let that shit go. I know you feel like you were done dirty and got the short end of the stick.

"I feel where you coming from, but it's time to let all that old shit go and be easy. Mia has done nothing but be good to us and try to reach back and pull us up with her. As she should to hear me tell it. You and I did a lot of shit to get her where she is today. You know how many people want to forget where they came from and the people who helped them out along the way? Well, Mia ain't one of them. And she's doing it more for you than me. Trying to make sure you good, my nigga. So let her."

I looked at Dip, frowning.

"Well, damn, tell a nigga how you *really* feel," I replied salty as hell. Why did everyone feel like they had an opinion on how I should be dealing with my breakup with Mia? Dip and my brother Cedric were quick to issue their opinions on how I should be feeling when both these niggas was hoes. They didn't know a thing

about truly loving a woman, being faithful, or
being a father. I knew about all three, even being
a dad, and I hadn't created not one child of my
own yet. *These muthafuckas!* I thought ruefully.
My brother Cedric would be in later tonight as
well so I knew when they got together they were
going to try to go in like they had the wisdom of
Gandhi, especially when they started smoking
weed.

"Well, nigga, since you asked, move the fuck
on! All these women after you, and over here,
you acting like Mia's pussy is made of gold . . .
Wait a minute, is it? Is the pussy so good you
can't forget?" Dip asked. The expression on
his face reminded me of a curious little kid. I
couldn't stop myself from laughing.

"Nigga, if it is, I ain't telling you about it!"

"Look, all I'm saying is this. I seen for myself
how good you were to that girl. I mean, dang, I
never knew Jacobi wasn't even your baby until
all the shit went down. I know I'm telling you to
get on out there and get ya dick wet and shit, but
I know you ain't no dog-ass nigga—"

"Like you?"

"Yeah, like me, muthafucka! Ain't no shame
in my game! I'm just saying this to let you know
that all the shit you did for Mia, another woman
is going to appreciate. All of it, the faithfulness,

dedication you had to her and her baby, all that shit. But you ain't never gon' have the love you want holding on to that bitterness. Mia did some fucked-up shit, but, man, she keeps trying to show you how much you mean to her. How much love she got for your ass. Cut her a break. You've punished her enough. And at the end of the day, you ain't hurting no one but yourself. She still gon' keep living and loving her husband when it's all said and done. And you gon' be bitter and alone if you don't let this shit go. Oh, and I'm still gon' call her to come through when I feel like it. Shit, Mia got a new album coming out soon, and I know she gon' have some bangers on that joint!" Dip said, walking into the club.

I stood outside the club thinking about everything he just said to me. I knew he spoke nothing but the truth. Dip wasn't the type of guy who, outside of business, spoke a lot. He was the type of guy who flew by the seat of his pants, liked his fair share of liquor and women but kept things light. So when he did drop some knowledge or spoke seriously with me, I had no choice but try to take it in. He always had my best interest at heart. It was crazy because we met in jail back in Texas. Dip had gotten into some trouble down there visiting and had landed in jail, and from the day we met, we'd been like brothers.

It was funny that he was so cool with Mia because when we'd first moved to New York, Mia couldn't stand him. She claimed he was looking at her funny. Hell, I'd almost ended our friendship behind the way she felt about him then. The Lord had surely been looking out because I would have been without the woman *and* the man who'd come to be my best friend.

Damn, this nigga right. Life is moving on for Mia, and here I am stuck. My mind ran to Nicole. When I was with her . . . and she wasn't acting fuckin' crazy are the only times I can honestly say my mind wasn't on Mia. How the hell have I even been functioning? Every single day I woke up and did what I was supposed to do, but my mind was always half there. I was brushing my teeth . . . and thinking about Mia. In a business meeting . . . and wondering what Mia was up to.

Yes. I had to let her go completely.

It was just hard to do when I'd always pictured my life with her and Jacobi in it. Not to mention I beat myself up on a daily basis wondering what would have happened between us if I had just forgiven her? If I had just set my pride to the side and listened to her all the times she'd reached out to me and begged my forgiveness. That's the part that haunted me these days. Because I know the outcome of the whole situation may have been different had I just bent a little. My pride wouldn't allow me to do it, though.

"Fuck!" I screamed, punching the brick wall of the building. Then I walked into the club. I just wanted to get back to my office and shut the door. Let me get my mind on work only. I don't want to think about Dip's guru advice-giving ass, Mia and that fuck-boy she married, and I damn sure don't wanna think about Nutty Nicole.

"Oh my God!" Tiny shrieked as I walked past her. I didn't bother to stop and see what the hell she was screaming about. I continued on to my office and closed the door, but it flew right back open.

"Boy, what happened to your hand?" Tiny pointed. I noticed she had a first aid kit in her hand.

I looked down to see my hand dripping with blood. Scrapes covered my knuckles. Shit, I guess I was so mad I didn't even feel the pain.

Tiny cut her eyes at me. "Sit down and let me fix you up . . ." she commanded, ". . . Now I got to clean you up *and* run a damn mop with bleach water behind your donkey-brain ass!" She cussed me out the entire time she was cleaning up my cuts and bandaging my hand for me.

"I'm sorry. Don't worry about it, I'll clean up after myself."

"Well, I can imagine how good of a job you'll do since you fucked up your good hand. Don't worry, I'll get it done. What's your damn problem anyway?" she asked. "What happened, you and Nicole fall out? I noticed she ain't been in here lately. Her girl Cherell stay up in here, though," she added sarcastically.

"Nicole, shit, I don't know what to say about her ass. I ain't with it, though. She ain't for me."

"Hmm. I can't tell the way you smiling every time you're around her."

"Tiny, let me ask you something, how much do you feel like you need to know about your man's ex?"

Tiny moved to my office chair and sat. "Well, I think there comes a time when we all have to lay our cards on the table. I know some people say don't discuss exes, but fuck that. I wanna know. I *need* to know if you've been screwed over so bad it's going to take me moving mountains and boulders and shit just to get into your heart. I wanna hear you speak on her so I can see the expression on your face and the tone of your voice when you speak that ho's name!" Tiny exclaimed, clapping her hands, getting good and ghetto.

"Why, though? What good is that going to do?" I asked curiously. "Why not just leave the past in the past and move on from there?"

Tiny looked at me, shaking her head at me. I could almost hear her saying, "Poor little Tink-Tink" in her head.

"Jeremiah, you can't really be that dense, can you? As women, we want to know because we need to see for ourselves that it's over. Now us women, if you didn't know, are fickle creatures. We can stand you having love for an ex. But when men say they're in love, for some reason, y'all harbor that shit forever. I think men in love, especially if he's a good man and don't be hoeing around and claiming he's in love with every woman he fucks with, y'all go hard. Then y'all treat the next woman like she can never live up to your ex."

I let her words sink in. Damn, Tiny was on point with everything she was saying. I ain't going to act like I was okay with Nicole's delivery, but maybe her feelings toward the situation weren't as invalid as I'd made them out to be.

"Is this the reason you and ol' girl are beefing?"

"I mean . . . yeah. Kinda," I said hesitantly. I'd told enough of my business for the day, and Tiny was Team Nicole, so I wasn't too sure if I wanted to add fuel to the fire by disclosing the reason Nicole was really upset about my ex.

"Yeah, *kinda?* Sound like you're trying to lie, nigga. Spill it."

"Look, Tiny, don't be overstepping your boundaries."

Tiny gave me a once-over through narrowed
eyes.

"*Boundaries?* Negro, once we decided to be
friends, the boundaries were erased, in case you
didn't know. So decide what you want me to
be. Strictly your employee or ya homegirl who
happens to also work for you? Choose carefully
too, nigga!"

I silently looked at Tiny weighing my options.
Then I sighed loudly—hell, it was more of a
groan!

"You my homegirl," I grumbled low.

Tiny leaned forward holding her perfectly
manicured hand up to her ear. "Huh? What did
you say? Nigga, you was mumbling!"

I burst out laughing. "Fuck you, Tiny. You
know you my girl."

"I already know! So what are you leaving out
of the story?"

I exhaled loudly. "Nicole is mad at me because I didn't tell her Mia is my ex-girlfriend.
Honestly, I didn't think it was a big deal who
my ex was—"

"Hold the phone, Negro! You mean to tell me
your ex is Mia, the singer? The very Mia who
is going to be performing here this weekend?
The Mia who's had this damn phone ringing off

the hook with people asking if they can make reservations so they don't miss the show—*that* Mia?" Tiny asked incredulously.

See, her exact reaction is why I didn't want people to know. I could tell the second the realization hit them about what all would go down.

"Damn! You're the boyfriend she had . . . and *dumped?*"

"See, that's the shit I don't want to constantly be reminded of. It was embarrassing enough when it happened—let alone always being reminded of the shit."

"Well, of course, I think she may have wanted to know, but I mean, it's no big deal who you dated in the past. If it makes you feel any better, you did get a raw deal. I thought it was fucked up. From what I read you were there for her from the jump."

"Thanks. I guess," I said dryly.

"Well, let me get out here and mop up after you. Look, as for Nicole, that's petty shit the two of you need to get past. Just be the bigger person and make it right. I mean, if you have no interest in her, just say fuck it, but I think you really like her, Jeremiah. Don't be so proud. Too much false pride is a muthafucka and ain't gon' do shit but leave you lonely and unhappy," she said as she walked out of the door.

Damn! It was freaky as hell to hear Tiny tell me the same shit I'd been beating myself over the head with for the last year. The thing holding me back was this, I knew for a fact Mia had been worth me setting my pride to the side. I couldn't exactly say the same about Nicole.

Nicole

"Girl, what are sitting over there looking all
crazy for?" Cherell asked between bites of her
salad.

We'd ordered in salads and sandwiches from
our favorite local deli and were having lunch in
her office. Shit looking crazy? That didn't touch
the way I was feeling on the inside. I kept picking up the phone as if I could magically make
him call me, but it wasn't working. I was also
too prideful to make the first move and call him.
I'd run over my conversation with Cherell in my
head a hundred times. She was right. What did
it matter who his ex was? He'd opened up to
me and told me how much she'd hurt him. He'd
confessed all his feelings. That should have been
enough for me.

Instead, I'd opened up my big mouth and
alienated him when I should have been comfort-
ing him the same way he'd done for me the night
at my house. We'd both been left feeling hurt

and abandoned around the same time. Yet, I was making my pain out to be more than his. My new therapist Lauren also helped me process my last exchange with Jeremiah.

Yes, the very next day I'd called Cherell's therapist stating I needed an emergency session. Thank God she'd been able to squeeze me in. What really shocked me was that the focus of my last few sessions hadn't been Kendrick. I'd gone in focused on myself and spoke about missing Jeremiah's company. I missed hearing his voice at night when we talked on the phone for hours before finally calling it a night and going to sleep.

"I miss talking to Jeremiah," I admitted.

"Well, do something about it, then."

"I can't. He doesn't want me, Cherell. I think I've completely blown it."

"Did he tell you that?"

"Yes. He did. Jeremiah thinks I'm a nut job."

"Well, I ain't gon' lie and say he was too far from the truth but prove him wrong. Ain't nothing stopping you from reaching out to that man but your ego. Reach out to him and tell him you miss his company. I think you should. The man showed up here bringing you lunch and making an honest effort, and you go and shit on him. You need to make it right. When you're wrong, you need to be woman enough to say you're wrong and make it right," Cherell said, picking up half of her turkey sandwich. I looked at her in amazement. Didn't shit stop this woman's appetite! It was a wonder Cherell didn't weigh 300 pounds with as much food as she put away.

I was just pecking at my food. Honestly, I hadn't eaten a decent meal since the day we'd had our falling out. If I didn't watch out, I was going to lose all my ass. I'd dropped twenty pounds when Kendrick broke up with me. My parents were worried as hell, especially since I hadn't been carrying any extra weight on me from the start. I'd just recently gotten back to my preferred weight of 135 pounds.

I picked up half of my sandwich and began to eat. The last thing I needed was to start falling off over a man that wasn't even really mine. Jeremiah felt like he could be mine, though, I thought to myself.

"Okay, look, I know your ass is stubborn as hell, so why don't you do this. Why don't you come with me to ladies' night over at Table 51 tonight? You can go in casually with me, no pressure involved, and check out the scene. More than likely, he's going to be there. If he avoids you like the plague . . . then you know yo' ass fucked up for good. But maybe, just maybe, both of y'all have cooled off, and you can discuss whatever the hell is going on between you."

My face was already screwed up at her bright idea.

"Cherell! Now you want me to seem like I'm straight stalking by going into his club all the time? That's going to make me really look crazy to him! I'm sure he doesn't want to see me in there all the time. And furthermore, you my girl . . . I think maybe you should stop going in there so much," I said meekly, adding the last part in.

It made perfect sense to me. We were friends well before that club opened! Cherell should just start going back to her old stomping grounds as far as I was concerned. If the shoe was on the other foot, she wouldn't have to ask me twice. I was loyal like that!

The sound of Cherell's uproarious laughter filled her office.

"Bitch, you crazy! Never that. Hell, I was in Table 51 last night, matter of fact, and spoke with Jeremiah. Whatever falling out y'all are having has nothing to do with me, girl."

I sobered fast, slowly setting my sandwich down.

"You saw him last night? Why didn't you tell me? Did he ask about me?" I inquired nervously.

"Yes. Because I'm not obligated to tell you. And, no, he didn't ask me about you. See how easily Jeremiah left me out of y'all personal bullshit? Try it!" she said, taking another bite of her salad and crunching loudly.

My heart sank.

He didn't care. I don't know why I thought he would.

"Look, heffa, you wanna go or not? I'm leaving straight from here to enjoy happy hour and get my free drink shit. Besides, I don't wanna get all in your business, but I do want to know how your sessions have been going. Shit, you had me canceling my damn session so she could fit you in. You're lucky you're my girl, and that I knew your crazy ass needed it. Shoot, I look forward to my weekly vent sessions." Cherell cut her eyes at me.

"I'll go," I said numbly. I don't know why the thought of seeing Jeremiah and not speaking to him made me feel so bad, but it did, and I couldn't deny it. I really didn't want to accompany Cherell to Table 51 tonight. There was only one reason I agreed. I'd had sex with Jeremiah multiple times already, I couldn't deny the fact I was interested in him . . . *very* interested. At the same time, I didn't want to revert back to the way I'd been once Kendrick and I broke up.

I didn't want to go back into hiding, ordering in takeout, and watching Netflix in my home like a recluse. The last month and a half had been very good for me. I'd noticed a change in myself, as well as the people around me I interacted with. My trainees noticed as well. My unruly trainee Khalid even mentioned me smiling more in class. Talking about he didn't even know I had teeth. I thanked him for the backhanded compliment—and then told him to get back to work.

"You don't want to go home and change first?" I asked, looking down at my outfit. I thought I looked way too conservative to be going out for drinks at a club. Hell, if it was going to be over between Jeremiah and me, I at least wanted him to regret it. I wanted him to look at me and wonder if he was making a mistake.

Cherell glanced up at me. "Bitch, you ain't slick. Go ahead and go home and change, if you want. You can just meet me over there. I'll save us a table because, girl, *everyone* is catching on to that place. It was packed as hell up in there last night."

"Cherell, you need to take your ass home sometimes. Do your neighbors even know who the hell you are, as much as you stay away from home?" I asked. I was serious as hell. Cherell never sat still for long.

"I know, girl! I'm working through all that with the damn therapist! I have a fear of being alone.

Plus, it's boring as hell. I like being around people and hate quiet. I told you I hated being an only child. Let me work though my shit at my own pace. Damn!"

I started laughing as we continued to make conversation for the remainder of our lunch hour. Oddly enough, as much as my head was dreading running into Jeremiah tonight, the butterflies in my tummy were fluttering with anticipation at the thought of simply laying eyes on him.

Later That Night . . .

I walked nervously into Table 51 around 6:30 p.m. Dang, Cherell wasn't lying. This place was crowded as hell. I navigated my way through the crowd looking for Cherell. During my hunt for her, I was stopped by two men trying to catch my attention, but I politely turned them down and kept moving. Besides, I wasn't too fond of men who felt the need to get my attention by catcalling and grabbing my arm while I was walking. Approach me respectfully or not at all. It had been a while since I'd dated, and granted, this was my longest stint being single since high

school, but I did know what I liked and didn't
like. It took me several minutes to spot Cherell
seated in the corner booth, and I headed on over.

Cherell looked me over.

"Bitch, I'm jealous! You done took your ass
home and got fly as fuck, and here I am feeling
like Raggedy Ann!" she said, laughing.

"Girl, hush! I did what I could," I said slyly. I
did feel good. I'd raced home and practically
dove into the shower. I pulled out a little black
two-piece skirt outfit I'd never worn before. The
outfit was sleek and fitted. The top was long-
sleeved but was cropped, showing my lithe, flat
stomach, and the skirt hugged the curves of my
hips and stopped at the ankles. I'd paired it with
some strappy, six-inch sandals and a red clutch.
I decided to give myself a dramatic smoky eye
along with a bold red lip. To make my face
stand out, I'd taken some light molding gel and
sculpted my bob back away from my face. No ifs,
ands, or buts about it, I was feeling myself. I just
hoped Jeremiah was feeling me too.

"Girl, here . . ." Cherell said, handing me a
glass, ". . . I ordered a bottle of wine. Hell, this
is quicker than waiting on the waitresses these
days. And we don't have to get up! I'm over
here checking out the scene for now. Shit, I ain't
trying to walk around yet," Cherell said, twisting
her neck around.

"Who are you looking for?" I asked, taking a sip of my drink.

"So, look, I really didn't want to speak on it earlier, but I had a bit of drama at my place the other night."

"Girl, what happened?" I was feeling nosy as hell. Especially since even with all Cherell's shenanigans, she seemed to always have it under control. At least on the outside, that is. I was still getting over the shock of finding out she was seeing a therapist!

"Girl, why Travis show up at my place the other night while I was in the room fucking Carlos?" Cherell said. Her wineglass was turned up to her lips, and her eyes were bucked as she looked around the room.

"Girl . . ." I drawled, ". . . I told you that was playing with fire! What did you do?" I asked, taking a sip my damn self. My eyes scanned the room looking for Jeremiah while I feigned interest in Cherell's story.

"Well, what was I supposed to do? I mean, we kept fucking! I was close to coming too. Girl, this man was banging all on the door, and then it got quiet after a while, so I was like cool, he's gone. So why fifteen minutes later Travis started back up again? Shit, Carlos and I were done and were lying there trying to cupcake and shit, and there Travis was with all this nonsense."

"Well, what was Carlos doing while all this was going on?"

"Just lying there looking stupid. I mean, he stopped midstroke and asked if Travis had a key to my place. When I said no, he just kept going," Cherell said, laughing.

I just shook my head. I didn't see a damn thing funny about the situation.

"You really need to cut that mess out, girl. I told you, you can't play with people's feeling like that. If you don't want him, end it. You're going to get yourself hurt."

"I know, girl. Plus, Travis had just paid my car note too. I mean, it ain't like he knew I was in there with another man. I just didn't answer the door for him or answer the damn near fifty phone calls and text messages he sent me."

I didn't bother saying any more to Cherell. It was obvious to me she didn't care what I had to say about the situation. I guess since she had more experience with men, she didn't feel like I had anything worthy to add to the conversation. But I knew she was inviting a world of trouble.

Cherell tapped me under the table.

"There go ya boy! So what did you decide to do? Are you going to talk to him?"

I glanced inconspicuously to my right. Jeremiah looked so good. I was glad I'd taken the time to run home and fix myself up. He wasn't suited up tonight like he usually was, just a button-down shirt rolled up to his forearms showing off his intricate tattoos and classy watch and pinky ring. Dark jeans and loafers. He was standing with I guy I didn't recognize, but the man stood as tall as Jeremiah, and he was rocking long dreadlocks. They were surrounded by a flock of women. My heart sank a little watching Jeremiah hold conversation with some woman. He was smiling at her, and I had to admit, I was jealous.

"Girl, who is the brotha with the dreads? With his fine ass! Shoot, I promise you I'm finding out!"

"Aren't you juggling enough men right now? Slow your ass down!" I snapped. Now, dammit, Cherell was bordering on ho behavior if you asked me! Shit had already crossed the line as far as I was concerned sleeping with two men, but adding a third? Uh-uh. Sit your hot ass down.

Jeremiah

I had no idea who this chick was skinning and grinning in my face, but she was trying to talk my ear off. Of course, I had to be cordial. Since I was an owner, it was my job to make everyone who walked in feel welcome, but to be honest, she was boring me. Nothing about her conversation was interesting to me. Being here in Virginia almost made me forget how things were when Dip was around. He loved the ladies, and they damn sure loved him.

So, yes, the minute he'd stepped into town, he'd already formed a harem of women around him. Two females he met at the airport even showed up, and they were standing around looking salty as fuck. I guess they thought they were special—only to show up to find they were one of many.

I was also a little off my square because I'd spotted Nicole the second she'd walked into the club. I was a bit shocked to see her for some reason. I'd fully expected her to steer clear of me or anything having to do with me since she was so mad at me. Evidently, she wasn't as mad as I thought. I was still on the fence of whether I was going to speak to her. I watched her get up from the booth walking through the club. Several men tried to holler at her, but she seemed to be turning them all down and wasn't giving them any conversation. My stomach was tightening as I watched her. What's this I'm feeling? I had to take a second to assess the situation. Am I feeling . . . jealous?

How the hell you gon' walk your ass up in my club and not say shit to me? Act like you're ignoring me? Nah, fuck that. I'm about to 86 her ass. Nicole gon' have to find somewhere else to go chill and pick up niggas! She got me all the way fucked up.

"Hey, Tiny, pour this young lady a drink," I called out. "Enjoy your night," I told the woman and walked off in the direction I saw Nicole go. She must have been headed to the bathroom. I strode through the crowd, nodding at a few people on my way. Luckily, when I got to the hall it was empty, so I posted up on the wall waiting for her to come out. I was waiting for what seemed like ten minutes before she finally reappeared.

"What the hell took you so long? You out in a public bathroom shitting or nah? Take your ass home to shit," I said sarcastically. I was heated. I'd gotten madder as I waited. She gon' bring her ass out here in that tight-ass skirt with her damn belly all out for the world to see! I don't like that shit.

"*Excuse* me? I was not shi-shitting!" Nicole stammered, looking around to make sure no one was in earshot.

"Well, you took long enough," I spat.

"Whatever, Jeremiah. Did you follow me just to harass me? What do you want? Your ass following me, I'm surprised you noticed with all those big booty hoes in your face! Those girls look hideous! Asses all lumpy, you can tell they're fake."

I started laughing.

"If I didn't know better, I'd say you were jealous. But that couldn't be . . . jealous over *me?* Jeremiah, the no-good, lying-ass nigga?"

"Look, about all that . . ." Nicole started, looking down the hall nervously. She stopped talking as a group of women came loudly down the hall.

"Ohhhh, this nigga know he fine!" one of the passing women cackled.

Nicole rolled her eyes. They looked at me, and I simply smiled and issued them a head nod.

"Look, can we talk, Jeremiah? In private, please?"

I shoved off from the wall and began walking down the hall toward my office, Nicole following closely behind. Once inside, I perched on the edge of my desk and waited for her to speak. Nicole rocked slowly from leg to leg. Damn! She looked good as hell. I didn't try to hide the fact I was checking her out. What for?

"You look nice tonight," I said, breaking the silence since she hadn't.

Nicole smoothed a hand down her thigh.

"Thank you. So, okay, I wanted to apologize about the other day. I may have overreacted—"

"You *may* have? You *did!* Don't give me no half-assed apology if that's what you're trying to do. I deserve better than that with your rude ass. I bring you lunch, and you gon' shit all over my damn efforts like you don't even like the food when I know damn well everything I brought up in that muthafucka you liked!"

"I know! I'm sorry, Jeremiah! It's just that girl, Paige, she approached me and told me all this stuff about how you were never going to really like me. That you were still in love with Mia, and I didn't stand a chance with you. I thought maybe you didn't tell me who your ex was because you really *were* still in love with her. Are you? I just felt stupid. I thought we were being completely honest with each other and to find out you weren't hurt me."

I threw my head back and exhaled loudly. This woman was going to drive me crazy. I couldn't even rationalize in my mind why I was still talking to her ass. Maybe *I* was the one who was crazy.

"Nicole, what reason would I have to lie to you? I told you everything that went on with the situation except her name. When Mia and I met and fell in love, she was a senior in high school. When all that shit went down, she was so much more than that. You gotta understand it's not the same as having an ex no one knows. I've been trying to stay under the radar. Mia is a celebrity, I'm just a regular guy out here trying to live my life, have some things, and eventually find a woman that loves me completely.

"I would have eventually told you, but you gotta understand, you didn't exactly make it easy. Look at how you were acting the day we first went out and she came on the radio. I don't wanna talk about her. Or answer 101 questions about her, either. I just don't. People love Mia as a singer, but for me, she's just the woman who broke my heart. Period."

"I know. I realize that now. It took me a minute to see that, but I understand. Can you just forgive me? Can we start over?" Nicole asked. I could see the sincerity in her eyes, but, damn, she was a lot to take.

My immediate reaction was just to turn her down flat. I didn't need the drama.

"Please say yes, Jeremiah. I said I was sorry," Nicole pleaded.

I started chuckling aloud. "Ma, I think you might be crazy, though . . . I mean I really do think your ass is nutty." There. I said it. Ain't no sense in tiptoeing around the way I felt now.

"I might be. I can admit that. But if I'm only crazy about you, what's wrong with that? I love hard—"

"Aww, shit! Now I know you are! 'I love hard' is code for 'I'm crazy!'"

Nicole started laughing her damn self.

"Jeremiah, just listen, okay? I mean, if you really aren't interested in me, I'll just have to accept that. I just want you to know something about me. Birds of a feather don't always flock together. I have colorful friends. They're wild and outgoing. But all I ever wanted was one man to love me and want to build a life with me. I told you all this. I've only had two boyfriends really, and I gave my all in both of those relationships.

Everything. I'm coming to realize that I did myself a disservice. The times I should have walked with Don Travious I held on. But you gotta understand, I feel like when you love someone you don't walk away. You try to make it better. I realize now that I didn't know Kendrick as well as I thought I did. I can also acknowledge now that I read way too much into that situation. But I loved him too. I can honestly say I feel like I held on to these men so tightly I have their DNA under my fingernails from just holding on to what I loved when I should have let them go."

Hearing her speak about Kendrick and her attempt to come clean did make me feel slightly guilty. There *was* one thing I'd actually withheld from her.

"Look, can I tell you something without you going all the way off on me?" I asked.

Nicole's eyes narrowed like she was already preparing to be mad.

"Look, if we're going to do this, let's keep it completely one hundred. Let me start by saying the only reason I didn't say anything from the jump is because . . . you act fuckin' crazy! I didn't know if it would make you feel worse; plus, you kicked me out of your house that morning so I didn't know if I should say anything. I know your ex, Kendrick. Nah, let me clear that up. I met him again that Monday you kicked me out of your house."

Nicole's shoulders slumped, but she didn't say a word, so I continued on. I revealed to her that Dip and I actually purchased the club from Kendrick and Antonio. I also told her about the conversation we had discussing her.

"Nicole, look, he's not a bad guy, and he obviously still cares about your well-being. I'm starting to realize that in life you can't ask for more than to have people around that care about your well-being because that nigga was ready to tear into me if I was just fucking with you. To answer your earlier question, I love Mia, but, no, I'm not in love with her anymore. I have a few unresolved issues with her, but I do intend to wrap all that up with her so that I can move on the way I need to. Not for you, but for myself."

"Let me tell you something too. I'm well . . . after our argument the other day, I started seeing a therapist. So I guess if you're already calling me crazy, you'll really think it now, huh?" Nicole asked nervously, looking at me.

We stood there looking at each other silently before I beckoned for her to come to me. When she was standing in front of me, I finally spoke, pulling her into a hug.

"I don't care if your crazy ass needs to go lie on the couch and talk to some little old white lady. Nicole, just don't lie to me, cheat on me, and as long as all that crazy you got is just for me, okay," I whispered in her ear. Nicole wrapped her arms around me tightly, and I could feel her shoulders shaking.

"Don't cry . . ." I said, rubbing her back. "We both got some shit with us, but we'll be okay."

Jeremiah

They may have taken you for granted, but they had no clue that they would end up looking for you in others and finding nothing but fragments.

Mia was here. The muthafuckin' plane had landed, and I was actually at the airport waiting for her to come to the baggage claim. Dip was shocked as hell when I told him that I'd go pick her up. I was shocked my damn self, but it was time. There were some things I needed to get off my chest, and after a year and a half of avoiding it, it was finally time to confront the situation. You could tell several planes had landed by the swarms of people now flooding the baggage claim area. Mia was expecting Dip, so I already knew she was going to be shocked as hell to see me. I don't think I'd laid eyes on Mia for at least eight months.

I looked around wondering what type of disguise she'd be wearing today. I knew she usually did the whole big glasses and hat thing. After a fifteen-minute wait, I started checking my phone to make sure there weren't any missed calls from Dip. Had she missed her flight?

"I'm here," I heard from behind me. I was shocked, but I fought to keep my composure, even though my heart was beating rapidly. I turned around to face her, and sure enough, Mia had a floppy hat on her head, a scarf, and a pair of huge glasses covered her face. I don't know why every time I did happen to see Mia, I wanted her to look fucked up, but I did. A huge pimple would be nice, unsightly weight gain would give me something. God! It was petty as hell, I know, but I still didn't want Quinton having the woman I once thought was perfection.

I reached out and grabbed her suitcase and led the way to my car. Once we were settled in, I turned to look at her.

"Take that shit off and let me see you," I shocked myself. A month ago I would have been adamant I didn't want to see her ugly face. I knew she was nowhere near ugly, but she was when my heart was hurting. Mia slowly removed her disguise and turned in her seat to face me, smiling.

"It's good to see you, Jeremiah," she said, smiling brightly. "So I guess Dip must have been on his deathbed, and you couldn't find anyone else to pick me up, huh?" she asked softly.

"Nah, I offered to come," I said, weaving the car into traffic. It was almost 9:30 p.m., and it was Friday night, so traffic was thick, even leaving the airport.

"Are you hungry? You want me to run you by a Chick-fil-A?" I knew she loved their waffle fries and chicken nuggets.

"Actually, I am hungry. Yeah, let's go there," she said, rubbing her forehead. I knew she did that when she was nervous.

"How is Jacobi doing?" I asked, trying to relax her by speaking about someone who made us both happy, even though I didn't feel like I could fully express that to her these days.

"He's good, getting so big, and, man, can that boy talk. He runs me ragged. I brought you a ton of pictures."

"Thank you. I appreciate it."

"Do you, Jeremiah? Because you've pulled away from him completely, and I think that's fucked up on your part. I know you're mad at me. I just never thought you'd take it out on him."

I gripped the steering wheel tightly. Here she go with this shit. Granted, I hadn't had much to say to Mia since we broke up, but the one thing I thought I was being very clear about was my concerns about Jacobi. This man had spent three years without his child, had his son calling me daddy. I didn't have a problem with that at first. Once I found out the circumstances of Jacobi's conception weren't what Mia had led me to believe, I felt it only right to let that man have his spot in his child's life without any interruption from me. As a man, that's what I would want. Mia seemed to be the only person in the equation fighting me on the issue. Of course, Quinton didn't want me around his son, confusing him.

That's exactly what it was with those first few visits as far as I was concerned. Jacobi was just a little boy and didn't know the pain he inadvertently caused calling me daddy in front of Quinton. He didn't see the hurt in Quinton's eyes, but I did. It looked like he'd been punched in the gut. Even though I hated everything Quinton stood for then . . . and now, I wouldn't wish that kind of pain on any man.

"Mia, I know you don't understand where I'm coming from with keeping my distance, but Jacobi is too young to completely navigate the fucked-up situation we . . . or rather *you* . . . put him in. Let him get to know his father completely. Does your husband know how hard you're fighting to keep me around his son?" I asked.

"Yes."

I balked. I couldn't believe she had the nerve to say it so plainly, with no reservations. Couldn't be my damn wife!

"You're kidding me, right?"

"Absolutely not. Quinton knows I consider you to be family. Regardless of how bad things have been between us, I need you in my life. My world doesn't feel complete with us at odds this way."

I swerved into the drive-thru, my mind jumbled with thoughts. I automatically placed the order already knowing what she wanted and pulled forward in the line before I turned to look at her.

"Please don't tell me you think of me like a brother. Ain't that about a bitch!" I said, cutting my eyes at her evilly.

Mia exhaled loudly. "Jeremiah, don't talk stupid, please. After all we've been and done to each other, how could I ever think of you like a damn brother? I grew up an only child, but if I did have a brother, we damn sure wouldn't have fucked!"

I jerked my head back. Shit, how the fuck I know that? She didn't have no issue laying up ready and willing with her mama's boyfriend. I didn't know what boundaries Mia wouldn't cross to be really honest.

"Don't talk like that; it sounds nasty."

"Well, don't ask me stupid-ass questions, Jeremiah! People can break up with each other and still be in each other's lives as friends is what I wish you'd understand," she cried. I looked over and could see her chest heaving; she was getting upset. Once we got her food, we drove in silence to the Sheraton, got her checked in, and I escorted her up to her room. We both stood at the doorway to her room nervously.

"Look, can I come in so we can talk?"

"Of course."

"I don't mean to disrespect your-your husband," I stammered, choking on the word. I still couldn't believe she'd married that clown-ass nigga. My mind flooded with the image I saw looking through her window that night years ago.

"Come in, Jeremiah," Mia sighed, sounding annoyed with me.

"Damn, this is nice," I said, looking around the suite. "I can't believe Dip said he'd pay for all this with his cheap ass!" I said aloud.

"He better! Shoot, I don't mind doing a free show for y'all, but the least you can do is put me in a nice-ass room," Mia said, stuffing her mouth with fries.

I sat down on the love seat and composed my thoughts. I only wanted to have this talk one time and one time only. I didn't want to leave any stone unturned or have unanswered questions when I walked out of this room.

"Look, Mia, I know you tried to talk to me about this situation a hundred times . . . maybe more, but I think I just needed to deal with this in my own time, but I'm ready. I'm not trying to fight with you. None of that because at the end of the day, the damage is done, but I do have some questions for you," I said, clasping my hands before me, elbows resting on my knees.

Mia took a long sip of her lemonade, wiped her hands and mouth, and nodded her head.

"Okay. I agree, this talk is long overdue," she said, her voice low.

"Why didn't you just tell me the truth about what was going on in that house? Why did you tell me everything to pull me in and make me go so hard for you, but left out the most important parts? The things I really *needed* to know."

"Jeremiah, I was so confused then. I don't know why I did half the things I did. I couldn't stand Quinton when my mom first moved him in. He was always there, watching me, lurking, but at the same time, he protected me too. I didn't notice it at first, but he was the buffer between me and Terri. Many times. I didn't know why my mom acted like she hated me and that started long before Quinton even came on the scene. He was just there for me. Then I met you. I don't want you to ever feel like the feelings I had for you weren't true, because they were. But things between Quinton and me just escalated quickly, and to add to the confusion, I knew it looked bad. He was my mother's man. How could I just tell anyone that? When I stepped out the door to my house, you were all I needed to make it through the day. I was a normal teenager with a boyfriend I loved, and who loved me back.

"But when I walked into my house, Quinton was also there. Loving me and protecting me in ways I didn't realize. I know you think he's all bad, Jeremiah, but he isn't. Even then, Quinton was supportive of me; he encouraged me in school. He did a lot of things in that house that made my life easier."

I sucked my teeth loudly and jumped to my feet. "That nigga ain't nothing but a child predator! If the nigga is that good and caring, why didn't he call child protective services on Terri? And that still doesn't explain why I seen the nigga trying to fuck you when you were dead to the muthafuckin' world that night! What was all *that* shit about?" I asked, outraged. I couldn't believe after a few measly vows being said Mia would forget that shit.

Mia shook her head sadly. "I have no idea. I've asked him countless times, and he won't answer me. I've just let it go. One day he'll tell me, but for now, I'm choosing to take him for the man he is and has always been to me. He's the one who has never left my side, Jeremiah. Even when I've hurt him, lied to him, and took his child away. I've played my part in the lies and deception with both of you. I'm not innocent. I was an empty well using both of you to fill what was missing in my life. I hurt him just as much as I hurt you."

"Oh, please! He was a grown-ass man preying on little girls," I said, refusing to believe any of that shit.

Mia laughed lightly. "Quinton is only a few years older than we are, so stop it, Jeremiah."

I cut my eyes at her and walked over to the huge window overlooking the city. "Okay, even with all that, Mia, it was just me, you, and Jacobi, for three years. You made me feel so fucked up behind this shit because then you go and marry this nigga."

"Jeremiah, had you just talked to me, if you would have just picked up the phone one of the hundreds of times I called you . . . How many e-mails did I send you that you never even opened? Text messages. Had you responded to me at all, I would have waited. Now, don't get me wrong by saying this, but I'm going to be honest because I don't want to live my life with lies and regrets any more. But had you just talked to me . . ." Mia said, her voice cracking with tears, ". . . even if it was to say, 'Mia, I'm mad at you, and right now, I need a break, a year, something,' I would have taken my punishment as long as you gave me some type of hope, Jeremiah, but you didn't. So I did what I had to do for me and Jacobi."

"Nah, you ran right into that nigga's arms. You wasn't waiting for me."

"I *was!*" Mia screamed. "I was alone! Me and our son, Jacobi was crying every day for you, and you didn't care, Jeremiah. And, yes, once again, Quinton showed me that he was the only one who was going to be there for me. No matter what. I moved on when you didn't give me any hope."

"I still think you ain't telling me everything. You never fucked him, not even *once* while we were together? You weren't calling him, none of that shit?"

"No!" Mia said hesitantly.

"You don't sound so sure to me," I chided.

"Okay, since we're telling the truth, I did sleep with him one time when you first broke up with me. You had broken up with me, and Terri had just taken Jacobi. I slept with him *one* time."

"*Now* we get to the truth. There it is, Mia. I guess there was a reason my heart wouldn't let me forgive you because your ass still been lying! Not only had we only been broken up . . . what hours? . . . and you was fuckin' the nigga. When you should have been worried about Jacobi being taken, you was busy giving that nigga pussy that should have only been for me. You know what? I'm good. I know everything I need to know to finally let you go in my heart. We good. I've spent the last year looking inside myself for the answer as to how I could have been so wrong about you after I put so much time, love, and effort into loving you, and right now, right this second, I realize God wants me to have a woman that loves me a little harder than you ever could."

Standing there in that very moment, I could see Nicole's face clear as day. Open, loving, and waiting for a man to give her all the things I'd freely given to Mia. Yeah, she'd been hurt before. So had I. The simple things I'd wanted from Mia and that Nicole wanted from the men in her life were qualities we'd both been seeking in the wrong people. If we gave each other an honest chance, maybe we could stop looking.

"Okay, I messed up that time, but we were broken up! You ended it, Jeremiah—"

"Oh, no worries, baby girl. We're good. From this day forward, you and I can be cool. Quinton married you, so obviously, you're everything he's ever wanted in a lover, wife, and mother of his children, but right now, at this very moment, I just realized I'm the type of man who deserves more. Even when we're down and out, I need a woman that's gon' be as sick without me as I am without her, you feel me? My woman ain't gon' never do some shit to me where I gotta walk around ashamed. Looking like a fool and feeling lied to. The woman God has meant for me is going to mourn me when I'm gone, and I don't mean that in no morbid type of way either. I mean in the way another man can't fill my shoes easily when it comes to her heart, her body . . . It's all mine, and I don't have to question it. We're good, Mia, I promise you that. I'm so good on you," I said, shaking my head. "Thank you, Jesus, for looking out me. Thank you, thank you, thank you!"

Mia stood there frowning with her hands on her hips. "Now, wait a minute! I don't think I like how you're trying to make me sound. It's like you're calling me a ho—"

"*Like?* I can't make you out to be nothing, baby. So let me gon' get out of here and let you get some rest. It was nice seeing you. Do you want me to swing by and pick you up early tomorrow morning? I know your band should be showing up in a few hours. We have people picking them up. Just let me know, and Dip and I will fall through," I said, ready to leave. I'd told Nicole I was stopping by after I got done with all this, and I, of course, wanted to keep my word to her. I felt like a weight that had been pressing down on my heart for over a year had finally lifted.

"Okay, I'll call you in the morning . . ." Mia sounded confused as hell, but it wasn't my problem. She could go and talk to her crazy-ass husband about how she felt. I walked out of the hotel room and kissed my fingers to the sky.

Mia

I stood there watching Jeremiah walk out of the hotel room confused as hell! Did he low-key call me a ho? I mean, I knew I was wrong to sleep with Quinton that one time, but I still wanted Jeremiah at the time. I knew that if I confessed everything, he'd never consider taking me back. I grabbed my cell phone, flopped down on the love seat, and called Quinton. I felt dirty and low-down for some reason.

"What's going on?"

I smiled at the sound of his sexy Southern twang.

"Well, I don't know . . ."

"Your talk with Jeremiah didn't go well?"

I sat up ramrod straight.

"How do you know Jeremiah decided to talk to me today?" I asked, really feeling played now.

"Because he called me and asked for permission to speak to my wife privately. I gotta give it to the nigga, I was worried as hell about him trying to snatch my wife up and fuck her, but he came at me with nothing but respect."

I was curious as hell.

"When was this? What exactly did he say?"

"He called early this morning and said that he had some unfinished business he needed to settle with you. Asked if I minded if he picked you up from the airport and spoke with you. He said he wouldn't feel right being alone with you without your husband knowing. I ain't gon' lie, he had me feeling less than because I would have never considered asking him if the shoe was on the other foot."

I couldn't do nothing but shake my head at that, because I knew it was true. When it came to me, Quinton didn't see any right or wrong.

"I know you wouldn't. That's the difference between you and Jeremiah."

I could hear Quinton sucking his teeth loudly through the phone. "That don't mean he's better than me!" he spat.

"I know, baby, you two are just different. Very, very different. Kiss Jacobi for me, okay? I'm tired from the flight. I'm going to get some sleep, okay? I love you," I said before hanging up the phone. I was drained. More from the talk with Jeremiah than my flight. He'd definitely brought out some old feelings I thought I'd buried and

let go. When I married Quinton, I thought I
reconciled within myself that there were things
he'd done I would never know or understand.
Hearing it out of Jeremiah's mouth tonight only
made me wonder even more. I could imagine
how in Jeremiah's mind seeing what Quinton
was doing that night did make him seem like no
more than a sick, depraved man. Shit, how did
it make *me* look *marrying* him? Because there
had never been a doubt in my mind that what
Jeremiah said he witnessed was true. Jeremiah
was honest to a fault.

I stepped into the shower sure of one thing.
I didn't want any secrets between Quinton and
me. He was going to tell me what the fuck he was
doing to me that night, or else. I was going to see
if he loved me enough to tell me the truth. When
I was done showering, I sent him a text.

Since your sister is there visiting, ask her to
watch Jacobi and catch the next flight here. I
need to ask you something face-to-face, and it
can't wait.

Quinton started blowing my phone up.

I wasn't answering him tonight. I was going
to go over my set for tomorrow night's show
and get some much-needed rest. I also made a
quick phone call to my first signed artist under
my own record label. Her name was Daya, and,

damn, this girl could blow. When this little impromptu show came up, I thought it would be the perfect time to let her get her feet wet. We'd been working hard on her material so we could get some organic feedback from the crowd. I flicked on the lamp on the nightstand and dug under the covers, a feeling of dead filling me. This damn Quinton better tell me the truth, I muttered to myself. I guess I gave up honesty when I chose his ass.

My talk with Jeremiah also revealed something else to me. Quinton was, without a doubt, right. There was a part of me that would always be in love with Jeremiah Wilson. It made me think about what Quinton said. Would I have ended up with him if Jeremiah had forgiven me? I'd chosen to believe that things just fell into place with us.

Now I wasn't so sure.

Nicole

*** *It's hard to wait around for something you know might never happen, but it's harder to give up when you know it's everything you want.* ***

Shoot, well, maybe he just couldn't make it tonight, I thought, padding back to my bedroom. Jeremiah said he'd be busy for most of the day but had promised he'd stop by when he was done tonight. Suddenly, I heard my doorbell ring and began jumping up and down with excitement, stuffing my fist in my mouth to muffle the sound of my screams. I blew out several quick breaths on my way to the door trying to calm myself before I swung open the door, trying my best to appear calm.

"Hello," I smiled.

"What are you giving me that fake hello for? You look crazy!" Jeremiah said, crossing the threshold of the door.

"Boy, shut up! How do I look crazy? I'm just happy you came. I didn't think you were going to show. I was just about to go to bed." A week ago I would have been embarrassed to let Jeremiah know how much I looked forward to being around him, but what had trying to front gotten me in the past? Absolutely nothing. So if I wanted something different, I had to be different. I had to be myself for a change and not what I thought men expected me to be. I learned that in therapy. I wanted to just be myself and have that be enough.

"Nicole, you're smiling like the Joker right now, you know that, right?"

I couldn't stop myself from laughing no matter how hard I tried. I was doubled over. Once I composed myself, my shoulders were still shaking.

"That's fucked up, Jeremiah. I'm adding you to my list of things to talk to the therapist about next week."

Jeremiah raised his eyebrow at me. "Look, now, I don't care about you seeing a therapist but don't be telling that white lady all my damn business!"

"It's a sista, thank you very much!"

"Aww, hell! Y'all ain't doing nothing but sitting around talking shit for an hour! Probably over there sipping Moscato too! I'm sure you could have run your mouth at Cherell's loud-mouthed ass for free!"

"Jeremiah, be quiet. I probably shouldn't tell you this, and you better not repeat it either, but I found her *through* Cherell! I had no idea she was seeing anyone."

"Well, it's private. You weren't supposed to know, nosy self!"

I could see Jeremiah yawn and stretch. I was disappointed because I knew he wouldn't be staying long.

"I'm sleepy, baby. You said you were going to bed. You inviting me to the slumber party or not?"

I couldn't say yes quick enough. Jeremiah kicked off his shoes at the door and followed me back to my bedroom where he stripped down to his boxers and climbed into my bed. I stood there looking at him snuggled under my comforter, and I couldn't deny it. I wanted him here with me, not just tonight, but the night after and the night after that. My mind was shouting at me not to rush and get ahead of myself. I'd gotten it wrong so many times before I just didn't want to make another heartbreaking mistake.

"I'll be right back," I said before turning on my heels, cutting off the light to my bedroom, and walking back into the living room where I sat in the dark and I . . . well, I just prayed. That's all I could do. I prayed not to make the same mistakes. Prayed that God would send me exactly who I was looking for to take this journey called life with. I also prayed that if Jeremiah wasn't him, that God left me with just enough pieces of my heart to put it back together and try again if I had to. I just prayed.

All of a sudden, my living room lights flooded the room.

"What are you in here doing, Nicole? Bring your ass to bed!" Jeremiah was standing over me frowning. I looked at the clock. I'd been on the couch for a solid hour. Before I could even rise up from the couch, Jeremiah had bent down, scooped me up, and was carrying me to the bedroom like I weighed no more than a rag doll. He laid me down in the bed, climbed in after me, and pulled me close.

"Where have you been tonight, Jeremiah?" I asked through a yawn. "I expected you earlier."

"I picked Mia up from the airport and went up to her room so we could clear the air on a few things."

I couldn't help it. My body stiffened, and my heart began beating erratically.

"I see. Um, how did that go?"

"Nicole, cut it out."

"Huh? I didn't say anything," I cried indignantly. I was thinking shit . . . but I was pretty sure I hadn't blurted anything out loud. I think. Did I? I know one thing, though, I'm throwing out all Mia's CDs and clearing her out of all my playlists tomorrow!

I could feel Jeremiah's grip on me tightening, and his hand firmly gripped my left breast.

"Nicole, I can feel your heart beating hard as hell. There's going to be a lot of things I do where you'll have this reaction, this ain't one of them, ma. I promise you. I just had some unanswered questions. We cleared the air, just like I told you I was gonna do the other night. Remember?"

I turned around to face him, but his eyes were closed. I still looked. Jeremiah was a gorgeous man, and Mia may be a great singer and beautiful, but she was a fool. An outright idiot to hurt a man as special as him, but I was so glad she did. In all honesty, after finding out about her being Jeremiah's ex, I'd done quite a bit of digging around to find out what all went on. Google was my new best friend, and in a word—*eww!*

I know the Lord says we shouldn't judge people, and I hadn't walked a mile in Mia's shoes, but *eww! Eww! Eww!* I cringed at the thought of it all. Why in the hell would she want to marry a man that had touched all parts of her mama's pussy? Good Lord. I didn't get it. Yeah, her husband was fine and all, but those two dirty birds could have each other!

Obviously, they were meant to be.

Just like Kendrick and Tierrany were meant to be. Who knows, maybe in a year or two I could say the same about Jeremiah and me. No pressure or anything, but who knows? Anything is possible.

"Please take your ass to sleep and stop staring at me," I heard Jeremiah mumble.

"Nigga, if you were really sleeping you wouldn't know I was looking!" I said, laughing.

"I can feel your eyes boring into me. Damn, Nicole. I know a nigga rich and handsome . . . and you ain't had no man this good. I mean, I know ya' ex. He a'ight, I guess—" I didn't even let him get the rest of that nonsense out of his mouth before I was beating him with my pillow. Jeremiah was laughing, and it was music to my ears. He leaned back in my bed fluffing my pillows behind his back. Before he cut his eyes at me, he said, "Look, it's clear to me you ain't letting me get no damn sleep tonight, so come on. Sit on daddy's lap." He patted himself. I could see his hard dick peeking out from the waistband of his boxer shorts.

I shook my head vigorously. I was shy but not that damn shy.

"Don't even try to play me like that. If you want me, just say it and make a move."

It seemed I hadn't blinked good and I was flat on my back with Jeremiah between my spread legs kissing me, grinding his hard dick against the crotch of my now-soaking-wet panties.

"I want you. Don't ever question it. Just believe me when I say I want you, Nicole."

"One more thing, Jeremiah . . ."

"What's that?"

"Don't you ever take your ass in Mia's room again! You better sit your behind in the lobby and talk next time," I said. I knew my face was frowned up something terrible! I tried to hold it in and not say anything, but uh-uh. He had to know I wasn't cool with that at all.

Jeremiah just laughed, shaking his head.

"Understood," he said before leaning down to kiss me again.

Jeremiah

Today was literally off the chain. Dip and I had all the staff working overtime. We'd opened the club up early today because the place had to be decorated, special caterers were due to come and take over the kitchen, and both bars were stocked to the brim. I was glad to hear our radio promos playing every hour on the hour, but they'd been hyping us up for the last three weeks anyway, so I wasn't surprised. I'd swung by Mia's hotel and picked her up to check out the club, and we could hear her and the band practicing their set. Her little protégé sounded damn good. Mia seemed a little sullen when she got in the car, but I didn't even bother asking why.

For the first time in over a year, I didn't even care how she was doing. I welcomed the transition from her completely ruling my every waking thought to nothing. I'd awakened next to my crazy Nicole, and I was feeling happy. For the first time in a long time, I felt at peace. From looking at the contented look on Nicole's face while I watched her sleep for a few minutes, I was pretty sure she felt the same way. Nicole asked if I wanted her to come up to the club to help get things ready, but I told her it wasn't necessary. Everything was under control, and it wasn't like we were running a small operation. We'd paid plenty of money to have this event run smoothly. Plus, Nicole's ass wasn't slick. I knew she was hesitant about having me around Mia, even though I'd assured her the past was now officially in the past.

I knew it was going to take some time for her to completely trust that she could rest easy with me. I wasn't out to break her heart. I was confident she'd get there in time. My phone buzzed in my pocket, so I pulled it out to find a text from Nicole. She'd sent me a picture of herself still lying in bed, covers pulled up to her chin with a message that she missed me already.

"Well, someone sure is putting a smile on your face."

I looked up to find Mia staring down at me nosily with her hands on her hips. The shit kinda made me want to laugh. Granted, I'd made my peace with Mia, finally, but I hope that didn't make her think we were going to act like best friends, and I was going to be telling her all my damn business! Never that. At the end of the day, Mia was a liar and a cheater, and the way she went about everything was dead-ass wrong. You don't treat people who you consider "family" or a "friend" that way. So we could be on some "hi and bye," "how are you" type shit. Hell, even business, but it would be a long time before I considered her a friend again.

If ever.

"Yeah," I said with a quick smile and glance up at her before I sent Nicole a text and put my phone back in my pocket.

"Well, who is it? Tell me about her," Mia asked eagerly.

"Why? Mind ya business, girl," I said, laughing.

Mia sighed loudly.

I just shook my head.

"She'll be here tonight. I'll introduce you to her. Actually, she's a fan of your music," I said. I honestly wish I could avoid doing that, but it would be weird if I didn't, so fuck it. I knew Nicole wasn't going to ask me to introduce her, but I knew damn well she'd notice if I didn't. I knew Nicole's self-confidence had taken a beating, and I was going to make it my business as her man to change all that.

Damn—her man? I thought to myself, but, yeah, I said it, right. I was her man.

Mia's face fell.

"Hmm. You told her about me?"

"I sure did."

"Well, how bad did you make me sound, Jeremiah?"

I was a bit caught off guard with the question. It actually sounded more like an accusation.

"I told her the truth. What do you think, I'm supposed to sugarcoat things to make you seem how? It is what it is. You did what you did. As long as you're happy with the way your life is right now, fuck what anyone has to say about it, right? You ain't never cared about no one else but you all this time. Why you worried about how you look now?"

Mia hung her head. I could see her chest rising and falling.

"Hey, look at me, Mia. What the hell is wrong with you?"

Mia picked up her head but avoided looking at me. "I don't know, Jeremiah. I just have wanted you back in my life for so long, you know? But being around you, talking to you, for some reason, you remind me what a freak show my life is, you know? Don't think for a minute I don't know it. I do. I just choose to overlook it. Ever since things went down, I don't do the social media thing like I used to, and I never read the comments. Because as much as I like to think people are over it, they always remind me they haven't forgotten. People bring up Terri, how Quinton has had sex with both of us. I see the ugliness of the situation, even though I try to look past it. But you, Jeremiah? Being around you just puts it smack-dab in my face," Mia said, swiping her cheek.

Damn. Is she really standing in front of me having a pity party? Ain't no damn cake and balloons coming, Mia.

"Mia, it sounds like you still have some things to work out in your mind." I didn't know what to say to her ass. Because the one thing I wasn't going to be is her confidant about Quinton and the choices she'd made for her life. Like she said out of her own mouth, I gave her an alternative, a good one, and she chose to stay in a bullshit, dirty-ass situation. Mia had choices, and she made hers. Honestly, I hated that Jacobi even had to grow up around all that because it was never going away. It was only a matter of time before he read about it for himself, or some of his friends told him about it. Kids were cruel.

"You know why it's hitting me so hard, Jeremiah? It's because when I see you, you represent everything I wanted for my life. It's all wrapped up in you. I wanted a normal boyfriend, I wanted to date like every other teenager. When we left Texas, and with your prompting, I kept Jacobi. I wanted to have the family I never had. I wanted that with you because you made me feel normal and loved. Even when you pushed me to do music, you knew I wasn't going to pursue this. You gave me my life, Jeremiah, and I owe you more than I could ever repay you in two lifetimes. I know in life you're lucky to meet a person who loves you unconditionally, and for me, that person was you. I just know I'm never going to have you in my life that way again because I know how you are. I fucked up too much," Mia said regretfully.

Why was Mia laying all this shit on me now? Especially when I'd put the drama to rest.

"Well, Mia, you know damn well I'm no fan of Quinton, but he's your husband. He should be that person for you. You shouldn't have to look to the outside for anyone to make you feel the way I did. He should be doing it." I heard the words coming out of my mouth, and I could only hope she couldn't tell how fake I was being. That nigga couldn't never be even half the man I was. Fuck that.

"Jeremiah, please stop blowing smoke up my ass."

I busted out laughing, and so did she.

"Please stop acting like I don't know your sarcastic ass because I do. I know you'll never believe me, but Quinton *is* a good man. But I know what my husband is, and what he isn't. Look, speaking of Quinton . . ." Mia said, finally taking a seat next to me, ". . . I called him last night and told him I needed him here."

I cut my eyes at her but didn't say a word. What was the use? It was her husband, and he had the right to be anywhere she was. I hated calling his ass yesterday, but I felt as a man it was the proper thing to do. That nigga sounded dry as fuck when he realized it was me calling him. I can't deny it made me feel good to know he was intimidated. As he should be. I believed in Karma, and the same way he got Mia is the way he was going to lose her. Bet on that.

"Like I said, you make me see things clearly. I've let him get away with not answering my questions about what you saw that night. I want to know. So I told him I needed to see him, and it couldn't wait. Plus, I know his ass at home going crazy because I'm here with you anyway. But I need answers. I got a lot of shit going on inside of me, Jeremiah. You just don't know how hard it gets sometimes. My mama ain't shit, in jail for kidnapping my child, and even with all that, she's the only one I have. I don't have anyone I consider family but you, Jeremiah. That's why I cling to you so hard, but I have to know what really happened," she sobbed.

"Now? After all this time? You married the nigga knowing he did some foul shit. Why the need to know now?"

"I've been *wanting* to know! I just thought I could let it go, but I can't."

"I think the nigga drugged you, to be honest. You were out of it. That nigga was moving you all around and positioning your legs. It was some sick shit. I almost fell off the goddamn roof I was so shocked. Oh, well, Mia, do what you gotta do. But you better know, no matter how much you may love him or not, that's the type of man you've hitched your wagon to. For better or worse," I said, standing up to stretch. This was her problem, not mine. "So, look, Dip is in the back if you need anything. I gotta run to the airport and pick up my brother."

"Ugh! I didn't know Cedric was going to be here," she said sourly.

"Yep. Don't be sounding like that about my brother. He ain't never did shit to you but call you out on your shit," I said, gloating. My older brother had seen through Mia from the jump, but I was so in love at the time I wouldn't listen to reason. We were closer than ever now, though. Instead of me thinking he was seeing life through a weed-smoking haze, I was all ears now. Am I my brother's keeper? Hell to the muthafuckin' yes! It was my new motto.

"Whatever. Bye. Hey, real quick, what do you think of Daya? She writes all her own songs and plays six instruments. You've always have a good ear for music. I don't know why you didn't come into the business with me. You've been still getting your money off cowriting 'Ballad Of A Bad Bitch,' right?"

"You better know it," I said with a smile. I never really put it out there like that, and on the credits, I just listed my initials, but I'd actually written three of the songs on Mia's first album. It's how I had the money to invest in the club with Dip. That was as far as it went, though. I was pretty good at it, obviously. They were her three number one songs on the album. Other artists had tried to find out who I was, but I wasn't into it like that. I only did it then because it was Mia. I thought we were in love, and that was going to be the "family" business, so to speak.

"Mia, I didn't want to because at the time we were engaged and I didn't want to be riding off my woman's fame. I'm my own man, Mia, so you already knew I wasn't going to do that full time. I think she sounds damn good, though. Just market her correctly and she's going to be big."

Mia nodded her head thoughtfully as I walked away. Once I was in the car, I called Nicole and asked her if she wanted to ride with me to pick my brother up. Nicole sounded nervous as hell but excited too.

Nicole

I'd been running ragged from the second Jeremiah asked me to ride to the airport with him. His brother Cedric was a stone-cold fool! In a good way, that is. He had me laughing from the second we picked up him up and all through lunch. He was just as handsome as his younger brother, but his complexion was a deeper shade of chocolate.

"Now, what did you say Jeremiah's brother's name is? Cedric? Hook me up because I think I need to clear all these niggas I know out of my phone and start fresh! This Cedric will be perfect. He's out of town, and I don't have to be bothered," Cherell said, snapping her fingers. "Ouch! That hurt, Choi! What in the world are you doing to my damn feet?" She yelped loudly.

We were in the midst of getting some much-needed manicures and pedicures in preparation for tonight's festivities. I'd had Jeremiah drop me off at Cherell's place once lunch was done.

He still had a ton of things to get done, and I'd wanted to make sure I was looking my best as well. I wasn't too sure about what I was wearing tonight, but Cherell and I had shopped prior to coming into the salon, so I had two choices.

I couldn't deny the fact it was on my mind that Mia would be there tonight, and she was absolutely gorgeous. I kept thinking about that bitch Paige telling me I looked like Holly Hobbie, or whatever the hell she said. That bitch had some nerve! I was so glad Jeremiah had gotten rid of that pesky houseguest.

"Cherell, I am not introducing you to Jeremiah's brother! I mean, you'll probably meet him anyway since he'll be there tonight, but as in hooking you two up? Ain't no goddamn way. You have too much going on. You said you've still been avoiding Travis, and the nigga still coming by your house all crazy! You're not handling this situation correctly at all if you ask me—"

"*And I didn't!* Thank you very much, heffa! Look, Travis is a grown-ass man. He needs to learn to roll with the punches. Sometimes shit just don't work out. Move the fuck on," Cherell stated, her face was scrounged up.

"Cherell, you can't just do people like that. How is that man supposed roll with the punches when you won't even break up with him? All he knows is he's being treated badly. You're my friend; you've been by my side this last year and have seen firsthand how being left in the dark affected me. I didn't know Tierrany even existed. If I had known, maybe I would have made the choice to not date Kendrick."

Cherell sucked her teeth. "Girl, miss me with all that! You *still* would have been with him."

"But I would have known! It would have been *my* choice. Travis is in love with you! You've led him to believe he's the only one. So to cheat on him and run behind his back knowing damn well you don't want him is wrong as two left feet. So what his dick is the size of a Vienna sausage and he comes in two seconds? Let him go find a woman who doesn't mind all that. What you don't want someone will. Shit. Every woman ain't no damn size queen like you! Then you don't like the dick, but you're taking all his money and got him paying bills. You're wrong, Cherell!" I said. I was going to speak my damn peace. I'd been cheated on so many times with Don Travious, I knew how it felt—and it didn't feel good.

"Shit, he owes me money and gifts as compensation for even letting him get a whiff of my sweet stuff."

I just rolled my eyes at her and let it go. It made me wonder exactly what the hell she was talking about in her therapy session. She obviously wasn't trying to be a better person on all levels.

Jeremiah

Holy shit, I thought walking around the club. Dip and I couldn't have prayed for a better turnout tonight. Table 51 was filled to capacity, and there was still a line of people outside waiting to get in. I hated to break it to them, but I didn't see that happening. It was standing room only, and even the folks standing didn't seem to have a problem with it. They were mainly fans of Mia's standing at the roped off area near the stage, dancing and swaying to the beat of the music. Daya's opening set was smooth and soulful, providing the perfect introduction for Mia. The crowd was primed and ready the second she took the stage. I glanced over to the table where Nicole was sitting with her group of friends. I noticed in addition to Cherell, her one crazy friend Meka was in attendance and some white chick I hadn't met before. I'd gotten Nicole and her friends seated, made sure they had three bottles of Champagne at the table, and plenty of appetizers. It was so packed I didn't want Nicole to have to move around asking for anything if she didn't absolutely have to. She looked gorgeous tonight.

Dip and I even hired bathroom attendants for the night. That's just how packed and crazy it was in here this evening. Despite the madness, everything was running smoothly, and everyone appeared to be having a good time. I milled around the crowd a bit when my eyes landed on Quinton. I couldn't stand his ass, but business was business. Besides, Mia was doing the show off the books as a favor to us, and who knows? Maybe we'd need her again. I may as well be cordial to this muthafucka.

"She sounds good, doesn't she?" I asked, approaching him. Quinton was standing at the side of the stage gazing at Mia adoringly. I couldn't deny the nigga did look in love. In my opinion, it was a sick, demented, child predator type of love . . . but who was I to judge?

"Yeah, she does. She works hard at her craft, but you already know that, don't you?"

"That's right, I do."

"So did you clear up all this old shit between you and my wife? I ain't trying to start no shit tonight. I just wanna make sure these talks aren't something you need to keep having with my wife," he dryly stated.

I also caught him cut his eyes at me real quick before he pinned his eyes back to the stage. Mia was crooning a slow tempo song that had the crowd mesmerized. I almost laughed in his face. *Nigga, I'm the last man you got to worry about,* I thought to myself but held my tongue. I don't backslide, and I knew without a doubt, any future I thought I could have had with Mia would have been based on nothing but lies. Her lies. Quinton could have that.

"Nah, man, we're good. Once again, I appreciate your understanding in regard to that. I know this entire situation hasn't been easy. I'm still hoping to make arrangements on how to be in Jacobi's life. Man to man, it's been hard for me not seeing him, but I completely understand the fact that you two have a lot of time to make up for. It takes time to bond, and I felt like me still coming around a lot to see him would only add confusion. He's just a little boy."

Quinton looked at me and nodded. "Well, man, I really thank you for letting things play out this way. Don't think I don't know if Mia had her way, your ass would be flying in every weekend. Thank you for being understanding and giving me the time I need to solidify a spot in my son's heart. I appreciate that shit. I respect it."

I just gave him a nod. Okay, that was enough of this shit! I'd humbled myself enough, dammit!

"All right, man, I'm about to go check in with my lady but just let me know if you need anything tonight. You know Mia has a reserved table in VIP, so it's going to be easier to get some drinks over there."

Quinton's eyebrow raised, and he smiled.

"All right, then, she's almost done with this set, so we'll head over. By the way, congratulations on the new club. It's a good look."

"Thanks, man," I said before walking off. I exhaled deeply. *That wasn't as bad as I thought it would be.* I guess I just needed to let all that old baggage go so I could let some new things into my life. It felt good too. Let me go check on my lady in red. Nicole looked good as hell when she walked into the club tonight. A figure-hugging, off-the-shoulder red dress bodycon that stopped at the calf. I almost had a damn heart attack when I saw her walk in, then she was looking at me all shy. I made sure to tell her how good she looked, and she really knew it when I took her hand and sneakily brought it to my groin. Oh, the monster was damn sure awake! Nicole made me laugh, acting all shy. I'd met Kendrick and actually thought he was cool. The nigga just got caught up in a situation, but who was this fuck-boy Don Travious that had played with my baby's heart? Shit, Nicole said the nigga was in a wheelchair now. What I tell you about that bitch, Karma?

"Jeremiah!"

I turned at the sound of my name to find Paige and her coven of witches staring in my damn face.

"Paige! What is your ass doing here?" I asked, frowning.

Paige stepped up closer to me.

"Well, that's what I was trying to tell you, Jeremiah. I love you. Of course I'm here to support you," she said, rubbing my arm slowly and looking over at her friends.

I was stunned, but, shit, what could I do? It was a free country, and as long as she paid the cover charge to get in, that was on her.

"Don't start all that love shit. You know it's not happening. But y'all enjoy the club tonight," I said loudly enough for her friends to hear. They both broke into wide grins.

"Hi, Jeremiah!" they said in unison.

"Well, y'all enjoy yourselves," I said and attempted to walk away when Paige grabbed my arm, getting all in my personal space.

"Jeremiah, so look, they made us pay at the door—"

"Okay, and? There's a charge to get in tonight," I answered dumbly. I didn't get where she was going.

"I mean, do you think we could get some refunds? I mean, we're together, after all. I wouldn't even be here if it wasn't to support you. I tried to jog the memory of the lady taking the money at the door. Shoot, she saw me twice last week when I was here," she pouted.

"No, Paige, I will certainly not be getting you a refund. Grab yourself a drink and enjoy the show. You have to pay to play just like everyone else. You ain't special," I spat, frowning my face up. I was mad at myself for ever sliding up in her ratchet-ass coochie. Just goes to show what a man will fall for when he's feeling down and out.

"Ewwww! Paige, why is your fiancé treating ya girls so shady?" Chantal piped in.

"I know, right? We just like family. Our names should have been on the list at the door, and we should have been escorted straight to VIP," Desiree crowed, rolling her eyes at me. "I mean, damn, Paige you ain't got your man trained?"

"Be quiet, you two!" Paige hissed. "Look, Jeremiah, can you just do this for me and get us a table and a round of drinks?" Paige looked at me, her eyes pleading with me to go along.

Fuck that.

"Look, Paige, I don't know what kind of show you're putting on for your friends, but I am *not* the one. I don't play these type of games, and you know that shit. Which is *exactly* why I put your ass on a plane back to New York when you showed up here uninvited. Why you're even back here, I'll never understand. I made it crystal clear to you that you and I are nothing to each other. We hooked up sometimes to fuck. That's it."

"What! Paige, your lying ass told us y'all were engaged!" Chantal gasped.

"Chantal, I told you the shit she was saying didn't add up! *I told you!*" Desiree said, clapping her hands, punctuating each word. "When she called talking about she needed the money to reserve the motel room for us, I knew something was fishy. Talking about a convention was in town and if we wanted to get a room, Western Union her the money. I *knew* it was some bullshit!"

The lights were dim in the club, but I could see Paige's high-yella ass turning red from the neck up.

"Now, y'all in here, so I do hope you enjoy yourself, but all this other mess needs to cease. Chantal and Desiree, since y'all were hood-winked down here, I'll have my waitress get you two drinks each, and, of course, the appetizers are free for everyone tonight. Try to enjoy yourself despite your friend's lies," I said, looking at Paige. Shit, I was calling my girl Nicole crazy, but she didn't have shit on this one right here. I went in search of a waitress to hook these two birds up with a drink. Paige could die of thirst for all I cared.

I glanced over to the VIP to check on Nicole and saw she wasn't at the table. Cherell and the white chick were there talking, along with Carlos.

"Whassup, my man!" I turned around to find Kendrick and Antonio standing there with their spouses. I'd seen Kendrick's wife Tierrany before, but Antonio's wife? Gahhhh damn! I mean *gahhhh damn* her ass was fine! Even in the dimly lit room, I could see her bright, sparkling green eyes. She had this long, thick, auburn-colored hair and . . . just *damn!* I had to make myself look up and keep my eyes trained elsewhere before I disrespected that man! They both introduced their wives to me, and I greeted them in return.

"Well, baybee, it's so nice to finally meet you!" Tondellya, Antonio's wife, drawled. Her Louisiana accent was thick as hell.

I immediately broke into a grin because the sound of her voice reminded me of home. I needed to make a trip back to Texas real soon. Every part of Texas was filled with New Orleans transplants since that bitch Hurricane Katrina hit.

"Well, I'm sure glad y'all could make it. I have your table ready in VIP. You ladies enjoy the show," I said and started to walk off.

"*Kendrick!*" Tierrany, Kendrick's wife yelped.

"Aye, man, Jeremiah, hold up," Kendrick said, glaring at his wife real quick.

"Look, man, do me a solid. My wife over here acting like a damn groupie and shit, acting like she gon' go crazy if she can't meet Mia and get an autograph. Do you think you could get us an introduction?"

I just laughed. I was used to Mia causing this type of reaction when she was around.

"No problem, man. Look, let me just do a few things and I'll join you in the VIP. As soon as Mia's done for the night, she'll be up there. Her husband Quinton might already be up there. Oh, and make sure shit is straight because my girl Nicole is up there too, so I don't want no friction," I said, giving a slight nod toward his wife.

Kendrick cocked his head back, smiling.

"Your girl, huh? So you went on 'head and handled that, I see. I'm happy you're making her happy. That's what's up, my nigga." Kendrick leaned in close. "This some bullshit, though! I feel slightly uncomfortable. I did my research on you too, nigga. I know you used to be with Mia and what went down with ol' boy she married. Shit, I been with Nicole. I mean, goddamn! I gotta hurry up and get my ass outta here! This is just a little too close for comfort, you know what I mean?" he said hesitantly. The nigga even had the nerve to pull a handkerchief out of his suit jacket and dab his brow.

Both of us broke out into laughter.

"Go sit yo' ass down, nigga. I'll be back in a few."

I looked around real quick for Nicole and still didn't see her. Shit, let me do this running around so I can chill with her for a little bit.

Nicole

The crowd was so thick in here tonight I could barely navigate my way to the bathroom, but what I couldn't do is sit in the VIP watching that bitch Paige drape herself all over Jeremiah. Out of all the people in here tonight, I'd noticed her walk in with some friends. I just knew she was asking him to come into the VIP section. I wanted to trust him so badly, but I knew for a fact he told me he'd dropped her off at the airport. Was he lying, or did she come back? If he made it clear to her that he wasn't interested in her, why would she come back?

It didn't make sense to me.

Surprisingly the bathroom was empty with the exception of an attendant who was sitting in the main lobby area of the bathroom. It was odd to find it empty given the number of people in here tonight. But Mia was in the middle of her second act, so I shouldn't have been shocked. No one wanted to miss hearing her sing. Hell, a few days ago, I would have been the same way. I still liked her music, I couldn't lie and say I didn't. I also didn't throw out her CDs or delete her from my playlists either. I tried, but hell, some of those damn love songs helped me live to see another day after my breakup with Kendrick. But I wasn't as all in as a fan the way I had been.

I guess it was because now I knew she was just as flawed as the rest of us. Instead of me viewing her as this superstar with an amazing life and this fine husband, I knew the dirty side of her.

I walked into the stall, quickly handled my business, and walked out to wash my hands. I was zoned out thinking about Paige and Jeremiah. Calm yourself down, Nicole, and don't go accusing him of anything or jumping the gun, I coached myself as I rinsed my hands and turned to grab some paper towels.

"Humph! If it ain't Raggedy Ann herself. And she got on a red dress too! Ain't that . . . Well, it's cute, I guess. You tried," Paige said, glaring at me evilly.

I groaned inside. Not this bitch. Please, not tonight. Instead of letting her get too wound up, I caught her off guard by speaking.

"Hi, Paige. Are you enjoying the show? I love Mia's music," I said, rubbing my hands dry, tossing the towels, and pulling out a small tube of hand lotion from my purse. Paige just glared at me.

"Hello, I'm Nicole," I said, extending my hand to both of her friends who spoke back and shook my hand.

"Don't be shaking this bitch's hand!" Paige spat, turning on them. "This the ho who been down here stealing my man from me!" she fumed.

"Whatever, Paige. I don't know what to believe at this point with the shit coming out ya mouth! Got us all the way down here and Jeremiah says he don't even fuck with you like that," Chantal said.

"Your ass was lying. I guess she was right," Desiree said, leaning into the mirror to fluff her 24-inch wavy Malaysian weave.

Paige stood there turning red in the face.

"I don't have to lie to either one of you hoes . . ."

"Well, why are you then? Please believe you better have $160 in my hand before we make it back to the motel tonight, or your ass will be sleeping on the street. I'm about tired of your nonsense. Even my mama asked me why I was still hanging with your trifling ass. And your ex-roommate showed up at my damn job yesterday too! You better get your life straight, boo! Chantal, come on; let's find us a damn seat if we

can and enjoy the rest of the show since we paid
to get in! At least Jeremiah was nice enough to
give us two free drinks each," Desiree spouted
off through narrowed eyes.

"I know, right? Shit, let's get 'em before he
change his damn mind. You foul as fuck for
leaving out here like this, Paige. I thought we
were better than that. I guess not," Chantal said
before following Desiree out of the bathroom.

"Excuse me, but is everything good over
here?" the bathroom attendant asked, peeping
around the corner with a small walkie-talkie up
to her mouth. Her hand was shaking like a leaf.

"Bitch, gon'! Ain't nothing going on over here—
yet," Paige snarled, turning back to me.

I leaned forward in the mirror, checked my
lipstick, and ran my fingers through my hair to
fluff the waves I'd worn my bob in tonight.

"Bitch, you ain't cute! I don't know what
Jeremiah sees in you."

I chuckled lightly. "Everything he *didn't* see
in you," I said confidently. I was surprised to
hear the words coming out of my own mouth. I'd
come in here disturbed at seeing Jeremiah even
speaking to Paige, but it dawned on me finally. If
I saw through Paige so quickly in what . . . two
or three meetings, I was sure Jeremiah had too.
Paige raised her hand as if to slap me.

"Bitch, I really wish you would. I wish you would! Don't let the fact I seem quiet make a fool out of you," I seethed.

"Girl, they did a real nice job in here! And it's jam-packed! Almost made me wish the guys hadn't gotten rid of the place," I heard a woman say upon entering the bathroom.

"Nawl, baby, never that! It's nice in here, but I didn't like Antonio putting in all that time coming over here at night to check the damn books."

I'd know that voice anywhere. I turned toward the sound of her voice, and when did, I was hit with a blinding slap across the side of my face so hard it jarred me backward.

"Aww, hell, nawl, bitch!" I heard Tondellya yell before I could gather my wits. All I saw was a blaze of red hair snatching Paige up and her screaming as I heard the sound of a loud crunch.

"What in the hell is going on?" I looked up to see Kendrick's wife looking around wildly. I quickly scrambled up from the ground to pull Tondellya off of Paige. The last thing I wanted was for her to get in any trouble.

I grabbed Tondellya around the waist and tried pulling her off, but it felt like she had the strength of ten men inside of her. I had the top part of her body pulled off, but she was steady stomping Paige on any part of her body she could reach, cussing her out the entire time.

"Bitch, you got me fucked up putting ya damn hands on my friend!"

"Are you being paid to just stand there? Call security, girl!" Tierrany yelled at the attendant who stood there glued to one spot with the walkie-talkie in her hand. I guess Tierrany's voice snapped her out of it because I heard her asking for security in the ladies' restroom. Paige lay on the bathroom floor moaning, holding her bloody nose.

"Now, what are you doing in the bathroom by yourself? Fighting at that, Nicole. Got me out here roughhousing over your ass, and you don't even speak to me no more!" Tondellya yelled, looking down at Paige. "Bitch, act like you wanna get up and see what the hell happens!" she ground out.

"I'm sorry. I didn't want you out here fighting for me," I said low. I hadn't seen my friend in over a year. Tondellya had gotten married, had her first child. Actually, she was a mother of two, including the daughter Antonio already had, and it hit me hard that I'd missed it all. I'd been so selfish, only thinking about myself at the time that I'd wanted to deny my friend all the happiness she had in her life. Had I had my way at the time, Tondellya would have been left feeling as empty as I had felt all this time. I felt so ashamed of myself that I burst into tears.

I raised my hands to my face trying to hide it because I was in full-fledge ugly cry.

"I'm sorry, Tondellya. I'm so sorry about how I acted," I sobbed over and over. "I missed you so much, but I didn't think you'd wanna speak to me again . . ." I stuttered between my tears, ". . . and-and I-I wanna see your baby!" I wailed loudly.

"Lord have mercy!" I heard Tierrany say from the background, but I didn't even care. I was just glad to be able to apologize to Tondellya regardless of whether she accepted. I completely understood if she didn't accept it. Tondellya had every right to want nothing to do with me. I'd behaved horribly toward her. Even my own mama tried to tell me, but at the time, I just didn't want to hear it. I'd even missed a month's worth of Sunday dinners at the time, accusing my own mother of choosing Tondellya over me.

"Girl, stop all that damn crying and come give me a hug. You know damn well I love you. I prayed on this shit a long time ago, and I knew you was gon' get your mind right one day soon," Tondellya said, smiling at me.

I grabbed her tight, still sobbing, only now my tears were happy.

"You stupid bitch! I think you broke my nose!"

"Girl, shut up down there before I go in on your ass. Don't you see these two hoes over here having a tender moment?" Tierrany said, peering into the bathroom mirror and fluffing her thick curly hair in coils. I inhaled deeply, quickly making a decision. What the hell? I was on a roll.

"Tierrany, I'ma apologize for barging into your house that day. I'm sorry I called Kendrick all those times and that he had to change his number. Twice. I can admit I went a little crazy. I just, well, umm . . ." I was going to say loved him, but I didn't know if it was appropriate seeing as how I was in the middle of an apology.

"He's easy to love. You ain't gotta tell me. I fell for him when I was a kid. And I tried to stay away from him for three years and couldn't do it. You came at me sideways, but I understand . . . I mean, as long as you have a handle on that shit now, I mean," Tierrany said with a raised eyebrow.

"I do. I promise."

"Is anyone going to help me?" Paige screamed out.

The bathroom door burst open, and Jeremiah and Dip rushed in looking at all of us.

"Nicole, what the hell is going on in here?" Jeremiah asked.

"She attacked me. My friend defended me."

Minutes later, security escorted Paige out of the building. Paige was kicking and screaming the entire time, threatening to sue, but no one paid her any attention. Jeremiah assured everyone he'd handle the situation.

"Are you okay? She didn't touch you, did she?" Jeremiah asked, inspecting me from head to toe.

"I'm fine. My cheek is a little red, but my hair with cover that. It'll be gone in a few hours," I said shyly. Tondellya and Tierrany were not hiding the fact they were checking Jeremiah out and watching the interaction between us.

Relieved, Jeremiah smiled. "Now, can y'all get back out there, please? Stay out of trouble, ladies," he said jokingly as he held the door open and we filed out of the bathroom.

Mia

"These wings good as hell, babe! Damn, I didn't realize I was this hungry," Quinton said.

Daya and I had finished all the live music we were going to do tonight. The DJ took over, and I took pictures with as many fans as I could. I, of course, couldn't take one with everyone, but we'd established that at the start there would only be forty people allowed back in the room the club had set up for a little meet and greet. Besides, I'd done the same thing before the show as well, so in total, about eighty fans had gotten up close and personal. Shoot, everyone else was free to take as many pictures as they wanted with their cell phones if they could get me.

"Well, there's plenty of food and drink here, that's for sure," I said, sitting down to relax a bit. Now that I was off the stage and my main reason for being here was complete, my mind went straight to the reason I called Quinton to come here in the first place. I knew this wasn't the time or place to discuss it, though. If I'd learned anything since being in the public eye, it's that nothing was private. There were eyes and ears everywhere. The only place you could speak freely was in your own home, and even there, I had Douglas, my security guy, do regular sweeps to make sure nothing had been planted. I also didn't let just anyone in our home. Delivery staff, hell, anyone . . . This life made you suspicious of people, and I'd already been through enough.

"So I talked to ya boy Jeremiah earlier. I mean, it ain't like me and the nigga gon' ever be friends or no shit like that, but—"

"Quinton, is that you, nigga? You curly-haired muthafuckin' bandit!"

I looked over and groaned. It was Jeremiah's brother Cedric who has never liked me. Shoot, let me stop lying. I just don't think he liked me with his brother because he knew what was going on with Quinton and me.

Quinton jumped up from his chair, wiping his mouth and hand.

"Cedric, man, I didn't know you were going to be here!" he said excitedly. I could tell by Quinton's entire demeanor he was happy to see his old friend. Sometimes I forgot just how much Quinton had given up for me as well. I always gave Jeremiah all the glory for getting me out of Texas and away from my mother and Quinton, who, at the time, I wanted to run from as well, but honestly, Quinton was still sacrificing for me. Quinton had stepped right into his role as a prominent businessman in the city of San Antonio, Texas. He now had a huge board of directors and a team of people making sure the more than twenty group homes he owned all over the city and in Austin ran smoothly and provided exemplary care to the residents his company served.

Quinton had flipped the money his father had left him so many times it wasn't even funny. He'd told me from the start he would always take care of me and provide me with a good life. But I hadn't been so sure of that at the time.

When we got married, I had to be in New York or Los Angeles where we also had a place. Quinton didn't like it, I knew, plus, he was a mama's boy, so someone from his family was constantly with us, but I knew at the end of the day he missed Texas. I knew he's definitely going to be homesick after hanging with Cedric tonight, I thought shaking my head.

"How you doing over there, Ms. Lady?"

It took me a second to realize he was speaking to me. It's not like he ever went out of his way in all the years Jeremiah and I dated. But I guess neither did I.

"Oh, hey, Cedric, how are you doing?"

"I'm good. You sounded nice out there tonight. I always thought you had a beautiful voice," Cedric said, smiling at me.

I don't know why that pissed me off, but it did. Cedric ain't never had a kind word to say to me. Even about my singing.

"Man, don't leave! Let me run to the bathroom real fast," Quinton said. The rest of the VIP area was empty. Everyone was on the dance floor enjoying themselves. I walked over to the railing and looked out at the crowd dancing.

"I seen you roll your eyes at me. What was that all about?" Cedric asked, standing next to me.

"I mean, why be fake, Cedric? You don't like me, and you never have."

"I ain't never disliked you, Mia. I just knew you weren't the one for my brother. And let's not play any games here . . . You knew why I felt the way I did. Hell, you ended up marrying the nigga. So why you drug my brother's heart through the mud is beyond me. But now that everything is as it should be, we can be cool now. You're happily married to Quinton, and my brother is going to have the same kind of happiness," Cedric said, pointing out to the dance floor. My eyes scanned the floor to find Jeremiah wrapping his arms around a woman in a red dress.

"Who y'all talking about?" Quinton asked, standing next to me. "Oh yeah! Jeremiah got himself a new lady! Shit, I'm happy for him. We all deserve to be happy. See, bae, I told you that man was going to be just fine without you," he said, kissing my cheek.

"Uh-huh. I'll be right back," I said, twisting out of his reach and plastering a fake smile on my face. For some reason, I wasn't as happy seeing Jeremiah in the arms of another woman as I thought I would feel. I'd prayed for him to find the love I had with Quinton all this time, but when it looked like he might have it, all I felt was scared.

Nicole

"So, where is she?" I asked, gazing up into Jeremiah's eyes. I was relaxing in his arms, swaying to the beat of the music on the crowded dance floor. Tonight had been hectic, to say the least. It never occurred to me that Tondellya would be here. I couldn't even put into words how good it felt to come clean with her and apologize for the way I'd treated her. I had so much to talk about with my therapist this week I'd probably have to schedule two sessions!

I tried to play it cool while Mia was performing, but I couldn't help myself. During her time on stage, I went just as crazy as everyone else in the building, but the second she walked off, in my mind, she went right back to being my man's ex. Damn, it felt good to say that. I was trying not to jump ahead of myself, of course, but we had established that, yes, we were together and working toward building something.

"I don't know. Last I saw she was up there with her husband," Jeremiah said, nuzzling the crook of my neck. "You still want that autograph?"

I tried to hide my grin, but, shit, I *did* want it. You know, just to say I had it. The song ended, and we walked off the dance floor toward the VIP section. It was actually crowded. Tondellya, Antonio, Kendrick, and Tierrany, along with my friends, not to mention the other people who'd paid a hefty fee to sit there this evening, and it wasn't exactly "quiet" over there either. But it added to the festivity of the night.

"What the fuck is going on over here?" I heard Jeremiah say aloud as we entered the area. Something in his voice caused the hairs on my arm to stand up as we broke through the crowd.

My heart sank when I saw a man standing in front of Cherell screaming.

"You see the shit I have to go through to get your attention, huh, bitch?"

"Travis, leave me alone! Nigga, get a clue! If a woman don't want you, she just don't want you! Learn to take a clue," Cherell yelled back just as loud.

A crowd was forming trying to watch the scene play out, and I saw Jeremiah pull a walkie-talkie out of his suit jacket and call for security to come to the area before he turned to Travis.

"Look, man, I don't know what problem you have with her is, but you're going to have to solve it outside of my club, my man. I'ma need you to leave."

"Nigga, I paid my money to get in this mutha-fucka just like everyone else! I ain't going no-damn-where. You see the shit I have to do just to find your ho ass, bitch?" he said, turning to Cherell.

"Cherell, come on, let's go to the bathroom," I said, motioning for her to leave the booth. Maybe if Cherell got out of his sight, he would cool down a little. Or better yet, security would have him removed from the building by the time we got back. I'd only met Travis once or twice, and he was such a nice guy, but I knew all too well everyone had their limit. I'd been warning Cherell about this shit. Now, here she was out in public arguing with this man like a typical hoodrat.

"This bitch ain't going no-damn-where—not until she gives me back every dime I've spent on her ho ass. Every dinner I've paid for, bills and car notes . . . until I get all that shit back, she ain't going no-goddamn-where!" Travis raged, stepping in front of Cherell, who was standing at the edge of the booth.

"Whatever, nigga! Deal with the fact you got tricked off. I ain't paying you back shit!" Cherell said, laughing in his face. I don't know if it was because some of the childish people in the crowd were hyping her up, making her feel bold, or the fact she'd been drinking, but Cherell definitely wasn't diffusing the situation.

"Man, look, just let this shit go and leave on your own before I have to call the cops," Jeremiah said once again, trying to reason with Travis without creating more of a scene.

Kendrick and Antonio walked over. "Man, what's going on? You need some help gettin' this nigga out of here?" Kendrick asked. Just then, a voice came over the walkie-talkie informing Jeremiah security was on the way up but there was a string of fights they'd had to intercept out in the parking lot.

"I swear, niggas don't know how to act! Everyone was having a good time—now this shit. Nigga, get your ass the fuck on," Antonio spat, shoving Travis.

"Nigga, I don't give a fuck about no damn cops. This bitch made me love her! I didn't make that shit up on my own. This ho told me she was in love with me. I introduced her to my family, asked her to marry me, and she took my fuckin' ring, and here I'm finding out she's fucking anything moving," Travis said.

"Nigga, I had to! Your dick game ain't hittin' on shit, do you *hear* me? I don't know how you made it this far in life without anyone just letting you know straight out! Ain't no woman gonna ever love your ass or be faithful to *that!*" Cherell said, pointing to his crotch. People in the crowd started laughing, and I cringed at the entire scene. It was getting so nasty between them. Where the hell was security? It seemed like this had been going on forever, but in reality, I knew no more than a minute or two had passed.

Enough was enough.

I was going to drag Cherell's ignorant ass to the bathroom and let Jeremiah's security team handle Travis. I swear to God this was going to be my last time going anywhere with Cherell if this was the type of drama that would be following us. There was a bathroom in the VIP area so we'd just go in there and let this blow over. I walked over to Cherell, grabbed her by the arm, and started leading her away. Stupidly, Cherell was still hurling insults at Travis.

Travis stood there shaking his head. "You know what, bitch? Your ass ain't no good to anyone I'll bet." He reached under his shirt, pulled out a gun, and pointed it at Cherell.

"Man, don't do this . . ." Jeremiah said.

Everything seemed to move in slow motion at that point. I heard Jeremiah screaming my name, three shots rang out in rapid succession, and I was tackled to the floor. I saw Cherell drop to the ground next to me, and the entire VIP broke into pure chaos.

Epilogue—Six Months Later

She was a little all over the place, that was for sure. But the good news is that when she loved, she loved big. And if she loved you, you knew she loved you. You never had to wonder.

Every man has two men in him. A king and a fool. How do you know when you've found a queen? When she speaks to the king in you.

Jeremiah

"Jeremiah, if you don't hurry up and get out of that shower we're going to miss our flight!" Nicole yelled.

"Calm down, we're going to make it on time," I said, turning off the water and stepping out of the steamy shower. There Nicole sat perched on the toilet seat waiting on me to step out holding my towel. I almost laughed at her ass, she was such a mother hen. I stood on the bath mat dripping wet. Nicole jumped up, rubbing me down.

"My mama is so ready to see me. I never thought I'd miss home so much," Nicole said, rubbing the towel over my back.

"I'm bringing her baby back to her," I said with a laugh.

For the past two months, Nicole and I had been in New York. Like I told her from the start: if things worked out with us, we were going to make it work. That was an understatement.

"Your scar is barely noticeable," Nicole murmured, running her hand over the slightly raised bullet hole scar on the front upper right hand side of my chest. It was identical to the matching scar on my back where the bullet exited.

"Yeah, I wouldn't care if you did see it, though," I said thoughtfully, running my fingers over the scar. Our grand reopening of Table 51 made the papers of Richmond, Virginia, all right—for all the wrong reasons. I'd jumped in front of a bullet to protect Nicole, her friend Cherell was murdered, and her crazy boyfriend killed himself like a coward. It was a wonder my damn business survived that whole episode, but a week later, it was business as usual.

I got chills every time I thought about that shit. It could have all ended so differently if that bullet hadn't hit me and made it to Nicole.

"You have a nice ass, Jeremiah."

"I know. You keep telling me that," I said, walking into the bedroom to throw on the clothes she had laid out for me on the bed.

"Ma, you know you don't have to keep laying my clothes out, you know."

"I know. I like taking care of you, though."

"Well, why do you seem to like doing all that, but you're taking your time about becoming Mrs. Wilson? We live together now. I asked you to leave your job so we don't have to ever be apart.

You did. You have full reign over my houses here in New York and Virginia. You love me, right?"

Nicole nodded her head slowly.

"I need you to help me understand, Nicole. I mean, in two months you're giving birth to my son. I kinda just assumed we were going to all walk out of the hospital with the same last name. I proposed to you, I'm in love with you, but I don't know where your head is with all this, and I ain't gon' play no games with you. I'm getting impatient with all this," I said. And I was.

So much shit had gone on after that night at the club, but in that one moment, the second I saw that nigga raise that gun and put his finger to the trigger, I didn't see anyone in that room but Nicole, and all I knew was I didn't want her hurt. So I jumped in front of a bullet for her.

I was laid up in the hospital for a minute, but I was okay. Despite her friend being killed and having to deal with telling Cherell's parents their only child had been murdered, Nicole never once left my side. Matter of fact, she and Mia even had some words at the hospital. Then a month later, we found out Nicole was pregnant. The only thing I can say about the whole incident is that God truly ordered my steps that night. Because not only was I protecting Nicole, I was protecting my unborn son.

Nicole

Your king. You'll know your king not by how he dresses or what he spends on you. No, you'll know your king by how he leads and loves you.

Fall in love with someone who doesn't make you think love is hard.

I was looking into Jeremiah's eyes, and I could see the frustration building. As a matter of fact, I could see it building every month my stomach protruded a little more with his baby growing inside of me. I wanted to wait to get married. I never in a million years would have thought I would be the one saying I wanted to wait. Especially since I'm pregnant, but I had to be sure. I had so many thoughts running through my head, and if I thought I'd been confused before, it was even worse now. These last six months had really opened my eyes.

I'd been so scared the night Jeremiah had been shot. One minute I was trying to drag Cherell to the bathroom to prevent the argument between her and Travis from escalating, and suddenly I heard my name being screamed and was knocked to the ground with Jeremiah on top of me. Cherell dropped next to us seconds later, and then another shot rang out. I was lying there covered in blood—Jeremiah's and Cherell's. The club was in complete pandemonium. Strangely enough, I don't know how I would have made it through if it wasn't for Kendrick and Antonio. Jeremiah's brother, of course, was at his side, but he'd just gotten to town. They totally took over everything, with their wives right at their sides, as they should have been. Tondellya never left me either. Meka? The second she saw a gun, she ran. In fact, I didn't hear from her until two days later when she had the nerve to text me to see if I was okay. Tondellya told me so many times Meka wasn't about shit. After that incident, I finally listened. I mean, it wasn't like I wanted her hurt too. I knew she had a child that depended on her, but, damn. Two days later? I could have been in there dead.

It was horrible digging through Cherell's phone trying to find her parents' number to contact them. I'd never wanted a Xanax so much in my life as in those first few hours.

Jeremiah's injuries weren't life threatening, but he was hurt, and to top it all off, guess who tried to get bold with me at the hospital? Mia!

I mean, there I was, a total wreck, and Mia tried to have me put out of Jeremiah's room, talking about I barely knew him, and he needed his rest—that I could call him once he was released from the hospital. I never thought the saying "seeing red" was true until that night!

I cussed that bitch out from the rooter to the tooter. I mean, it was ugly. Mia was really trying to stand her ground too . . . until Cedric stepped in and defended me. Since he was the only blood relative, he had the final say on who stayed and who had to go. But what was even crazier was the way her husband Quinton went off on her ass!

When that nigga started going off on her is when hospital security got involved and had them escorted from the building.

Long story short, I was a wreck. I took time off work. I just couldn't go back in that building knowing Cherell wouldn't be there with me. I was seeing the therapist more than ever to work through the grief of losing her. Jeremiah was recuperating himself but was taking care of me because I was so depressed.

I didn't even notice I'd missed my period. Hell, every time I thought about Cherell, I got nauseated, so I didn't even pay that any attention. I started dropping a few pounds, and Jeremiah was the one who noticed I'd missed my cycle. He took charge of everything . . . doctors' appointments, all of it.

I couldn't believe how excited he was about an unplanned pregnancy. I was happy about the baby, and I couldn't have asked for more from Jeremiah—but now I was terrified.

Did he just want me because I was pregnant? If there was no baby, would he still love me? Did Jeremiah think this son was going to replace Mia's son? I just didn't want to make an even bigger mistake now that a baby was involved. Hell, I was just starting to get myself together. Some things I was scared to speak about with Jeremiah. He already thought I was crazy as it was.

"Jeremiah, if I wasn't pregnant with your baby, would you still choose me? Just be honest with me," I said, my voice shaking. I was trying do the right thing for both of us. Trying to make a good decision. I didn't want to be a single mother. It's not how I imagined it would be when I had my first child, but if I had to, I could do it. I could always go back to work. I had a family that loved and supported me, no matter what.

"Nicole, bring your ass over here," Jeremiah said, throwing the shirt he was about to put over his head on the bed. I walked over and sat down.

Jeremiah sat at the head of the bed and spread his legs. I eased up between his legs, leaning my back against his chest. He began rubbing my belly. See, this is what I was talking about. I knew he loved the baby, but how much did he love *me?* He only told me he loved me once he knew I was pregnant! I was mad already.

"Look, we need to catch this damn plane. Finish getting dressed, please," I said, standing up. Lord, my stomach was getting so big! Jeremiah pulled me back.

"Sit your ass down. I ain't worried about that damn flight. Everything I need and want is right here in this damn room. We about to lay whatever you have on your mind to rest, Nicole. I know you've been through a lot. I've been as patient as I can be with you. But don't think I don't see how you've been walking around here creating all this extra shit in your head. I see your wheels of crazy turning in your head even when you don't," he said, tapping the side of my head.

I wanted to slap him!

"Nicole, you standing there with a straight face asking me if I would chose you. I've been choosing you since the day I laid eyes on your rude ass! If you ain't my woman, I don't know who the hell is or ever was! I made the choice to cover

for you that night with Kendrick. I didn't have
to, I could have sipped my drink and minded my
own damn business, but I saw you there, struggling, and I chose to be there. You've cussed me
out, called me a liar, and every-damn-thing else,
and I *kept* choosing you. Every time I've been
with you, it's been a choice. Right down to the
fact I chose to slide inside you without a condom
and make this baby with you. I can tell you the
exact date and time we made this baby, because
I ain't never in my life, outside of Mia, been with
a woman without a condom on.

Nicole, I ain't one of these niggas who thinks
love is all lightning bolts and stars and cupids
and shit. I think love takes work. Everything
involved in love is a choice. You gotta choose to
not lie, choose to not fall on another nigga's dick,
or in another bitch's pussy!"

"*What?*" I yelped, turning around as fast as
this big belly would let me.

"I'm just saying, ma! That's real shit! But I
already chose you to be the only woman to have
my babies. I chose you to spend the rest of my
life with. Now, shit, all I'm saying is choose me
back! Why you acting like I'm holding all the
cards here, Nicole? You got choices, so make
yours. Choose me back, Nicole. Don't make me
beg for you when you know I love your crazy

ass. I mean, it ain't shit. I'll do it, no problem. I jumped in front of a bullet for you, so that's the least I could do is get on my damn knee."

I busted out laughing.

"Jeremiah, you're nuts, do you know that?"

"I didn't used to be until I started fuckin' with you. Ain't no sane woman gonna want me now, so you gotta take me."

Jeremiah said everything I needed to hear from him. I could see the truth in his eyes, I felt the love he had for me and our baby, and a calmness . . . A sureness spread over me that I'd never felt before. It felt like God was telling me right then and there Jeremiah was the one. That he was the reason it had never worked with anyone else because he was the man meant for me. Unlike times before, my heart and mind was suddenly sure. Better yet, I finally felt secure.

"Why are you crying?" he asked, wiping my cheeks.

I hadn't even realized I was. I wrapped my arms around his neck, never wanting to let him go.

"Let's do it. As soon as we get to Virginia, we're getting married."

*****You owe yourself the love you so freely give to other people.*****

Mia

*** *Don't ask for signs, and then ignore the signs.* ***

The last six months of my life have been a living hell. I'd just had the nanny take Jacobi to the park because last night, Quinton and I had gotten into it again. It had been a rough night, and I knew we were gearing up for round two of World War III. Why? Because I ain't gave that nigga no pussy in six months. These legs were staying closed until he told me what the hell I wanted to know.

But let me back up.

It all started the night of Jeremiah's grand reopening. Shit hit the fan with that crazy man killing that woman, and Jeremiah got shot. I thought I was going to literally lose my mind on the spot because I was on the other side of the room when it happened. Jeremiah jumped in front of who I guess was his li'l girlfriend, and it looked like it was happening in slow motion. I started running toward Jeremiah, and Quinton was trying to hold me back.

At the hospital, me and this Nicole girl got into it, which just escalated the entire situation. I'm still hot as fish grease about that. I can't stand Jeremiah's brother Cedric. That night I also started to hate my husband a little bit too. How the fuck are you going to stand in front of all those damn people and take another woman's side over mine? Talking about some damn, *"Get out of their business. She's his woman. It's her place to be by his side. You don't even need to be here—period—Mia."* That just set me all the fucking way off. Security had to escort us out of the building we starting fighting so bad.

So when Quinton and I got back to the hotel room? Oh, it was on!

I asked him what the fuck he was doing to me in my room that night all those years ago. This nigga had been running his mouth talking shit, but when I asked him *that,* you could have heard a rat piss on cotton it was so damn quiet. We fought all night. Flew back to New York in silence, and basically, things have been fucked up ever since.

Quinton called himself flying back to Texas several times for work, but I think he just thought I was going to come running after his ass. He had me all the way fucked up. Quinton never stayed gone longer than a week and was right back in New York staring in my face. It's been this way for six months now. Yeah, we're still married . . . for now. But he's got a week to tell me what I want to know. If he doesn't? That can change too. Because the more he resisted telling me, I knew it was some really fucked-up shit he'd done.

Quinton

I walked into the kitchen to get a glass of water. Mia cut her eyes at me and turned her back. This is the shit I been dealing with for the last six months. I was at my breaking point with her.

Don't get me wrong, wasn't nothing in this world going to ever make me leave her ass.

Ever.

When we exchanged vows and that judge said "Till death do you part," I meant that shit. Literally and figuratively. But Mia was pushing me to the point she was going to see a side of me that I'd never shown to her. Mia might wanna visit her mama in jail and ask about me. Every man has a breaking point, and I was just about at mine with her.

All of a sudden, she was pressing me about old shit that should have been left alone a long-ass time ago. We been married for how long now? All of a sudden after going to Virginia and seeing Jeremiah, now she wants answers to things we'd left in the past? I said it before, and I'll say I again . . . Everyone has a chapter in their life they don't want read out loud. The muthafuckin' book is closed on all that mess. But if Mia keeps pressing me about this old shit . . . I might have to give her ass a li'l excerpt on just how far her husband went to get her.

And how far I'll go to keep her ass.

The End

Thank you for reading this novel. If you enjoyed this book, please consider leaving a short review where you purchased your copy.

Thanks, again,
Ms. Bam, aka Candace